HELLDORADO

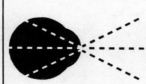

This Large Print Book carries the
Seal of Approval of N.A.V.H.

A LOU PROPHET NOVEL

HELLDORADO

PETER BRANDVOLD

WHEELER PUBLISHING
A part of Gale, Cengage Learning

GALE
CENGAGE Learning™

Detroit • New York • San Francisco • New Haven, Conn • Waterville, Maine • London

GALE
CENGAGE Learning

LIBRARY OF CONGRESS CATALOGING-IN-PUBLICATION DATA

Brandvold, Peter.
  Helldorado : a Lou Prophet novel / by Peter Brandvold.
    p. cm.
  ISBN-13: 978-1-4104-3502-6 (softcover)
  ISBN-10: 1-4104-3502-4 (softcover)
    1. Prophet, Lou (Fictitious character)—Fiction. 2. Large type books. I. Title.
  PS3552.R3236H465 2010
  813'.54—dc22
                                  2010045412

Published in 2011 by arrangement with The Berkley Publishing Group, a member of Penguin Group (USA) Inc.

Printed in the United States of America
1 2 3 4 5 6 7 15 14 13 12 11

This book is for Diane Nygren,
though she deserves a hell of a lot more.

1

"Looks like we have a visitor heading to our humble casa," said Rurale Sergeant Rafael Santangelo, pointing across the sunblasted rocks and cactus toward a boulder-strewn ridge. "A tall hombre on a sway-backed mule."

Corporal Hermano Alvarez squinted his good eye while holding a hand over the one that a Nogales whore had ruined with a razor-edged stiletto. "*Si, si!* Should I shoot him off his mule?"

"Shoot him? From here?" Sergeant Santangelo gave a mocking laugh. "You can't even see him from here, you one-eyed, whore-mongering idiot! How do you expect to shoot him?"

"I can see him fine," insisted Alvarez, who stood half a head shorter than the tall, gangly, and mustached Santangelo. Closing the ruined eye through which he could see only a perpetual blizzard even in the bowels of a hot Mexican summer, the corporal raised his Springfield Trapdoor rifle to his shoulder and aimed it out from the guard tower where both he and Santangelo had been posted since sunrise.

He racked a live round into the rifle's breech and grinned. "Watch this, Rafael, and prepare to kiss my ass."

Santangelo, who had been made a sergeant less than a month before and who kept his dove gray, gold-buttoned tunic well laundered and freshly brushed even here in the dusty Mexican desert, angrily doffed his leather-brimmed hat and swiped it three times against Alvarez's head and shoulder, knocking the corporal's straw sombrero down his back. "I told you, pig of a bastard peon, to never call me by my first name again! I am 'Sergeant Santangelo' or simply 'Sergeant,' but never again shall I be addressed by you as Rafael! Do I make myself clear, you half-blind cur of a two-peso *puta?*"

"*Si, si!* I apologize, Raf . . . I mean, Sergeant Santangelo!"

"Besides, if you could see farther than your ugly hawk's beak of a nose, you would see that the big bastard on the mule is a man of the cloth, you fool."

Alvarez squinted into the distance.

"Really?"

"If you shot God's servant there, the Devil would reach up and tickle your toes."

"I am not afraid of the Devil."

"Oh?" Santangelo smiled cunningly. "Go ahead, then. See if you can shoot the padre's hat from his head. Let's see what you can do, eagle eye."

Alvarez looked up at the taller man and gave a devilish chuckle. Licking his chapped lips, he drew a deep breath, raised the Springfield to his shoulder, and sighted down the barrel.

The rider was about a hundred and fifty yards out from the Rurale fort, which had once been a mission school before being taken over and used for a prison by a northern Sonora contingent of the Mexican rural police force. The sprawling adobe structure, surrounded by a stone stockade bristling with a brush-roofed wooden guard tower at each corner, had been built on a rolling bench between two craggy sierras. The man moving toward the fort now had one ridge behind him, and his long, chocolate-brown robes were clearly defined against the ridge's sunbaked, adobe-colored wall.

A large, straw sombrero shaded the padre's face, and his rope-soled sandals jostled

9

down beneath the mule's ribs. He rode lazily on the mule's bare back, swaying easily, keeping his chin dipped low against the merciless Sonoran sun that winked off the silver crucifix hanging from his neck on a braided rawhide thong.

Alvarez brushed a buzzing fly away from his nose, then pressed the Springfield's stock tight against his cheek, lining up the rifle's sights on the padre's high sombrero crown. He chuckled to himself, then frowned, getting serious, and squeezed his bad eye closed. Keeping the sights steady on the bobbing sombrero that was a hundred yards out and closing, he held his breath and took the slack out of his trigger finger.

The rifle leaped and roared.

The echoes flatted out between the ridges.

The slug blew up a dogget of sand and gravel just right of the mule's right rear hoof, causing the beast to hump its back and leap, braying, as high as any mustang stallion with its tail on fire.

The padre's head snapped up, tossing his sombrero down his back, and his free hand flew high as the mule reached the apex of its leap, dropped, and hit the ground on all four hooves. The padre threw himself forward, clinging for dear life to the animal's bridle reins and its shaggy mane as the frightened, angry beast took its God-fearing benefactor on a wild, crow-hopping, sunfishing ride around the bench fronting the fort.

Santangelo, Alvarez, and the two guards in the other west-facing tower whooped and hollered uproariously, thoroughly enjoying the mule-and-padre rodeo.

As the mule headed toward the fort in the most roundabout way possible, several times the brown-robed gent was nearly tossed from the squealing, braying mount's hurricane deck only to save himself at the last second by grabbing the flying reins or buffeting mane. He slipped down the mule's right side, then its left side, half-dragged across the sand and cactus. Then he was hugging the beast's neck before another violent buck and lurch would have sent him flying ass-over-teakettle off the hysterical mount's pitching ass if not for his last-second grab of the reins.

Santangelo roared, forgetting his rank and slapping his thighs like a drunken peon.

"A hundred centavos in gold dust he doesn't make it to the gate!" shouted one of the guards from the other tower, his white teeth flashing in the sunlight.

"You're on!" roared Santangelo. "I think

he's going to make it!"

More laughter as the mule brayed and thumped its hooves wildly and thrashed the poor man on its back like a wicked child shaking a rag doll in a dirty clenched fist.

"Here he comes!" Alvarez squealed as the mule and its thrashing rider drew within twenty yards of the fort's open front gate. "I think he's going to make it. . . . Ohh . . . *ohhhhh, noooooooh — and here he* came so *cloooose!*" the corporal lamented just after the mule had deposited the padre in a sand patch a few feet in front of the fort's gaping doors, dust wafting around the poor man who lay writhing on his back, mashing his sombrero into the ground beneath him.

"The poor bastard," said Santangelo, gaping down from the guard tower. "Look there, Hermano, you old heathen. Look what you've done! To a man of the cloth, no less."

"I guess you're right, Raf . . . I mean, Sergeant Santangelo. I guess my aim isn't as good as it was before I visited Nogales." Alvarez chuckled deep in his throat, showing his cracked, tobacco-stained teeth.

"Come on, you hell-bent son of a demon lobo." Santangelo slapped his partner's chest before looping his own rifle around the handle of the Gatling gun that each of the four towers was armed with and dropped down the rickety wooden ladder. "We'd better see how badly you've injured the padre. I have a feeling forgiveness isn't in the cards for you, my friend!"

Santangelo leaped from the ladder's third rung to the ground. As Alvarez followed close behind, the sergeant pushed through the half dozen Rurale guards who'd gathered inside and outside the open front gates to enjoy the show. The heretics were laughing amongst themselves, slapping each other's chests or pounding shoulders, while the faithful, of which there were far fewer, stood around in hushed awe, crossing themselves and lifting forgiveness-beseeching gazes skyward.

"Back, swine, get back!" Santangelo ordered, shoving a couple of the gaping men back away from the padre — a big, raw-boned, unshaven man with sandy hair and light blue eyes. He was flat on his back, groaning and grunting painfully, but as Santangelo approached him, the big padre pushed up on his elbows and shook his head as if to clear it.

"I apologize for Corporal Alvarez, Father. He has been stationed so long out here in these rocks that he's gone a little off his nut." Santangelo glanced up at Alvarez, who was standing behind him and staring sheepishly down at the disheveled stranger.

The big man grunted, stretching his lips back from his teeth.

"Hey, Father, you speak English?" Santangelo squatted beside the man, wrinkling his brows suspiciously. "You know — you don't look like a Mexican priest to me. You look like a gringo. You speak Spanish? Uh? Let me hear you say something in Spanish."

The big man's bleary eyes rolled up toward Santangelo. As though suddenly understanding what the sergeant was saying, he held up the finger of one hand while reaching into a pocket of his robe with the other. He pulled out a wad of small, scribbled notes. He peeled the top note from the wad, and offered it to Santangelo, who took the note brusquely and held it up to his face.

" 'I apologize for not speaking, but the Yaquis cut out my tongue.' "

A couple of the men standing around behind Santangelo and Alvarez clucked or muttered regretfully.

"So you have no tongue, uh?" Santangelo chewed his lower lip. "Really? That's true?" He shoved his head down closer to that of the padre. "Let me see."

The padre tipped his head back and

14

opened his mouth about halfway. Santangelo lowered his head still farther and sort of cocked it to one side to see inside the stranger's mouth. Alvarez did the same, peering over the sergeant's shoulder while holding one hand over his bad eye and squinting his good one.

"Open wider," Santangelo ordered the priest. "I can't see a damn thing in there."

The priest muttered something. It was like a gargle.

"Huh?" Santangelo said.

Another gargle as the padre's lips moved slightly while he held his mouth half open.

"What's that? I can't hear you, damnit!"

The priest's blue eyes flickered devilishly. They acquired a cool, bemused cast as he cleared his throat and said in perfectly enunciated English, "Open yours, you smelly son of a bitch!"

Santangelo's heart leaped into his throat when he saw that the padre had opened his robes and was aiming a sawed-off, double-barreled, ten-gauge shotgun up and out from his broad chest clad in skin-tight, wash-worn red longhandles, at Santangelo's suddenly gaping mouth. The sergeant had only seen the brief flash of the gut shredder's left barrel when, on the heels of the cannon-like blast, his head was ripped from his shoulders to fly up and over the still-staring Alvarez, spraying blood and brain goo in every direction before hitting the dirt behind the corporal and rolling up over one of the stunned onlooker's high-topped black boots.

Alvarez lowered his hand from his milky brown eye, screaming and fumbling with his Springfield Trapdoor. Lou Prophet snarled like an enraged bobcat as he slid his sawed-off ten-gauge slightly left and tripped the second trigger.

Booommmm!

The melon-sized spread of double-ought buck blasted through the scrawny corporal's filthy tunic, lifting the man three feet off the ground and punching him straight back into three others, laying one out flat before Alvarez hit the ground in a bloody, lifeless, quivering heap just inside the fort's broad double doors.

He leaped to his bare feet — he'd lost both sandals during the joyride that he'd managed to prolong by grinding his heels into the mule's flanks, wanting to keep the Rurales as entertained for as long as he could. Now he swept both sides of his billowing robe back to allow access to the two Colt .45s bristling from holsters and a third one wedged behind the two cartridge belts crisscrossed on his waist. The Rurales standing around him were just now recovering from the shock of seeing the sergeant's head whipping through the air like a Cinco de Mayo rocket and were fumbling pistols from their holsters or raising old-model rifles to their shoulders.

Prophet dispatched one of the soldiers — a fat corporal with a long, tangled beard — before the man could slip his Remington from a shoulder holster, sending him into a bizarre pirouette across the bench. The robe-wearing bounty hunter killed two more with a single bullet each before the Colts leaped and roared four more times, and all seven Rurales were either down or going down bloody, screaming and yipping like coyotes, one blindly triggering his revolver through the cheek of a bellowing compatriot.

As powder smoke billowed around him, Prophet quickly aimed his cocked Colts at the guard tower just left of the open doors, where a Gatling gun bristled like a giant, deadly mosquito, flashing brassily in the late-morning sun. He ratcheted back both hammers but held fire when he saw the guard who'd been manning the tower turn a somersault off the tower's rickety wooden rail, losing his sombrero and rifle and hitting the ground with a dull thud that clipped his horrified shriek.

His rifle landed with a clatter a half second later.

Two familiar figures stood in the tower — peon-revolutionarios in their traditional white pajamas, serapes, and wagon-wheel sombreros. The younger man held a machete while the older one, known as Tio Largo, or "Big Tio," grinned delightedly down at Prophet while turning the Gatling gun toward the fort's courtyard with a squawk of its dry cylinder swivel and squatting down behind it.

Prophet lifted a hand to his temple in salute and dropped to a knee to reload his gut shredder. When he'd filled both tubes and closed the ten-gauge with a loud clack, he jerked with a start as Tio shouted, "Here they come, Lou!" and opened up with the Gatling gun, laying down a deadly line of fire on the courtyard where Rurales in all stages of dress poured out the doors of the prison buildings and stables.

A second later, one of the other Gatlings in another guard tower began roaring as well. Looking up as he shook spent casings from one of his .45s, then filling the empty chambers from his cartridge belt, Prophet saw a dozen or so peon-revolutionarios —

all Big Tio's men whom Prophet had thrown in with in the scrubby hills around Del Rio — whooping and hollering as they spilled down the fort's east and north walls.

They dangled from ropes or dropped into the courtyard while the men behind the deadly Gatling guns turned the Rurales spilling out of the guardhouses and barracks and big central prison block to a wheeling, screaming mass of bloody carnage tumbling down stone steps or rolling in the hard-packed, straw- and dung-littered dirt of the yard.

Above the din rose a girl's shrill scream.

Prophet gritted his teeth as he spun the cylinder of his third filled Colt, wedged the gun behind his cartridge belts, grabbed his shotgun, and sprinted between the fort's gaping doors and into the bloody, smoky melee of the courtyard, bellowing, *"Loooeeeezzzz-ahhhhh!"*

2

Running through the gate's open doors and into the prison courtyard, Prophet threw a hand in the air, signaling Big Tio to hold off with the Gatling gun.

He heard the Mexican revolutionario leader shout the cease-fire orders to the other towers, all four of which had been overtaken by the nimble, mountain-bred rebels while Prophet had diverted the guards' attention outside the front gate.

The angry, ragtag bunch led by Big Tio had been chomping at the bit to take out the corrupt Rurale contingent stationed here at San Cristobal for several months. The Rurale officer overseeing the headquarters and prison, Major Rudofo Montoya, was in the business of kidnapping young women from the nearby mountain villages and selling them into prostitution in the mining perditions of southern Chihuahua, where isolated rock breakers, more savage than any Apache or Yaqui, paid good money for female companionship. The younger the better.

But while they paid good money for the young women and girls — some as young as eight — they went through them quite quickly, always needing more. Prophet's sometime partner, sometime lover, Louisa Bonaventure, had been caught in a trap sprung by Major Montoya three weeks ago in the village of Del Rio, and she and the young peasant girls she'd been captured with had been brought here where they were awaiting transportation by mule train into the Sierra Madres.

All this Prophet had learned from Big Tio's spies. And that was when the American bounty hunter, who'd met Big Tio on a bounty-hunting expedition to Mexico several years ago, had helped the revolutionario leader organize the raid on the prison here at San Cristobal.

Now, as the Gatling's cover fire died, leaving countless Rurales sprawled and groaning around the big monastery building that Montoya had converted into a prison, Prophet dropped to a knee and extended the sawed-off shotgun from his right side.

Two Rurales had just bolted out of a low, arched doorway in the officer's headquarters

21

in front of him, one extending a rifle toward Big Tio's guard tower, the other clamping a hand to a bloody shoulder while cursing loudly in Spanish and raising a pearl-gripped Remington. Prophet tripped both triggers, and the stout weapon leaped and roared in his hands, blowing both officers off their feet and piling them up on the floor of the low stone stoop just outside the door from which they'd emerged.

Big Tio's roaring laughter carried down from the guard tower. "Lou, remind me to buy that savage popper from you before we part ways again, amigo!"

Prophet snorted and, realizing he was still wearing the cumbersome brown robes, shrugged out of them, letting them drop to the dust. Beneath he wore only his long-handle top and denim trousers, which he'd rolled up nearly to his knees to give the impression that the robes were all he had on. Jerking the cuffs down to his bare ankles, making it easier to run, he leaped a dying Rurale as he headed past the officer's headquarters, making for the prison's main doors.

With rifles, pistols, machetes, sickles, and any other weapon the peasants had managed to get their hands on, Tio's men were cutting down the Rurales who'd dodged the

Gatling fire. The gunshots were sporadic but furious. Men screamed and cursed and one dying Rurale was down and wailing near horse stables, from which the frightened screams of the horses sounded above the shooting.

The prison's main, double doors stood at the top of high stone steps that fairly glowed in the midday sun. At the bottom of the steps, a Rurale guard who'd been shot through the belly was crawling toward his dropped rifle. Prophet drilled a .45 round through the guard's head from point-blank range then took the steps three at a time, his bare feet slapping the hot stones as he heard once more the shrill scream of the girl inside the mission/prison.

Hearing several of Big Tio's men running up the steps behind him, Prophet pulled one of the heavy, brass-handled doors open, throwing it wide so the revolutionario behind him could catch it. He bolted inside, his shotgun dangling from the wide leather lanyard around his neck, holding a cocked Colt pistol in each big, calloused hand.

A ways inside the door, a girl sat on the floor against a cracked stone pillar. A tray, a broken bottle of clear glass, and two shot glasses lay nearby. The senorita, only fourteen or fifteen, was barefoot, and her shabby gray skirt was pulled up around her dark brown thighs. Silver hoop rings dangled from her ears. She wore no blouse. Her small, tan breasts peeked out from behind her long, mussed hair, which was the color of dark chocolate.

Her brown eyes flashed in terror when they found Prophet, and her entire body quivered as she crossed her thin arms on her chest and loosed another scream.

Prophet looked around quickly. Spying no other movement in the broad, dark foyer and atop the flagstone stairs that rose on his right, he lowered his pistols and moved inside, gesturing to the revolutionarios behind him to spread out. They needed no further orders; they all knew that their mission here was to kill every Rurale they ran into and to free the prisoners from the dungeon moldering in the bowels of the hideous place.

As the men ran off, some up the stairs, their sandals or bare feet slapping the floor, the barks of pistols sounding presently, echoing up and down the halls, Prophet dropped to a knee beside the girl. "You're all right, senorita. No one's gonna hurt you. *Comprende?*" He switched to his cow-pen Spanish, gesturing with his hands. "We're here to set you free."

The girl stared at him in awe, her brown eyes wide. Relief washed over her round features, and her thin lips shaped a shivering smile. "You are the one called Prophet!"

She grabbed his arm with both her small hands, digging her fingers in. "You have come like she said you would!"

"Who?" Prophet asked, unable to control his own excitement. Only one person could have told the girl about him. "Who said I would?"

"La muchacha rubia!"

The girl's voice was nearly drowned by more gunfire inside the building, the shots echoing loudly with the screams and shouts of fighting, dying men. Prophet set his pistols on the floor and grabbed the girl's shoulders, shaking her gently, unable to contain his own excitement.

Ever since he'd heard that Louisa had been taken, he'd been sure he'd find her ravaged body along the trail. Or worse, he'd never find her at all and he'd have to finish out his days, wondering what had happened to the beautiful, persnickety, young hazel-eyed blond — beautiful like a stalking panther, some would say, for there were few deadlier bounty killers than Louisa Bonaventure — who'd been born and raised in Nebraska Territory by a family she'd seen mercilessly butchered by cutthroats.

"Where, senorita?" Prophet pleaded with the girl. "Where is the *muchacha rubia?*"

She pointed up the stairs and prattled off Spanish too fast for Prophet to follow beyond gathering that Louisa was two flights of stairs up and on this side of the building. He stopped another of Big Tio's men making his way into the foyer and ordered the man to give his serape to the girl and to stay with her until it was safe to take her out.

As the older, fatherly gent quickly lifted his serape over his head and knelt down beside the girl, Prophet holstered his pistols and hustled up the stone steps, breeching his shotgun and replacing the spent wads with fresh. He quickly checked out the second story, finding nothing but empty rooms, before heading up to the third, where, as he strode slowly along the dim hall, his ears sharply pricked, he saw a shadow move under a door.

The door was not latched, and as Prophet stopped in front of it, it moved slightly.

He stopped, squared his shoulders, and rammed his right boot against the heavy door. A man gave a cry as Prophet bolted into the room, his shotgun in one hand, a Colt in the other, and saw a scrawny, curly-

hips, noting the scrapes and bruises on her long, pale legs. He set his guns down on each side of the girl, noting that her chest rose and fell faintly.

Tipping his head over her chest, he was grateful to hear a heartbeat, albeit a faint one.

"Louisa." His voice was low and thick with restrained emotion. "Jesus, girl, what in the hell'd that old bastard do to you?"

He choked back a sob as he inspected her face — her beautiful angel's face that was now puffed and bruised, eyes swollen shut, the rich full lips cracked, her cheeks torn from the slaps of powerful, be-ringed hands. Louisa's breasts were red mottled, chafed. There were even knuckle-shaped bruises on her flat belly, and on her hips were what could only be cigar burns.

Prophet reached up to pull his big bowie knife from the sheath tethered behind his neck and cut the girl's right wrist free of the poster.

"It's okay, Louisa. You're gonna be all right. Ole Lou's here, and he's gonna get you outta here."

He reached over to free the girl's other wrist and stopped. He'd heard something. Looking around quickly, he saw a cigar smoldering in a stone ashtray on a table

29

beside the bed, near a half-filled glass of clear liquid — probably tequila. His gaze continued roaming and stopped on the heavy drapes over the windows. They were billowing ever-so-slightly.

Might only be the breeze through the window, but . . .

Prophet's eyes dropped to the floor beneath the moving drapes and bored angrily into two pale, bare, bunion-gnarled feet that appeared between the drapes and the floor.

Prophet hardened his jaw and, scooping up both Colts from beside Louisa, stepped down from the bed.

3

Prophet ratcheted back the Colts' hammers and held them out before him as he crossed the room and stopped six feet away from the drapes. He looked down at the bare feet. They hadn't moved since he'd first spied them from the bed, and for a moment he wondered if they weren't part of some ugly stone statue.

The velvet drapes moved again slightly, as though a round paunch was pushing against them from the other side.

Suddenly, one of the feet moved, and a voice snarled as a bare arm shoved the drapes back to reveal a naked man with a large, bulbous belly and long, birdlike, blue-veined legs lunging toward Prophet with a pearl-gripped knife raised high in his right hand.

His silver-streaked hair was thin, his face hawkish, with eyes so deep-set it was impossible to tell their color. He reeked of smoke and tequila and sweat, and as he lunged toward Prophet, whipping the knife toward Prophet's neck, the bounty hunter triggered both pistols.

The booms thundered in the close quarters, the maws flashing brightly.

The naked man — it had to be Major Montoya himself, who always kept the prettiest of his prisoners for his own sick pleasure — jerked back against the drapes and the wall flanking them, between the two tall windows. Squeezing his eyes closed and sucking a sharp breath through gritted, yellow teeth, he twisted around, dropping the knife and clamping his hands over the twin bullet holes in his belly, just above his pale, limp pecker.

He dropped to his knees, threw his head back, and loosed a tooth-gnashing scream. When the scream's echoes had died, his wide, pain-racked eyes raked Prophet venomously. "Who are you, gringo bastard? And what are you doing in my private quarters — you who have the manners of a backstreet cur!"

Prophet would have loved to keep the man alive for a while, to let him die slowly as his blood and guts leaked out on the polished flagstones around his bony, white knees. But he had Louisa to tend to.

"Love to stay an' chat, but I gotta run, Major. Suffice it to say that girl over there's a real good friend of mine. So when you see El Diablo, which you're about to do in about three seconds, tell him his old friend Prophet said to crank the furnace up."

The major's eyes opened wider, as did his mouth, but Prophet rendered the man's scream stillborn by drilling two .45 slugs through each temple, hammering him back into the wall behind him with a sharp thud and then a groan of the man's released final breath.

As he hit the floor, he gave a loud fart, and kicked his spindly legs wildly. Prophet holstered his pistols and hurried back to the bed, where he cut Louisa free of the other posters, wrapped her up in a blanket, and picked her up in his arms.

"You with me, girl?" he said, turning toward the door he'd blown open. "Stay with me, all right? Wouldn't hurt if you said somethin' or opened your eyes a little, let ole Lou know you know I'm here."

As Prophet passed through the door, Louisa gave a groan. Her eyes fluttered, and she rolled her head toward him, burying her face in his bicep.

"Good enough," Prophet said as he moved through the office toward the dim hall beyond. "That's good enough for now."

He found his way to the door through which he'd entered the building and stood blinking in the sunlight at the top of the steps. Two covered wagons had been driven into the yard and stopped amongst several Rurales lying dead in the dirt.

Big Tio's revolutionarios were scurrying about the wagons with the group of young girls standing nearby, sobbing and shading their eyes against the sunshine. Just led up from the dungeons in the prison bowels, they all looked disheveled in their sackcloth dresses, their hair hanging limp and luster-less. Several showed bruises on their young, pretty faces and on their bare legs. That some had been forced to walk from where they'd been captured was evident by their bloody, swollen feet.

The revolutionarios in the yard were led by Big Tio's daughter, Chela. The scrappy, hot-blooded Mexican woman would have passed for one of the men in her peasant garb — red calico blouse, red neckerchief, baggy duck trousers, and rope-soled sandals — if not for her nicely curved hips and the two swollen mounds pushing out from behind her billowing blouse. She was direct-ing several men to carry the released girls up into the wagons as she gave each a cursory inspection for injuries.

The youngest was a little, round-faced, black-haired girl of eight or nine, and this one Chela picked up in her arms, cooing to the child as she led one of the revolution-arios with another child in tow to the second wagon around which the wind lifted a tan-colored dust cloud.

Meanwhile, Big Tio was directing a small contingent of his men to haul the Gatling gun down out of the guard tower he'd oc-cupied. The big man, corpulently regal with his gray beard, deerskin leggings, and red sash, shouted Spanish epithets while point-ing up at the tower, where three men were rigging the gun with ropes. One, a square-faced gent called Benito, gave back the old revolutionario as good as he was giving, pointing and grunting curses.

Prophet carried Louisa down the steps and over the dead Rurale at the bottom. Hearing hoof clomps, he turned to see a string of saddle horses being led through the open gates by one of the peasant boys, Ramon. Only ten years old, Ramon was as good with horses as any full-grown man Prophet had ever known.

The bounty hunter moved past the small group of battered, terrified senoritas toward his own horse, which Ramon was leading directly behind him on a short lead line, as the lineback dun, whom Prophet had appropriately named Mean and Ugly, did not get along with others. In fact, he'd fight like a grizzly at the challenging roll of another horse's eye. And if there were mares in the remuda, things could get dusty and bloody rather quickly.

"Where you going, Lou?"

Prophet stopped and turned around. Chela stood behind him. She'd placed the girl in the wagon, and her arms were free. She looked at Prophet now through big, brown eyes that were slightly almond-shaped in a flat, mestizo-featured face that owned the sizzling, exotic beauty of the untamed.

"She'll ride with me."

Chela jerked her head toward the wagon. "Put her in there with the others."

Prophet held Louisa more tightly against him, reluctant to let her go. He'd journeyed a long way for her, traveling countless miles all the while thinking she might be dead. He'd burned with that hollowed-out feeling of a loss you knew could never be made up again. Not if you lived a thousand more years.

"No." Prophet looked down at the battered blond in his arms and shook his head.

"Gonna put her on my horse."

Chela moved toward him, her red bandanna fluttering about her long, brown neck, and glanced between Prophet's face and Louisa's. "She's special, yes?"

"We rode some hard trails together."

"Then you want the best for her."

Prophet sighed. He knew Chela was right. He just didn't want to take his hands off Louisa's warm, reassuring form.

The young Mexican woman's rich lips quirked an understanding smile. "She'll be better off in the wagon, with me and the other girls. In her condition, she does not belong on a horse."

She snaked her arms under Louisa. Prophet found himself resisting, keeping his own arms wrapped tightly around Louisa's sheet-wrapped figure. Finally, he let her go.

"You can ride close to the wagon," Chela said. "You don't have to let her out of your sight. But she must ride in the wagon, you crazy gringo." As she turned with Louisa in her arms, the beautiful revolutionaria cast a flirtatious glance over her shoulder. "I'm jealous now, you bastard. I thought it was only me you had eyes for."

Prophet followed Chela to the wagon and watched as Big Tio's comely daughter wrapped Louisa in bobcat hides while the other girls sat around in starry-eyed shock, some sobbing uncontrollably into their hands or covering their heads with skins. Prophet was not encouraged that Louisa did not open her eyes. She groaned, sort of whimpered a couple of times, but otherwise kept her eyes closed, and she said nothing.

It hit him like a sledge, nearly buckling his knees.

She was going to die.

Rage like a flash fire shouldered out the dread, and he resisted the urge to go back into the building and fill Montoya's lifeless carcass with a few more .45 rounds. He ground his teeth but stepped back as Chela, cooing to the smallest girl, who sobbed uncontrollably, walked around the wagon and climbed fleetly into the box.

"Let's go!" she yelled to her father and Benito, who were wrestling the Gatling gun onto the back of a mule someone had hauled out of the Rurale stables flanking the prison. "They probably have a couple of patrols out, Papa. We'd best hightail it before they get back. I don't want any shooting around my girls!"

"Don't worry, my lovely daughter," Big Tio yelled as Chela turned the first wagon in a broad arc around the yard. "If we're pestered, we now have a lovely new Gatling gun to clear any and all lobos from our back trail!"

Laughing heartily and taking the mule's lead rope in his gloved left hand, Big Tio swung into the saddle of his Appaloosa mustang as his daughter's wagon thundered past him toward the open gates. The second wagon, driven by a young peasant boy in a broad, low-crowned sombrero and with a savage scar on his chin and a big pistol wedged behind his rope belt, followed Chela's wagon around the yard and out the gates.

Prophet rode up to Big Tio and several men mounting their saddled horses while a half dozen others continued to strip guns and ammo from the dead Rurales strewn about the yard as though they'd been dropped from the sky. Several other rebels were hauling loot out of the prison building's gaping doors. Mostly they carried burlap bags of meat, beans, and liquor including demijohns of wine and clear bottles of tequila, pulque, and bacanora. Some of the older peons were smoking good cigars.

They weren't lingering, but the anticipatory expressions on their Indian-dark, haggard faces — even the boys in their teenaged years looked like well-traveled men of thirty or so — told Prophet they'd have a tail-stomping good time this evening in their village of Rocas Altas, high up in the valleys of the Montanas Olvidadas, or "the Forgotten Mountains." A remote, forbidding range haunted by both the Apache and the Yaqui as well as many wild, dangerous animals including the puma, it was forty miles by way of several connected barrancas east of here.

"I'm gonna stay with the wagons," Prophet told Big Tio, looking around to make sure no Rurales had been left alive. He hadn't needed to. The old revolutionario leader's men had made fast, savage work of the corrupt rural policemen, leaving several of the worst offenders with bloody gashes where their privates had been.

Before Prophet could nudge Mean and Ugly's flanks with his heels, Big Tio said, "I see you got your girl back, eh, Padre?"

"So far."

"How does she look? Not so good?"

Prophet gritted his teeth as another burn of raw fury seared him, and he glanced toward the massive prison building from the open windows of which the smoke of set fires curled like fog. "Not so good. But she'll make it."

He wished like hell he could believe it.

As the bounty hunter gigged Mean into the sifting dust of the wagons rattling off across the bench fronting the courtyard, Big Tio yelled behind him, "I'll stop and say a prayer for her at the shrine of Guadalupe. The saint will look after your girl, Lou. You may want to stop there yourself."

"I reckon I better not," Prophet grunted to himself.

Yeah, you'd better not, he thought. *Your praying days ended the day you sold your soul to the Devil, you big dumb son of a bitch. Now what're you gonna do? Louisa needs help, and you don't even have a god to pray to for her.*

He tipped the straw sombrero low and put Mean and Ugly into a gallop, chewing up the sand and sage and looking around warily for returning Rurale patrols. He almost wished he'd see one. The day was still young, and there were still a good twenty, thirty Rurales from here whom he'd like to kick out with a shovel.

He didn't know which ones had sprung the trap on Louisa and the peasant girls — the senoritas had all been washing clothes at a stream when they'd been captured, with several older women killed outright — but as far as Prophet was concerned, there wasn't an innocent Rurale in all of northern

41

Mexico.

The next one he saw would die hard.

4

Prophet took a swig from his canteen as he rode, wishing he'd given Louisa some water. That might have brought her around. She probably wouldn't have drunk it, but he should have tried. Soon, he'd have Chela stop the wagon — by Pozos de Cobre, maybe, or Copper Wells — and he'd make sure she got water. He doubted that she or any of the other girls had been given much to drink or eat since they'd been carted off to the prison.

Prophet ground the cork into the canteen's mouth with the heel of his hand and cursed himself. He shouldn't have let Louisa part ways with him back in the Seven Devils Range on the Arizona-Mexico border.

He'd last seen her after they'd run to ground the Three of a Kind Gang, who'd killed her cousin and her cousin's family and burned the entire village of Seven

43

Devils to the rocky ground. Prophet, Louisa, and the young man from Seven Devils, Big Hans, who'd guided them into the mountains after the butchers, had killed the gang bloody, leaving their carcasses, including that of their demonic, beautiful female leader, to the diamondbacks and buzzards in a sunblasted canyon where their gnawed bones were likely now strewn like matchsticks.

Louisa had pointed her pinto northwest, with no destination in that stubborn, independent mind of hers. Just an urge to be alone and to ride. That had been two months ago.

Prophet and Mean and Ugly had headed down to Monterrey, and they'd both stomped with their tails up for a good week, Prophet spending most of his time playing poker and getting to know a big-breasted half-breed *puta* named Riget right down to the leaf-shaped birthmark on the back of her right thigh, just below the lovely globe of her smooth, tan butt cheek.

Mean and Ugly had torn a stable apart while expressing his affection for a buckskin named Linda. Prophet had had to rescue the ugly dun from a stableman's bullet twice. Still, he'd intended to stay with the sultry Riget for another week — he liked her digs and the sound of her lusty chuckles — and he'd likely still be tumbling with the girl, and drinking her liquor, if he hadn't gotten wind of a bank robbery just north of there.

Two young peasant girls had been killed in a hail of gunfire as the banditos had trampled a young pregnant peasant mother and headed north . . . toward the Montanas Olvidadas.

Prophet didn't know what it was that had warned him of danger. Maybe his own sixth sense acquired from years of man hunting on the western frontier after barely surviving the War of Northern Aggression. Or possibly a weird lining up of certain stars in his and Louisa's signs — though it was she who believed in such blather, not him. But a prickling between his heart and his spine told him that Louisa would be on the trail of those child-killing wolves, and that it wasn't a trail the lovely blond bounty hunter needed to be on alone.

Not in Mexico or anywhere else. Sure as hell not in the forbidding Olvidadas.

That's where he had picked up her trail, after he'd cut that of the banditos — all four of whom she'd taken down in a deep canyon not far from Rocas Altas. Prophet hadn't learned how she'd handled it. Knowing

Louisa, she'd used her charms as well as her guns, maybe even the razor-edged stiletto she kept in her boot. She might have shown up around the bandits' campfire like a vision straight from a young man's lusty dream, only to leave all four dancing with El Diablo behind the smoking gates of hell.

She'd laid over in Rocas Altas — coincidentally the village where Big Tio's revolutionarios had been holed up as well — and that's where Montoya had gotten her. Likely caught her off guard while she was enjoying a few days in the remote mountains with the innocent village children, tending her tack and gathering trail supplies while letting her horse rest before moving on. Having had her own childhood cut short by bloody murder, Louisa loved being around children — when she wasn't hunting those that killed them, that was.

Prophet kept Mean and Ugly close to the back of Chela's wagon, not minding that he was eating its dust. Occasionally, Big Tio's comely daughter turned to look through the covered wagon at him, over the jostling dark heads of the Mexican girls. Louisa's blond head was all but covered by the hides, but Prophet kept his eyes on the swatch of hair he could see of her, in case she needed him.

"We stop here," Chela said an hour after

46

they'd left the prison, the backside of which they could see in the canyon below them, black smoke rising into the brassy sky above.

Prophet also saw Big Tio's men galloping toward him and the wagon over the low, cedar- and manzanita-stippled hogbacks, their horses looking bulky with stolen Rurale loot.

Chela had stopped the wagon by a stream, and while the lovely revolutionaria and the boy with the horse pistol wedged behind his rope belt helped the Mexican girls out of the wagons, Prophet grabbed his canteen, stepped off Mean and Ugly and into the wagon in which Louisa lay unmoving beneath the bobcat hide. He dropped down beside her and tipped her face toward him.

Beneath the purple bruises, she looked paler than before. Waxy. Prophet's heart thudded. Had she died on him without so much as a parting word? He doffed his hat, lowered his head to her chest.

Faintly, her heart thumped.

He popped the canteen's cork and, snaking his left arm around behind her head, tipped the flask to her cracked, swollen lips. "How 'bout some water, girl? Huh? How 'bout it? Why don't you take a drink for ole Lou?"

Her lips didn't move. Her swollen eyes

remained closed. As swollen as they were, she probably couldn't get them open if she tried.

Prophet felt as though a sharp knife were poking around in his guts. Frustrated, he sighed and lowered the canteen from Louisa's lips. As if in response to his sigh, she gave a soft sigh of her own. Her head moved slightly, as though shaking her head. As if to say, *not now, Lou. I'll drink later.* At least, that's what he hoped she meant. That she was conscious enough to refuse the water.

"Okay," Prophet said, ramming the cork back into the canteen as hope softened the edge on that knife in his guts. "Maybe later. I'll let you sleep now."

He glanced over at the creek twisting through sycamores and poplars beside which the rescued girls sat with their knees up and staring or leaning forward to drink from the cool, running stream. Chela sat beside one of the girls, smoothing the senorita's hair back from her forehead with one hand while offering bits of jerky with the other. Another girl was sobbing against the shoulder of yet another, older child.

Prophet's heart wrenched. What misery they'd all been through. Yet, they had each other. Soon, they'd be home with their families. Louisa had no one but him. No one waiting for her with a warm fire and a hot meal.

Just Prophet himself — a down-at-heel, bounty-hunting saddle tramp. And all he had were empty pockets, a few pots and one change of clothes in his saddlebags, guns, ammo, tack, and a hammer-headed lineback dun.

That's all he had, and that's all she had. The last of her known family had been killed in Seven Devils.

He imagined the anguish being played out behind those swollen-shut eyes, and he groaned. He slumped down beside the comatose girl, wrapped his arm around her shoulders, pressed his lips to her forehead. "Gonna get you well again soon."

He stared off at the ridge above the stream. "Good as damn new, and then things are gonna change for us both."

The horseback revolutionarios, several of whom were passing bottles or stone jugs between them, caught up to the wagons a few minutes after the girls had been loaded up and they were moving again. Prophet hung back with Louisa, keeping an eye on her, as they climbed the zigzagging canyon high into the blue reaches of the Forgotten Mountains.

The cool air was a welcome relief from the heat of the desert below. As he rode, Prophet remembered he was barefoot. He reached back into his saddlebags for his socks and boots, and then he pulled out his battered, funnel-brimmed Stetson that was stained from salt sweat and the weather of many western lands. While it wasn't as good protection from the high-country sun as the broad-brimmed sombrero, he was more familiar with it.

He clamped it down on his head and adjusted the curled brim.

They crested the last pass just before sundown, and as Prophet followed Chela's wagon down the rocky two-track trail, he saw the small village spread out across the boulder-strewn bowl ahead of him. Rocas Altas had once been a small, sprawling city nurtured by gold and silver mines, but earthquakes over the past hundred years had nearly obliterated it.

Ancient adobe and stone ruins hunched in the sage amongst the cracked boulders and cedars, but it was only a dozen or so brush huts, quickly erected so that they could be just as quickly abandoned at the first sign of an Apache, Yaqui, or Rurale attack, that were occupied. On the steep slopes all around the village rode the tawny grass parks on which goats grazed. On the far side of the village, a high, massive stone ridge rose like a giant, dilapidated castle angling away. Its steep slopes were pocked with the tailings of long-abandoned mines.

Because of the frequent quakes, the place was too dangerous to mine. But it was a good place for Big Tio's band of revolution-arios to hide out from the Rurale and Fed-erale troops as well as the wealthy landown-ers they intermittently badgered in revenge for the savage exploitation of the landless peon.

As the wagons squawked and rattled into the village, the families ran out from their brush huts or horse stables or chicken coops, scattering chickens and goats, and screaming and yelling and sobbing their delight at having their children safely re-turned to them. The old men who'd re-mained in the village with the women shook the hands of the men and boys who'd rescued the girls, and Prophet himself endured many grateful slaps and hand pumps.

He had to refuse several bottles and jugs thrust at him as Mean and Ugly shied from the din of the growing revelry as the other horses, having their tack stripped away, nickered and rolled. The big bounty hunter yearned for a drink of the raw Mexican bacanora, as well as a smoke and a plate of carne asada, but he couldn't relax until he'd gotten Louisa into a warm bed and tended her wounds. Pushing Mean up through the crowd milling around him, he stepped down from the horse and into the wagon, in which only his blond partner remained, and gently scooped her up in his arms.

"What're you doing?"

He looked over the tailgate. Chela stood, hair blowing, against the rosy ball of the sun rimming the purple peaks behind her. "Gonna take her into the stable." He'd been holing up in the stable behind Big Tio's jacale while he and the revolutionario had devised their plan to rescue the girls from the prison.

"She needs more attention than you can give her, fool. Stay there!" Prophet eased Louisa back down to the wagon bed as he watched Chela climb back into the driver's box and release the brake. He sank down quickly, nearly being thrown down as the lovely revolutionaria shook the ribbons over the backs of the tired team, and the wagon lunged forward, the wheels squawking loudly once more.

They rattled off into the brush beyond the main village, past the ancient church that had been cleaved in two rough halves by an earthquake, and across two shallow arroyos. Mean and Ugly followed at an anxious trot, not wanting to be left amongst the revelers. Five minutes later they passed a small brush stable and stinky hog pen and pulled up at the base of the high ridge that bordered the village's northeast end.

Prophet stared over the driver's box and the mules at what appeared to be a glow emanating from a crack in the ridge's sheer rock.

There was a broad fire pit near the crack, and a dog ran out from the ridge, barking and snarling. The beast appeared part coyote; its ribs shone through its dull yellow coat, and its hackles were raised sharply.

"Silencio, Christos!" ordered Chela, setting the wagon's brake. "*Silencio* now, or I will give you the bullet you have so long deserved!"

"Don't shoot my dog!" a voice of indeterminate sex screeched near the base of the ridge that was a soft salmon color in the mountain gloaming. "He brings my rattlesnakes!"

She'd spoken so quickly in Spanish that Prophet must have misunderstood her. She must have said the dog *killed* rattlesnakes, not *brought* them. Anyway, he was only half listening while looking around curiously as the dog barked at him from the end of the wagon. Chela appeared at the back of the wagon, kicking the dog, who yipped and ran off, then beckoned to Prophet.

"Bring the girl. This is the home of Sister Magdalena. If your friend can be healed, she is the one to do it." Chela's eyes widened impatiently as Prophet stayed where he was, hearing crippled-up old feet shuffling along the ground on the other side of the wagon's dirty white canvas. "Come, I said. She's not getting any better in there!"

Reluctantly, Prophet picked up Louisa in his arms and, keeping the blanket and the bobcat hide wrapped around her, carried her to the end of the wagon and handed her down to Chela, who grunted a little under the weight. Prophet leaped to the ground and, seeing a hunched figure with a raisin face slouch toward him, took Louisa back in his arms.

Some old Indian healer, Prophet thought, trepidation a cool hand on the back of his neck. This crone might very well do more harm than good.

5

Chela saw the reluctance in the bounty hunter's face as the old woman — she was a good seventy years old, at least, though it was hard to tell a person's age up here in this tough country where folks grew old well before their time — shuffled up to Prophet and lifted her head to get a look at Louisa.

"Que nos tienen aqui?" the old woman asked. It was like a crow's hushed caw, rising from deep in her narrow chest under a heavy, black shawl.

"A gringa, Sor Magdalena," Chela told the crone. "One who has been badly treated by the Rurales."

"Montoya?" the crone growled.

"Si."

Sor Magdalena chuffed her disgust, then, heading for the ridge, threw up a spidery old hand for Chela and Prophet to follow her. Chela glanced at Prophet and fell in behind the old woman, who limped deeply on both hips. Prophet followed with Louisa hanging limp in his arms.

Ahead of him, he saw that the crack in the ridge wall was wider than he'd thought. It was about the size of a cabin door, but jagged-edged, the top slanting down on the right.

The old woman ducked under it, followed by Chela, glancing once more at Prophet, and then he had to nearly double over to get through the low opening. When he did, he straightened with a wince at the pain in his tired lower back and looked around at the cave, which was furnished as well as any cabin, with a charcoal brazier in a corner breathing smoke up through a crack in the ceiling.

The natural shelves in the walls contained a hodgepodge of provisions, from airtight tins to small burlap and rawhide pouches spewing what appeared to be roots and herbs. The place reeked improbably of horseradish and turpentine and several other things Prophet couldn't place. Talismans hung from the walls. Some were Christian while others — including deer and wolf skulls, snakeskins and fangs, and bones of every shape and size — were pagan. They reminded Prophet of the hill folks he'd known back home in Georgia.

His stomach roiling against the stench of the place, Prophet jerked with a start when the crone barked at him in Spanish as she stood over a pallet of deerskins, beckoning.

"Set the gringa down there," Chela ordered. "Sor Magdalena will see what she can do."

Prophet glanced at the old woman skeptically. She stared back at him through molasses-dark eyes set deep in wizened, brick-red sockets. Her thin lips were moving and she was frowning impatiently, sort of mewling and grunting like an animal.

Prophet wasn't sure he wanted to put Louisa in the care of this old she-cat, but he wasn't exactly overrun with options. Staggering forward, ducking to keep the crown of his hat from brushing the rocky ceiling on which weird, brand-like signs were etched, he crossed to the woman, knelt, and gently settled Louisa onto the pallet.

Louisa groaned. Her puffy eyelids fluttered. She licked her lips, swallowed, and made a sobbing sound as she rolled onto one side, raising her knees toward her belly.

She was in pain. Physical as well as mental agony. Prophet could feel it himself, and his trigger finger itched with the desire to kill Montoya all over again.

The old woman dropped to her knees

beside Louisa and began pulling down the bobcat skin she'd been wrapped in. Prophet remained where he was, his stomach burning with worry and dread. Chela gave his shirt a tug, and he looked up at her.

"Come," she said, canting her head toward the door.

"I wanna stay with her."

"You go, big gringo." Prophet was surprised to hear the well-spoken English issuing from the crone, who kept her head down as she removed the hide from Louisa's curled form. "I take care of your girl."

Maybe it was the familiarity of the woman's English or just the fact that she'd addressed him directly, sounding halfway sane, but he suddenly felt a little less apprehensive about leaving Louisa there in her care.

"All right." He sighed, pushing off his thighs and heaving himself to his feet. "Much obliged, Senora. I'm gonna hang around, and I'd appreciate it if you'd let me know how she's doing."

The crone said nothing but only continued mewling and muttering to herself as she worked, and Chela pulled Prophet over to the door. She ducked out, and glancing at Louisa once more, Prophet went out as well.

"I'll trust you on this, Chela," Prophet said, doffing his hat and slapping it against his dusty denims. "But I don't like how it smells in there."

"It smells like healing in there, idiot." Chela rammed her shoulder against his flirtatiously. "Sor Magdalena was a nun back before the last earthquake wiped out the church."

"A nun?"

"*Si.* But she learned from the Yaqui, who used to haunt these mountains, about healing. And from the Apaches, too, as well as several other tribes. Over the years, she's learned what works best in all the traditions she studied, and she's very effective. I once saw her heal a man whose arm turned black after a fox bit him."

"He lose the arm?"

"Does Big Tio not have two arms?"

"I'll be damned."

"*Si.* I treat you right so far, haven't I, Lou?" Chela smiled up at him. "Let's get a drink."

"Nah, I'm gonna hang around here." Prophet strode wearily over to where Mean and Ugly cropped bits of wiry brown brush near the wagon, his reins dangling. "Gonna stable Mean, give him some water and feed, and hang around the corral till I hear about Louisa."

Chela followed him, her hands in her back

59

pockets. "She really means a lot to you, huh, Lou?"

"We been up and down the river, Louisa and me." He grabbed Mean's reins and led the sweat-lathered horse toward the empty brush corral.

"Don't worry." Chela climbed into the wagon and released the brake. "Sor Magdalena can help her if anyone can."

Prophet swung the corral gate open. It chirped loudly in the gloaming's hushed silence, only mourning doves cooing in the far scrub. He stood staring toward the wagon as Chela turned the team in front of the cave's dimly lit door and started back toward the corral. "I'm much obliged to you, Senorita."

"My father and I are obliged to you, Lou." The revolutionaria shook her black hair back from her face as she smiled admiringly. "Or should I call you Father Prophet now?"

Prophet chuckled.

The girl hoorawed the mules back out of the yard and across a shallow arroyo, turning the team on the other side of the cut and heading off toward the village from which victorious whoops and hollers emanated, as well as the raucous strains of a mandolin.

Prophet led the dun into the corral and

shut the gate, securing the rawhide latch. He stripped the bridle and saddle from Mean and Ugly's back, then jumped away as the horse immediately plopped into the dirt and rolled wildly, snorting and kicking up dust in all directions. Prophet set the tack atop the corral, casting anxious glances toward the ridge that was darkening quickly as the sun fell, the jagged-edged door brightening with candlelight flickering inside the cave.

After the horse was done rolling and Prophet had stayed well back from the scissoring hooves, he rubbed him down carefully and thoroughly with burlap from his saddlebags, taking his time and letting the horse cool down. That done, and glancing over his shoulder lest the horse should give him a playful nip and tear out another shirt seam, he headed off in search of water.

He found a well near the ridge and brought a bucket of the achingly cold liquid back to the corral and filled the hollowed-out log trough. When the horse had drunk, Prophet draped a feed bag with a couple pounds of oats over his ears, then walked out into the brush to relieve himself, taking a long drink from the spring, pouring the cool, refreshing water over his head and then shaking his hair out, ridding himself of a couple of inches of trail dust.

Heading back to the ridge, he resisted the urge to poke his head into the cave. The crone might lop it off with one of the several big, bone-handled knives he'd seen lying about the place.

He removed Mean and Ugly's feed sack from the horse's head, then paced for a time in the yard while the horse stuck its head over the top corral slat, watching him while curiously twitching his ears. The sun died. Prophet could see fires flicking around the village a half mile away. Shadows moved about them. Mandolin and guitar chords rose above the din of the villagers' revelry.

Goats bleated. A dog barked. Someone pounded a kettle. In the distant hills, coyotes yammered as if joining the village debauch.

Finally, after he'd been pacing around the brush and rocks fronting the ridge for over two hours, he gave an impatient grunt and tramped over to the door. A rich fetor slammed against him, stopping him in his tracks. He grimaced and was about to continue forward when the crone's hunched silhouette appeared in the door.

"She sleeps," the woman squawked.

Then she reached up to let a grass mat fall over the doorway, and only a jagged-edged strip of darkness showed before him.

Prophet cursed. He went back over to the corral, dropped his saddle in the dirt near the gate, and unrolled his blanket roll. He was too edgy to eat so he rolled a quirley and smoked until Chela brought him a plate from the village, and the smell of the spiced goat meat and fresh tortillas and cactus syrup made his stomach bark for joy.

He ate with unexpected hunger, swigging tequila from the bottle that Chela had brought with the food. The revolutionaria said nothing but only sat beside Prophet, sharing the bottle with him as they rested their backs against the same corral post. When he was finished, scrubbing the last bit of goat gravy from the plate with a scrap of tortilla, Chela left the bottle and, grinding her quirley out in the dirt beneath her sandal, leaned down to give his cheek a tender peck.

Swinging her full, lovely hips, she strode off toward the village.

Prophet finished the bottle, smoking, then slept fitfully against his saddle. Near dawn, the sky just beginning to turn lilac, he rose to evacuate his bladder and to study the cave door. It was black, and no sounds issued from behind it.

He dropped down, pulled his blankets up

against the high mountain chill, heard Mean and Ugly snort wearily, then tumbled back into restive slumber.

Something prodded his side.

He jerked with a start, lifting his head up. The old woman stood over him, staring down at him. Behind her, the sky was bright blue though dawn shadows lingered amongst the rocks and cactus, and the ridge was purple. The sun was somewhere behind it.

He stared up at the woman who stared down at him, pursing her withered old lips. She shook her head grimly, then slumped back toward the ridge.

Prophet's blood jetted through his veins, and his temples hammered. He sat up, throwing his blankets back.

"What the hell does that mean?"

The old woman disappeared inside the cave.

"Did she die?" Prophet called, hearing his voice crack.

Quickly, he pulled his boots on and ran to the ridge. He pushed through the grass mat and stopped just inside the door. The old woman stood over Louisa, who lay under the bobcat hides. Her swollen features were pasty and horrifically inert, her cracked lips slightly parted. A small rawhide pouch hung from her neck.

Prophet moved toward her, balling his fists at his sides. His heart turned somersaults in his chest. His voice quaked with anguish and fury as he said tautly, "Did you let her die, you old . . . ?"

A soft voice said, "Lou?"

At first, Prophet thought it had come from the old woman. Then he realized Louisa had said it, though her lips had barely moved. Her right cheek twitched. That was the only movement.

The crone looked up at Prophet, frowning. "You are Lou?"

"She's not dead," Prophet breathed to himself, forgetting the harsh smell of the place — the fetor of scorched herbs. He dropped his knees, reached under the bobcat hide, and pulled out Louisa's right hand, enclosing the tender limb in his own large, sunburned paws.

His voice shook with fragile relief. "She's not dead."

He called her name several times, smoothing her hair back from her piping hot forehead. Sweat beaded her skin, glinting brightly in the light from the fifty or so candles the old woman had lit around the cave.

Prophet was still calling to Louisa when

the woman touched his shoulder. He turned to see her kneeling beside him, a hide necklace in her hands. The hide was strung with what appeared claws of some kind, and the small, dried skull of what appeared a coyote.

A coyote pup with tiny, sharp teeth. Skinless, it appeared to be snarling.

"What the hell's this?"

"Put it on."

"Like hell, you crazy —"

"You can save her. She died once, but she has returned. She has said your name, calling to you from the other side. She wants you to pull her back to you."

Prophet stared at the crone in disbelief, his mind reeling. He looked at Louisa, who lay with her swollen eyes shut, her smashed lips etched with pain.

"Christ!" Prophet grabbed the necklace, draped it over his head. "How in the hell is this supposed to bring her back?"

The old woman shuffled off to return wielding a big, bone-handled knife in her tiny but strong, brown fist. For a moment, Prophet thought she was about to try carving his heart out. He jerked back a little when she thrust the blade at him, and his brows mantled heavily.

"Hey!"

"Hold up your left hand," squawked the crone.

"Huh?"

She gestured again with the knife, spittle flying from her lips. "Hold up your hand." She gestured at the left one.

"Now, hold on."

"She needs your blood. Hold up your hand. I cut just a bit."

Prophet had no idea what the old bat was up to. Something told him, however, she meant no harm, only to help. He'd let her try a little more of her sorcery, and if Louisa didn't come around, he'd haul her out of there and tend her himself, though what that would entail, he had no idea.

He held up his left hand, palm out, and winced as the crone swiped the knife's razor-edged blade across it. He felt the icy nip, looked at the long, red line running from the base of his index finger to the opposite side of the heel.

The crone set the knife aside, knelt down with a grunt, and peeled the bobcat hide down to Louisa's waist, exposing the girl's bare torso. She gestured for Prophet to run his bloody palm from Louisa's throat to her belly button.

He did so, smearing a long path of the blood down between the girl's breasts, feeling like a superstitious fool but too frightened and full of dread to care. At this point he'd have danced a jig on his hands around the old bitch's smelly cave, if it had a chance of bringing Louisa back to health.

He looked at the crone. "What now?"

"Shh!"

She stared down at Louisa, hands on her thighs. Prophet thought she might be praying, but her eyes were open. Finally, the old woman slid the bobcat hide up to Louisa's neck and sighed. She turned to Prophet, lifted the necklace over his head, snaked it over Louisa's, letting the coyote skull rest on her chest with the hide pouch, and said, "Now, we see."

Prophet spent a miserable day waiting around the cave door, which the crone kept covered with the grass mat. He paced, smoked, walked around the ridge and the village, accepted another plate from Chela but only picked at the corn tortillas and beans fried with spicy chicken.

His stomach was too knotted up for food.

He curried Mean and Ugly several times, trimming and tending all four hooves, adjusting the horse's iron shoes, just to keep busy. When the sun fell behind the toothy western ridges again, and he'd heard nothing from the cave, he threw back several shots of tequila and rolled up in his blankets, forcing himself to sleep.

Early the next morning, he woke with a start, jerking his head up and poking his hat back off his forehead. He looked around wildly, his cocked Colt in his hand.

He'd heard something. What?

It came again, rising from inside the cave — a female voice so familiar in its insouciant demand and inherent priggishness that he felt as though the long, fine fingers of angels were caressing the strain from his heart.

"Lou!"

6

Six weeks later, Prophet reined Mean and Ugly to a halt at the top of a low bench between craggy ridges in southern Wyoming Territory, a stone's throw from the Colorado line. He shuttled his glance from a signpost standing bold and straight and backed by a flat-topped boulder along the trail's right side, to the town sprawled in the shallow valley beyond.

"There it is," the bounty hunter said, rising high in his stirrups, then easing his 230 muscular pounds back against the cantle. "Juniper. Damn fine-lookin' place, sittin' down there along that little stream."

He glanced at Louisa, who reined her brown-and-white pinto up beside him and stared sullenly down at the saddle through the strands of her blond, wind-tussled hair. "I said — damn fine-lookin' village in one right purty settin' — wouldn't you say, Miss Persnickety Bitch?"

They'd argued three-quarters of the trail up from Mexico, over everything from Prophet's snoring keeping Louisa awake at night to her intolerance of his poor dish-washing abilities. Thus his new pet name for her, which she'd been ignoring to get his goat. As irksome as she was, and intoler-ant of his unheeled ways, he was as happy as a front-tit calf that she'd regained her health during the two months she'd spent recuperating in Rocas Altas, with the singu-lar Sor Magdalena acting as her own private nursemaid.

"Kind of hard to tell from here," she said, lifting her canteen from around her saddle horn and plucking the cork from its mouth with her gloved left hand, always leaving the right one free in case she needed to reach for one of her pearl-gripped Colts in a hurry. "You know how you are, Lou. You get something in your mind in a certain way, it'd take the Devil's own hounds to wrestle it out of your craw."

Prophet popped the cork on his own canteen and arched a sandy, sun-bleached brow at her. "Huh?"

She hiked a shoulder as she drank from the canteen as gracefully, Prophet absently mused, as a sixty-year-old schoolmarm would drink from a teacup that had been in the family for over a century. Only, the schoolmarm likely couldn't shoot the eye out of a galloping border bandit at a hundred and fifty yards.

Louisa lowered the canteen, sucking the excess moisture from her rich, lower lip, brushing a gloved hand across her chin, and favoring Prophet with a cool, hazel stare. "If you suddenly got it into that big mule's head of yours that the Sonora desert at high summer was about to see a boom in the ice trade, it would take your drowning in a melted ocean of it to convince you otherwise."

"That ain't true!" Prophet took a quick sip then pulled his canteen down sharply, indignantly. "I just like to look on the bright side of things, and I don't see nothin' wrong in doin' so. You're too negative — you know that? In fact, if a golden waterfall suddenly appeared right before your persnickety eyes, Miss Bonnyventure, why, you'd . . ."

Prophet let his voice trail off.

He stared at the girl regarding him with cool haughtiness, and the anger leached from his eyes. A more beautiful, albeit snooty, face he had never seen. It was heart-shaped, with a perfect, pug nose and the rich bee-stung mouth of a high-priced china doll . . . and no less pretty for having been abused so badly by Major Montoya back in that infernal Mexican hoosegow.

And seeing the few lingering remnants of the merciless beating Louisa had taken — a little graying around her eyes, a pale white scar on her right cheek, a not-quite-healed scab on her lower lip — Prophet realized that no one had more reason to look at life through shit-colored glasses than his beautiful, young partner, who had endured more than her share of misery in her twenty short years.

A rose of tenderness blossomed just behind his forehead and between his eyes. He sidled Mean and Ugly up as close as he dared to the girl's pinto, wrapped a big arm around her shoulders, drew her to him, tipped her head back, and closed his mouth over hers, kissing her tenderly.

"Lou, dangit!" she cried when the kiss had continued for nearly a minute, pulling away from him, gasping and clamping a hand over the crown of her tan felt hat before Prophet, in his overzealous affection, knocked it off her head. "Did you save me from the Rurales only to finish me off by sucking all the air out of my lungs, you ape?"

Prophet donned his hat. "I'm just damn glad to have you back, girl. And I'm pleased as the queen's own punch you agreed to make a fresh start with this old saddle tramp."

"You're not a saddle tramp. You're a bounty hunter." She reached over to brush a dried seed from the three-day growth of sandy beard on his broad, hard-lined face — a face that some would say was far too big, weathered, and scarred to be called handsome. "As am I," she added.

"Not anymore. You, Miss Bonnyventure, are about to join the ranks of the good, respectable citizens of Juniper, a town every bit as well-heeled as its name."

"Juniper, huh?"

Louisa stepped down from her pinto, tossed Prophet her reins, and strode into the rocks and brush beside the trail, her brown wool riding skirt buffeting about her long, well-turned legs and the tops of her undershot leather boots adorned with silver spurs. She scrounged around behind the town sign and the boulder flanking it and held up a gray-weathered plank announcing HELLDORADO in badly faded letters that might have been green at one time.

Louisa smiled cockily. "It appears to me that the good town of Juniper was once known by another name entirely. One bespeaking nothing so much as a hotbed of frivolous behavior and corruption of the lowest kind. Painted women and murderous rogues. Just the kind of town you once favored, Lou. You and your friend the Devil, or Ole Scratch, as you call him."

She grabbed the reins back from him and swung up into her saddle.

"You're gonna like it here, damnit," Prophet stubbornly assured the girl as they set off down the bench, each taking a track of the two-track wagon trail. "Helldorado was what the place was called — right appropriately — back before it was cleaned up by an old buddy of mine, the mossy-horned town tamer, Hiram Severin. Or 'Hell-Bringin' Hiram,' as he's been called in the illustrated newspapers."

Prophet chuckled. "I picked Juniper for you an' me special, 'cause Hell-Bringin' Hiram assured me it's as tame as any in the Rockies — tamer than most — and it ain't likely we'll be lured back to our crazy, sharp-horned ways here."

"We've tried this before, Lou."

"Tried what before?"

"Living lives with pianos in them, and picket fences, and a red stable behind a white frame house."

"No," Prophet said. "You tried it. Back in Seven Devils. And that was one bad piece of luck, Louisa. As bad a piece as I've seen

75

— or had seen till I pulled you out of that Rurale perdition. But I haven't tried it. You see — that's the difference. Maybe if we both walk the straight and narrow road, we won't so easily veer off into the tall and uncut."

He glanced at the girl riding off his right stirrup. She held her head forward, saying nothing. She hadn't said anything about what had happened to her back in Montoya's private quarters, and Prophet hadn't asked. He wasn't sure he wanted to know, but if she ever needed to tell him, she would.

One thing he did know — it had been hell. Otherwise, Louisa wouldn't have let him talk her into giving settling down another try. She hadn't jumped into the idea with both feet, but she hadn't slammed the door on it, either.

When Prophet had mentioned it late one night outside Sor Magdalena's cave and mapped out his plan about heading for Wyoming — about as far from Mexico and all the horrible stuff that had occurred there as one could get and not find himself hip-deep in a Canadian winter — she'd merely hiked a shoulder, nodded, lain back against her saddle, and rolled up in her blankets.

It had been hell, all right. And Prophet had held her every night while she'd screeched and squealed and sobbed it all out in her dreams.

Maybe here in Juniper, he thought as the first corrals and stock pens and a clattering windmill pushed up along the trail, she'd find relief from those nightmares and could finally put all of her sharp-edged memories to rest.

The town was good-sized and sprawling, though obviously not planned out very well. The main street sort of zigzagged, and new buildings were going up amidst the rubble of the old. There were still tent shacks here and there and log buildings that were part canvas and that bespoke the days when Helldorado was a hell-stomping hiders' and miners' camp. Whores' cribs flanked the tent saloons, and miners' shacks stood along the stream that angled along the town's north edge.

But everywhere Prophet looked as he and Louisa clomped along the street, weaving around parked or moving wagons and pausing as two muddy drovers chased a runaway bull from one side of the street to another while a shaggy collie dog nipped at the bellowing beast's kicking rear hooves, there were big two- and three-story wood frame buildings with false fronts announcing hotels and saloons and sandwich shops and breweries and laundries and ladies' hat shops and general stores and even toy stores and entire stores given over to books! Most were so new that the resin in the wood made the town smell like a pine forest — albeit a pine forest near a stockyard.

In the midst of it, and planted right smack in the middle of the street, with an old saloon tent on one side and Machiavelli's Mining Supplies on the other, stood a tall, narrow, richly ornate building of red brick and sandstone, and which large letters formed of black brick across the second story identified as the Juniper Opera House.

Prophet stopped Mean and Ugly in front of the place, which was barricaded off from the street by boards and sandbags, likely to keep runaway cows from breaking out the windows, and poked his hat off his forehead, whistling his awe.

"What's the matter — you've never seen an opera house before?" Louisa said in her condescending way.

"Why, sure I have. Even seen a gent up in Leadville last winter — fella named Oscar Wilde — give a talk on some dead Italian fella in the Tabor Opera House. Sissiest damn fool I ever did see, but he could talk the corn off a cob. But I sure as hell never expected to find an opry place as fancy as this one here this far off the beaten Wyoming path." Prophet chuckled and narrowed a hopeful eye at Louisa. "I reckon this place is even more civilized than I thought it was."

A man screamed behind them, and Prophet and Louisa turned to see that the bull had run up onto the boardwalk fronting a men's clothing shop, pinning a tall gent in a long, clawhammer coat and beaver opera hat against the building while the two drovers yelled and waved their hats and the dog barked and danced.

"I'd say it's still got some Helldorado in it," Louisa said with a chuckle.

Prophet gigged Mean and Ugly around the opera house, continuing up the main drag. "Well, it ain't New York City."

"So what do you have in mind for us here, Lou? I can't sing, so that sort of precludes the opera house. And you can't, either, in spite of your best efforts while bathing. Thank god that only comes around once a year!"

"Very funny, Miss Bonnyventure."

"I've told you — it's Bonaventure, you lout."

"Look around," Prophet said, swinging his gaze from one side of the street to the other. "There's every kind of shop you can think of. And look there, on the door of that haberdashery place. 'Help Wanted. Query Within.' "

"I can't see you selling buttons to old ladies in picture hats, Lou."

Prophet glanced to his left, and a well-dressed gent waved to him from the covered boardwalk in front of the Federated Bank and Trust of Southern Wyoming Territory. Prophet flushed and turned away sharply but checked Mean and Ugly down.

"You got my funny bone, Miss Bonnyventure." He pointed toward a boxlike, nondescript building ahead and on the street's right side. "There's a bathhouse. Why don't you go on over and scrub some trail dust off your purty little hide without starting a riot amongst the men folk. I'll be along in a minute."

"Where're you going?"

Prophet hesitated. "I'm gonna look for a livery barn."

"We passed three."

"Will you quit?" He jerked his chin at the bathhouse. "Go on and get yourself cleaned up now, and I'll see if I can scrounge up enough pocket jingle to buy you a steak and one o' them sarsaparillas you love so much."

"You're broke."

"Then you'll buy me a steak and a beer."

With a haughty chuff, Louisa booted the

80

pinto up the street. As she pulled up to one of the three hitchracks fronting the bathhouse, Prophet reined Mean over to the bank, where the well-dressed gent who'd waved and who also wore the five-pointed star of a county sheriff on the lapel of his black frock coat stood with a man even better dressed though slighter in build and puffing a long, black cheroot.

"Well, look what the damn cat dragged in," growled Hell-Bringin' Hiram Severin, standing beside the gent with the cigar while holding the flaps of his coat back from the two ivory-gripped Colts positioned for the cross draw on his lean hips. Beneath the brim of his black derby, he had a face like a crumbling old barn, and his knife-slash mouth was capped with a silver, soupstrainer mustache through which a gold front tooth flashed in the afternoon sunshine.

"What cat?" said the man next to him, puffing his cheroot as his black eyes strayed across the street to where Prophet had parted with Louisa. "It looked like a blond dragged him into town, and a pretty one at that." Not quite as old as the sheriff, who was in his early sixties, this man was hatless, with elegant silver-streaked hair combed straight back from a prominent

81

widow's peak, and a heavy Spanish accent.

"Nah, she didn't drag me." Prophet reined up in front of the boardwalk. "I had to drag her, though fortunately she didn't kick and scream too damn loud. It'll be the gents in the washhouse who'll be kickin' and screamin' when she starts takin' her clothes off."

Chuckling, the big, trail-worn bounty hunter stepped down from his saddle and, lifting his double-barreled shotgun up over his head and hanging it from his saddle horn by its wide leather lanyard, extended his hand to his old pal, Hiram Severin. "How'n the hell you been, you old chicken thief?"

"Better'n you look, ya damn brush wolf!" Severin pumped Prophet's hand with exuberance, and turned to the well-attired Mexican. "Don Jose Encina, bank president and mayor of Juniper, please meet your new gold guard, Lou Prophet."

7

Prophet remembered Encina's name from the telegram he'd received from Severin in response to his inquiry about employment in the sheriff's fair town. "Don, pleased to make your acquaintance. Sorry for the trail dust and foul odor, but I aim to fix that situation over to the bathhouse in two jangles of a whore's bell."

"The pleasure is mine, Senor Prophet," Encinca said, tapping ashes from his smoldering cheroot. "I have heard much about you from Sheriff Severin. Your inquiry for employment came at a most opportune time for us both, as I'd no sooner heard you were looking for work here in Juniper than I lost my head rider to an unfortunate horse accident, and the sheriff strolled into my office with your telegram under his hat."

"Well, then, I reckon we're both dancin' in high cotton!" Prophet chuckled. "When do I start?"

"Would be tomorrow be too early? I need a short run from . . ."

The bank president's eyes drifted past Prophet and into the street behind him. Hiram's Severin's gaze had wandered in the same direction, so Prophet swung around to see what they were looking at so intensely and felt his belly tighten.

"Ah, shit," he muttered.

Louisa was riding over from the direction of the bathhouse, within twenty yards and closing and cocking her head to one side, a suspicious look sitting hard on her pretty, heart-shaped, hazel-eyed face.

Prophet set a gloved fist on his hip. "Louisa, damnit, I told you to go on over to the bathhouse."

Louisa blinked and curled her upper lip at him. "You're not my boss, you two-timing son of a muskrat. What are you up to?"

"None of your damn business."

Jose Encina cleared his throat meaningfully, and Prophet turned to see the man forming one of those smiles that Louisa's presence always evoked in members of the male sex — sort of an expressive throwback to when said male was eleven years old and he realized he could do more with the prettiest girl in the schoolyard than merely dip her braids in his inkwell.

84

Or thought he could.

Prophet shifted his gaze to Hiram Severin and saw that the old law bringer wore a similar expression as he quickly doffed his beaver hat to hold it before him, worrying the upturned brim with a couple of fat brown fingers with yellow nails thick as clamshells.

Prophet returned his glower to Louisa. "Don Encina and Sheriff Hiram Severin, this here is my sometime partner and all-the-time thorn in the ass, Miss Louisa Bonnyventure her own self."

"That's Bonaventure," Louisa said through a glassy smile. "There never has been a 'y' in it, though this uncouth brute has never managed to get it right and likely never will if he lives to be a thousand years old."

"Ahhh," Encina said as though he'd just sipped an unexpectedly fine wine and gave a courtly bow. "How wonderful to meet you, senorita. I have heard a lot about you. The sidekick of Senor Prophet and a formidable bounty hunter in your own right."

He must have seen the puzzled light in Prophet's eyes. Taking a short puff off his cigar, the banker shifted his hungry gaze back to the girl on the pinto and let the smoke dribble out with his words, "I have

85

read about the two of you in the *Rocky Mountain News,* whenever I've been so fortunate to have had one brought to me by business associates from Denver. Quite the pair, you've made, taking down many bad men that somehow managed to elude frontier lawmen and who would, no doubt, still be wreaking their black havoc if you had not brought them to justice."

"I'll vouch for that," Hiram Severin said in his burly wheeze that bespoke a lifetime of strong whiskey and harsh tobacco. "There ain't enough lawmen out here. Now there's sometimes too many bad bounty hunters, but if you ask me, we can't get enough of the like of my old friend Prophet here."

As Severin shuttled his gaze back to Louisa, he smiled so brightly that Prophet thought the old lawman's eyes were going to pop out of his skull and his false teeth would crack. "And, of course, his purty sidekick."

"Lou's my sidekick," Louisa growled. "And I thought my sidekick here always told me what was on his mind. Now, however, I'm fearful he's been dealing from the middle of the deck."

"That'd be the bottom of the deck," Prophet corrected her through gritted teeth.

"You'd know that if you'd ever played cards."

"A game for sharpies and saloon frogs."

"I've gotten a lot of tips on badmen and their hideouts over games of stud, Miss Fancy Britches."

"Suppose we get back to the subject," Louisa said, jerking her chin toward the bank behind the two older gents, who were admiring her through toothy grins. "You're working for banks now? Doing what? Sweeping the floors and emptying spittoons, or something more exciting?"

Before Prophet could speak, Encina said, "A bit more exciting than that, but not much more, Miss Bonaventure. Senor Prophet has hired on to lead the gold trains from the mines around Juniper, to my bank here in town. In the old days, before Sheriff Severin came to our fair city and swept it more or less free of crime, such a job guarding the gold was a dangerous one indeed. Now, with the country scoured of badmen, it is little more dangerous than a Sunday afternoon ride along Chokecherry Creek with an hombre's" — he gave another winning smile as his dark eyes gave Louisa the lusty up and down — "favorite senorita."

"Lou said he wanted a peaceful town to settle down in," Severin said, doffing his hat and poking his fingers into his vest. "And a job he was qualified for. Well, I didn't see a reason to waste old Proph here in a livery stable, mucking out stalls. So I referred him to Jose here. I'm sure, Miss Bonaventure, that if the good banker had another opening on his gold-guarding crew, he wouldn't think twice of awarding that position to you . . . uh . . . in spite of you obviously being a member of the . . . uh . . . much fairer sex an' all."

Severin grinned and let his adobe-brown eyes roam the same bewitching path which the banker's had taken.

"As a matter of fact," the banker said, "I could use an extra rider on —"

"Now, hold on!" Prophet interrupted the man but kept his angry gaze pinned to his partner. "That ain't how I planned this out at all. Not at all."

"Oh?" Louisa arched her brows. "You intended for me to sell buttons and sewing needles to old ladies while you guarded gold shipments?"

"That's right, I did."

"Why?"

"Because it's time you settled down and started acting like a lady instead of a man with . . . well, uh, with . . . a good-lookin' stride and bad case of pistolero fever. Time you settled down and settled in with a respectable job for a young lady. And me, hell, what am I qualified for besides bounty huntin'? About the only damn thing I can think of is guardin' gold shipments." Louisa opened her mouth to speak, but Prophet held a hand up, cutting her off. "And it ain't like you're gonna miss out on any damn rodeo. Like Don Encina done said, the country's been cleaned up."

The banker nodded and broke in with: "We haven't had any trouble with the shipments for over two years, haven't lost any gold in three."

"There, you see?" Prophet jerked his head from the banker to Louisa. "It's no more eventful than a trip to the shithouse. Probably downright boring, in fact — wouldn't you say, Don?"

The banker raised his brows and shrugged noncommittally, absently puffing his cigar.

"Then why didn't you tell me about it?" Louisa asked Prophet. "You'd have to tell me sooner or later, idiot."

Prophet nodded. "That was a mistake, I admit it. Just figured you'd think you was missing out on something, and I thought it best to ease you into a quieter life. But now you know, so why don't you ride on over to the bathhouse, and I'll be over just as soon as I get settled up with Don Encina and Sheriff Severin here."

A bell rang behind Prophet, and he glanced over his right shoulder to see the bank's front door open and a young man in a tailored brown suit step in, donning a brown derby with a silk band. He had a worn leather valise clamped under one arm.

"Oh, here you are, Pa," he said to Encina but without the older man's accent. "I was just going to head over to Mr. Walthrup's office to have him notarize these . . ." His gaze slid to Louisa like steel to a magnet, and his brown eyes narrowed charmingly, cheeks dimpling.

Quickly, he doffed his hat and stepped up beside his father, giving the girl a bow not unlike the old man's though a tad less formal. "Oh . . . hello. Didn't realize we had a visitor."

"Visitors," Prophet grunted. "There's two of us."

The man glanced at Prophet but, disregarding the big bounty hunter out of hand, returned his gaze to the girl, still obviously awaiting an introduction. "Miguel," his father said, clamping an arm over the young man's shoulders, "our new gold guard has arrived . . . with his lovely young companion, Miss Louisa Bonaventure. Senor

90

Prophet, Senorita Bonaventure, my son, Miguel Encina. He pretty much runs the bank for me while I come in only to make a pest of myself."

"Mr. Prophet," Miguel Encina said, reaching across his father to shake the bounty hunter's hand. "How nice to make your acquaintance." He sidled up to Louisa's pinto and extended his hand to the girl, his eyes twinkling like a sky full of stars after a hard, cleansing rain. Louisa, Prophet noticed, had colored up when the young man had stepped out of the bank, and her cheeks were still mottled red now as she removed her right glove and let the handsome young banker squeeze it gently.

"Mr. Encina," she said with a nod and a slow blink of those pretty hazel eyes that she wielded with as much facility as her matched Colts.

"Miss Bonaventure, I couldn't be more pleased to make your acquaintance." The younger Encina dropped his gaze to the pistols prominently displayed on the girl's hips and glanced at Prophet. "Are you here with Mr. Prophet to . . . ?"

"Guard the gold shipments?" Louisa said with a casual spread of her lips, not pulling her hand away from young Encina's lingering, gentle shake. *"Si."*

"Ah . . . well," the young man said, obviously pleased. "We could use another guard, wouldn't you say, Father? Especially when we have another here as qualified as Miss Bonaventure. . . ."

The elder Encina narrowed his eyes and dipped his chin approvingly.

"I have Mr. Prophet's contract inside, awaiting his signature. I can draw up another one straightaway, and you could sign yours, too, Miss Bonaventure." Miguel Encina glanced at Prophet. "Do you have a few minutes?"

Louisa's smile brightened as she swung gracefully down from her saddle. "Certainly, Mr. Encina."

Prophet rolled his eyes.

8

Apparently forgetting about the papers he'd needed notarized, the handsome young Encina ushered Prophet and Louisa into his private, richly appointed office at the rear of the bank, beyond the three teller cages and the desk of a loan officer and accountant, and next to his father's office. The elder Encina still considered himself the bank's president, Prophet saw, as a varnished, gold-lettered plaque hanging from a brass nail on his door bore the label, while Miguel's read VICE PRESIDENT.

The younger Encina was a handsome, well-attired gent who seemed very comfortable in his own skin but not arrogant. In fact, he was downright polite and deferring, and the warm smile never left his eyes, nor did the boyish dimples leave his cheeks as he got Prophet and Louisa settled into comfortable, upholstered chairs fronting his desk while he went about drawing up a fresh contract for Louisa.

Prophet figured most of the young man's graciousness could be attributed to Louisa herself. God knew, with her cool, effervescent beauty and tomboyish charm, she'd caused more important men to piss in their boots and choke on their food. Still, the bounty hunter, who owned the southern sharecropper's — as well as western frontiersman's — suspicion of men with more money and better manners, found himself liking the kid. And he was only slightly chafed by the younker's obvious admiration for his pretty, young partner.

For years, Prophet had been looking for a young man whom Louisa could settle down with. Why not the moneyed banker's son?

The girl's obvious attraction to young Encina was a little harder to take. It twanged several chords of jealousy deep within Prophet, but he'd known he'd have to work through that sooner or later. The truth was, while they'd partnered up right well, and he truly did love the girl, and he knew she loved him, they were meant to be together no more than a lovely young mustang filly was meant to be paired for life with a crotchety Missouri mule.

"I don't think we need to make this too complicated," Miguel said, lifting the paper on which he'd written out a contract and blowing on the ink. "I could have my secretary type this up on her typewriter machine, and get a witness, but I reckon it's just for the filing cabinet."

He gave Louisa another winning smile as he slid the contract onto her side of the desk. Then, almost forgetting Prophet, he pulled another paper from under his desk blotter and, chuckling with boyish chagrin and sliding his fetchingly bashful glance between the two bounty hunters, said, "And this is yours, Mr. Prophet."

"Obliged."

"Not at all."

When Louisa had signed her contract with her customary flourish, then raised the paper to blow on it, she gave the pen to Prophet. The bounty hunter took the pen awkwardly in his left hand then shifted it to his right. Damn, if he didn't hate scratching his signature with folks staring at him, making him feel the school dimwit.

He looked at Louisa, then at Miguel, who leaned forward over his entwined hands, his expression affable and patient. Prophet grunted and frowned his discomfort, dipping the pen in the silver-plated inkwell sitting between two Tiffany lamps on the young banker's desk.

Miguel, suddenly realizing the bounty hunter's angst, leaned back in his chair and ran his hands through his thick mop of brown, curly hair and lifted his mock-casual gaze to the ceiling. Louisa wasn't as polite. She regarded Prophet with barely concealed disdain.

"It would go easier if you'd take your glove off."

Prophet looked at his right hand. With another grunt, he set the pen down, started working the tight doeskin glove off with his teeth, then pulled it off with his other hand and set it down beside him. Taking up the pen again, he glanced at Louisa, who was still giving him that haughty, impatient scowl, and he frowned at her.

"Don't you know it ain't proper to look over a fella's shoulder?"

With a huff she leaned back in her own chair and let her gaze follow the young banker's to the pressed tin ceiling. When he was sure neither was watching him, Prophet leaned forward over the edge of the desk, lowered his head, pressed the tip of his tongue against his bottom lip, and carefully and anxiously scrawled his name onto the line of the contract indicated.

Scrawling his name was always a difficult maneuver; while he could empty his Winchester and Colts with finesse, for some vexing reason a pen or a pencil always turned his fingers to lead.

He'd learned to read well enough in the Georgia mountains he hailed from to decipher wanted posters and even newspaper articles, if given enough time, but he'd never learned to properly write his name, and he cursed himself now for not practicing. He could sense these two younkers sneering at him though neither said a word, but Louisa was breathing extra loudly and shaking her crossed leg.

When he'd crossed the T on his last name, his hand relaxed, and his tongue slipped back into his mouth. He sighed as though he'd jogged a fair stretch, set down the pen, lifted the paper, turning it upside down, and held it sheepishly across the desk to Miguel. The young banker offered another winning smile as he accepted the contract and, politely not looking at it, dropped it with Louisa's into a drawer, closed the drawer with a flourish, and leaned forward in his chair, smoothing his blotter with his soft banker's hands adorned with clean, immaculately trimmed nails.

"Well, now that that's taken care of, will you both be ready to start as soon as tomorrow? Say, seven o'clock?"

"Fine as frog hair," Prophet said.

Louisa nodded. "How many other riders?"

"Three. They're expecting a new ramrod, and that man will of course be you, Mr. Prophet."

"Best not remind him of that too often," Louisa said.

Miguel smiled, flushing again as his gaze washed over Louisa like a soft summer rain. "You two have been together for a while, I take it?"

Louisa glanced at Prophet. "It's been a few years, hasn't it, Lou?"

Prophet felt a bittersweet pang of nostalgia, knowing — or at least hoping — their partnership was coming to a close. He wasn't sure he intended to give up bounty hunting for good, but he knew it was time for Louisa to hang up her guns. "Three years, four months, twenty-seven days."

"You two must mean a lot to each other?" Miguel said, pressing his fingers down hard against the blotter and looking up at Louisa from under his brows.

She glanced at Prophet, the skin above the bridge of her nose wrinkling slightly. She smiled and bit her upper lip, which quivered slightly with emotion, and Prophet moved in quickly to buoy the mood with: "I reckon you could say I been Louisa's big

98

brother, past couple years. I look out for her, and she looks out for me. Time to settle down now, though. Gold guarding's enough excitement for me. Hell, I might just find me a little shack and settle down right here in Juniper, run a few chickens, and get me a coon for a pet."

Miguel's eyes were on Louisa. "Is that your intention, as well, Miss Bonaventure? Settling down here, I mean."

"If I've learned one thing, Mr. Encina," Louisa said, lifting her gaze to his, her eyes clear and bold once again, "it's to never intend much of anything. I just ride. But I guess for now I'm going to stop riding for a while, since Lou wants it so consarned bad, and I guess you could say I'm ready to try something else. I suppose gold guarding will be a sort of gentle easing into an easier life for both of us."

"I hope you like it here. It's a nice town — I assure you."

"We'll see," Louisa said, glancing at Prophet as she gained her feet and donned her hat.

Miguel climbed to his feet then, too, and extended his hand to Louisa. "So very nice to meet you, Miss Bonaventure. I've heard a lot about you."

He extended his hand to Prophet as the

big bounty hunter heaved himself up from his chair and stuffed his battered Stetson on his sweaty, dusty head. "And of course I've read about you, too, Mr. Prophet. The trails from the mines have been quiet of late, and I'm sure when word gets around that you and Miss Bonaventure are working for us now, they'll be even quieter."

"Hope so."

"May I inquire where you'll both be staying? The Muleskinner's Inn is where the other guards flop between jobs, but . . ." The young banker's concerned eyes swept from Prophet to Louisa. ". . . But . . . um . . . it's really not a place I think you'd enjoy, Miss Bonaventure. It's a bit on the rustic side. May I suggest the Golden Slipper? It's near the opera house, on its north side, in fact. A lovely place run by a German couple from Denver, and it's where the opera companies stay whenever they're in town. In fact, one such company should be here yet this afternoon, for a performance this evening. I'm sure they've reserved rooms for themselves, but the Slipper has at least thirty."

Prophet glanced at Louisa. She returned it. They normally slept together, in the same room, and he could tell she was reluctant to sleep alone. But that wouldn't do here in

Juniper. Especially when Louisa had already gotten a young man on her string.

Quickly, Prophet said, "The Golden Slipper, huh? Well, that sounds just your style, Louisa. And if the Muleskinner's Inn don't sound like mine, I'm a monkey's uncle!" He laughed and hoped Encina didn't see the look of consternation on Louisa's face. "If you could point me in the right direction, I'll go on over and toss my gear down."

"I'll be happy to, Mr. Prophet," the banker said, moving out from behind his desk.

"The way I see it," the bounty hunter said as the younger Encina showed him and Louisa out of his office, "you best call me Lou or Prophet. The last Mr. Prophet I knew I left back in Georgia before the Little Misunderstandin'."

"In that case, I'm Miguel."

"But you sign the checks."

"Please, Lou," the young banker said when he and Louisa were standing outside his open office door, looking up at the bounty hunter, who was a good head taller than he, "it's Miguel. And I hope it's all right if we, too, can be on a first-name basis, Miss Bonaventure."

Louisa flushed again, and Prophet was vaguely conscious of a little jab of jealousy in the pit of his belly. He'd be damned if

101

the girl wasn't tindering a fire for their young employer. "Of course," she said, dipping her chin and sliding a lock of wind-tussled blond hair away from her eye.

Miguel bowed again and lightly tapped his shoes together like a French soldier. "Louisa it is."

He gestured for her and Prophet to lead the way to the door, and when they'd all filed onto the boardwalk fronting the bank, Miguel pointed out a tall, narrow, false-fronted building on a side street about a block south of the main one. It was one of the older, shabbier buildings that Prophet had seen so far, and it announced itself as THE MULESKINNER'S INN in sun-blistered green letters.

When the young banker had pointed out the Golden Slipper behind the opera house, which couldn't have been more opposite to the Muleskinner's if that had been the builder's sole intention, he turned to Louisa while rubbing his palms together slowly, as though warming himself before a hot fire. "If you have no plans for this evening, I'd like to ask you out to dinner, Miss Bona . . . I mean, Louisa. We could dine right there in the Golden Slipper and then, perhaps, I could show you around town, start getting you acquainted with some of the good townsfolk of Juniper."

Louisa's eyes slid to Prophet. And then Miguel's did, too, and he said quickly albeit insincerely, "Of course, you'd be more than welcome, too, Mr. Prophet. . . ."

"Balderdash!" Prophet said, feeling a little heavy-footed as he crossed the boardwalk and grabbed Mean and Ugly's reins from the hitchrack. "You two younkers go out and enjoy yourselves. Me, I'll probably finagle a meal out of Hell-Bringin' Hiram and then fleece him at euchre."

Miguel turned to Louisa, and the relief was evident in his warm, sparkling eyes. "Shall we say six thirty? That gives you ample time for a nap, if you wish."

Louisa gave Prophet a fleeting, oblique glance.

"Six thirty would be fine, Miguel." She smiled sweetly, without a trace of her usual irony. "I'll be dressed and waiting downstairs."

When Miguel had bid them both farewell and headed into the bank, Louisa swung up onto her pinto. Adjusting the reins in her hand, she glanced at Prophet and said sort of shyly and noncommittally, "He's nice."

"Damn nice fella."

She narrowed an eye at Prophet, suddenly looking more girlish than he'd seen her since they'd first met on the bounty trail up in the Dakota-Minnesota country. "You sure you don't mind, Lou?"

"Why would I mind? He's a nice kid, and he's your age. What's more, he's got money."

She frowned as Prophet reined Mean and Ugly out away from the hitchrail. "You're not jealous?"

"I didn't say that." He winked at her. "You go on over to the Golden Slipper. You'll probably get a bath there in a golden tub or some such. Hell, they'll probably even bring you up a sarsaparilla in a crystal goblet!"

"I'm not sure I like this, Lou." She raised a hand to shade her eyes from the westering sun as she regarded him sadly, gravely. "I'm not sure I like this at all."

"What's not to like? A good town with a handsome suitor in it for you?" Prophet looked up and down the street. Not a sign of commotion anywhere. He had to admit, though, he felt as though a sharp stiletto blade was pricking the backside of his heart. He'd wanted change, and now it was happening.

He sighed and flapped his reins against his saddlebow. "Ah, hell, we gotta give it a chance, Louisa. Me — I'm gettin' too damn old to be shootin' you out of Mexican prisons."

He left her sitting on her pinto, staring after him, as he gigged the hammer-headed dun through the afternoon traffic, slanting across the street toward the Muleskinner's. He was so distracted, as was Louisa, that neither one saw the long-haired hombre with the eye patch staring at Prophet from a rain barrel a ways up the street, in the direction of the opera house, and lovingly caressing the hammer of the Sharps carbine resting across his lap with his thumb.

9

Louisa put the pinto around behind the opera house, weaving amongst the foot traffic comprised mostly of beefy workers carrying rough wooden planks of all shapes and sizes as well as buckets of paint through the ornate building's double rear doors.

Louisa had never been inside such a place before. She hadn't had time for that brand of foolishness when there were depraved men running free across the West looking to kill and maim and leave orphans such as herself in their blood-tinged wake. But she supposed, in a vague sort of way through the consternation she felt at parting with Lou, that they were building sets for the house's next performance.

Lou . . .

She pulled the pinto up to the broad front porch of the Golden Slipper, which boasted a painted golden slipper on either side of the large shingle stretched across the porch and bearing the place's name in large, cursive, black letters. The place was brick, with a mansard roof and upper-story balconies with wrought-iron rails twisted to form little golden slippers.

For a moment, staring up at the imposing place and seeing a couple of women in frilly gowns and long, pastel-colored gloves and feathered picture hats spinning parasols on the porch while speaking in hushed tones, Louisa felt sick to her stomach. She didn't belong in such opulence. Not alone, anyway, without Lou to temper the experience, to make it an adventure and something to laugh about rather than something she merely felt alienated from.

But the Golden Slipper certainly wasn't a place for Prophet. He would fit in here about as well as a brush-tailed mustang stallion would blend in amongst the tight aisles of the haberdashery.

Just the image lightened her mood some, made it more bittersweet than sharply sad and lonely. She still wanted to turn tail and run back to Prophet and hole up with him at the Muleskinner's — she'd grown accustomed to such low-heeled places — but her heart was just light enough now that she could not allow herself to make such a spectacle of herself. Besides, running back to him would be like running back to her old, bounty-hunting life, and on the trail up from Mexico she'd decided that Prophet was right — that life was no longer the life for her. She hated to admit it — and she wouldn't admit it to anyone but herself, not even Lou — but she'd been defeated.

Montoya had defeated her.

He'd turned her into a frightened little creature wanting only to burrow and hide. She hadn't even wanted to take the gold-guarding job but had offered herself only out of her innate defiance and to prove to herself that she still had a little sand left in her soul.

Quickly, to keep herself from thinking of that horrible time at the prison and conjuring the unbearable pain of it, not the least of which had been inflicted by the major's cigars which he'd ground into her hips or the small of her back after he'd taken his goatish pleasure, she grabbed her rifle and saddlebags from off the pinto's back.

She hurried up the Golden Slipper's broad porch steps. Ignoring the puzzled frowns of the two picture-hatted, parasol-twirling ladies, who were no doubt sizing up the pretty though trail-worn blond sporting a pair of pearl-gripped Colts on her narrow hips, Louisa fairly threw herself into

108

the dark, cool lobby.

The place was all dark wood and wine-red carpet with black and gold designs and heavy drapes tied back from tall windows. But Louisa wasted no time admiring the richly appointed digs. She quickly ordered a room from the mustachioed gent behind the long mahogany desk on the left, scribbling her name into the register. Hefting her rifle and saddlebags and heading for the broad stairs at the lobby's rear, beyond the richly furnished saloon where a few impeccably dressed gentlemen quietly whiled away the afternoon, she informed the man, who scrutinized her with the usual male fascination, that she'd like a bath.

"Of course, miss." From the corner of her eye, she watched him lean over the desk to watch her rump as she climbed the stairway, her saddlebags jostling down her back. "Two buckets of hot water or three?"

"Three. And a little alacrity, please," Louisa ordered as she topped the stairs and turned to tramp along the balcony that encircled the entire second story, exposing all the doors facing a stove-sized, opal chandelier. She felt a peculiar need to assert herself here in this foreign environment. "After the bath, I'll be napping before dinner."

The desk clerk stared up at her from below, his round spectacles glinting in the afternoon light from the tall windows. "Uh . . . of course, Miss Bonaventure."

She found her room and went in.

Louisa was cool as a mountain snow, but even she had to stand in the open doorway for a moment, lower jaw hanging slack, as she looked around at the finely appointed room. It was as large as a livery barn and furnished with a marble-topped oak wash-stand, marble-topped mirrored dresser, and a sprawling, canopied, four-poster bed. The carpet under her boots was so deep that her spurs caught in the weave; the first thing she did after she'd tossed her possibles on the bed was remove them and hang them on the brass hat rack, giving each an absent spin.

She was still looking around the room in awe when a light knock jerked her head to the door. It was a husky young man in a red velvet uniform, hefting a copper tub. Louisa let him in and, after he'd filled the tub with two buckets of cold water and three buckets of hot, Louisa told him she'd set the clothes she was wearing outside her door to be picked up for laundering.

When the young man left, she stripped and tossed everything except her hat and boots into the hall. Then, naked except for the tan felt hat snugged down on her wheat-colored curls — Prophet's reluctance to remove his hat had rubbed off on her, she realized with a self-castigating chuff — she tossed the hat onto the bed and dipped a toe into the lightly steaming water.

She stepped into the tub and stood there for a moment, calf-deep, and pinned her hair into a loose bun behind her head, thinking absently as she looked around the room lit by two tall windows over which heavy purple curtains glowed that she might be able to get accustomed to comfort, after all.

As she sank down in the tub, she found herself thinking about Miguel Encina. She felt a tingling throughout her body, thinking about him, and as she sank back against the tub, extending her legs as far as she could, she realized that she had been quite taken with the young banker.

What girl wouldn't be?

She supposed she'd seen other handsome young men over the past few years, but she hadn't considered any for suitors because she'd been partnered up with Lou for more than just bounty hunting. She wasn't exactly sure what Lou meant to her, though she knew she loved him and had always enjoyed having his big arms wrapped around her in their joined blanket rolls.

But she'd always known that Lou would never make a husband.

One, he just wasn't the marrying kind. Two, he couldn't be faithful if he were riding a golden, fleece-lined cloud with Mary Magdalene herself. And, because Louisa had been more intent on hunting killers down and either hauling their wretched hides to the nearest law or killing them bloody, she'd never been too concerned about that.

She herself had fallen into the arms of others, though nowhere near the number of others Lou had. But now that she'd found herself warming up to this idea of settling down in a peaceful place like Juniper, she found herself cozying up to the idea of Miguel Encina.

He was right handsome, and those warm brown eyes seemed to probe right through to her core. Most men as handsome as him were rakes, and when they looked at a girl they were wondering what she'd look like naked. But Louisa's female sixth sense, which was as stout as hammered steel, told her that Miguel wanted more than just a tumble. He honestly seemed to want to get to know her better, to discover her soul and, in so doing, expose his own soul to her.

There was nothing more appealing in a man than that.

Again, a shadow passed behind her eyes, and she stopped scrubbing her raised thigh with the lavender-scented soap that the bellboy had brought and scowled at the window in front of her.

Lou already knew her soul, and she knew his. . . .

A sound in the hall instantly scoured her mind of all thought. She glanced quickly at her shell belt and the filled holsters draped over the chair she'd positioned to the right of the tub. Then she swiveled her head to peer over her other shoulder. Under the door, a thin shadow moved. There was a faint rasp, like that of a spur rowel catching on carpet.

Louisa dropped the soap. It hit the water with a plop. Her hands tingled as she kept her gaze on the charcoal shadow that had stopped outside her door.

Beyond the door, the desk clerk's voice echoed up from downstairs. "Um . . . excuse there, but . . ."

The shadow disappeared from under the door. Louisa's heartbeat quickened as the shadow appeared once more. There was a loud boom as the door burst open.

Louisa threw herself over the tub's right

113

side, splashing soapy water in all directions, and continued over the chair beside her but not before she'd filled both her practiced hands with her pearl-gripped .45s. From the corner of her right eye, she watched two men blow into the room. As she hit the floor and rolled, she glimpsed the sharp flashes of the four bellowing guns in the men's hands, heard the sharp pings and pops of the lead storm crashing into the copper, water-filled tub.

Belly down on the carpeted floor between the tub and the bed, Louisa angled both her pearl-gripped six-shooters at the big men standing obscured behind the wafting of their own powder smoke and the flashes of their pistols and returned fire.

Louisa's Colts leaped and roared in her small, strong fists, her eyes unblinking and hard, her tender upper lip slightly curled in cold, clean fury. Both men were just turning their wailing guns toward her when her .45 rounds began drilling into them, beating dust from their leather vests and blowing their dusters out behind them as the men themselves stumbled back, screaming, hats tumbling off their shoulders.

Louisa emptied her Colts into both men until they'd both been punched out the door, leaving behind only lazily drifting smoke and spilled blood on the carpet and walls near where they'd been standing. Water gurgled from the holes they'd pumped into the washtub, turning the carpet around it dark and soggy.

Tossing away the empty Colts, Louisa sprang to her bare feet and grabbed her Winchester carbine off the bed. She strode into the hall, looking around, seeing nothing but more smoke and spent shells. The carpet in front of her room was torn, and blood was smeared across the balcony's scrolled rail.

Louisa racked a cartridge into the carbine's breech and, holding the rifle up high across her jostling breasts, strode forward. She peered over the rail and into the lobby below.

Her heart began to slow when she saw both men sprawled on the carpet in front of the mahogany desk, both hatless, one flat on his back, limbs akimbo, duster flaps open to show the three or four bloody holes in his chest. The other lay curled on his side, one hand pillowing his cheek, as though he'd lain down for a nap. He had long, black hair, and he was dressed all in black except for a white shirt.

At least the shirt had been white. Now it was red, and more red trickled down from the ragged hole in his right cheek.

There was a strange, warbling sound. For a moment, Louisa thought it was coming from one of the men she'd shot, and she was about to drill each once more, to make sure the demons were galloping back to hell. But then she saw the desk clerk standing about ten feet away from her bushwhackers, in front of a potted palm, looking down at them while holding his hands in the air as though beseeching a higher power.

Slowly, he raised his face, crumpled in exasperation, to Louisa who was staring down at him from the second-floor balcony.

His lips moved as he tried to speak, but he could only make incomprehensible sounds that were soon drowned by the thumps of boots on the boardwalk in front of the hotel. When Louisa saw several men with badges, including Sheriff Hiram Severin, bolt into the lobby with their pistols drawn, Louisa remembered she was standing there in nothing but her birthday suit.

"The furnishings are right splendid," she told the desk clerk, who was still staring up at her in awe. She held the rifle across her soapy breasts. "But the clientele leaves much to be desired."

With that, she lowered her rifle, walked

back into her room, and closed what was
left of her door.

10

Almost an hour earlier, having bought a room at the Muleskinner's Inn and hauled his saddlebags including a sliver of lye soap over to the bathhouse, Lou Prophet scowled at the Chinaman in a red wool cap sitting at a dilapidated rolltop desk in the washhouse's shabby front room. "Eight bits for a bath? You gotta be joshin', amigo!"

Six kittens were drinking from a pie tin near a cabinet that had been nailed together from tomato crates and was sagging under the weight of many wash-worn cotton towels. The kittens' mother lounged on a burlap sack against the wall, licking a front paw to clean her face with.

The Chinaman held up eight pudgy fingers and jostled his Fu Manchu mustache as he said, "Eight bits or go! Eight bits or go!"

"Hold your damn horses," Prophet growled, tossing the silver to the squat bathhouse proprietor, who caught the coins against his shabby gray underwear top. "But, by god, the water better be hot!"

"Eight bits!"

"There's your eight bits. Now show me a room and bring some hot water. And for eight bits it better be *damn* hot."

"My water hot," intoned the Chinaman, dropping the coins into a lockbox. "My water hottest in town. Hey, cowboy," the man hailed Prophet, who'd drifted through the bead-curtained door in the office's back wall. "You want whore? I bring you whore. Best whores in town!"

"No, thanks," Prophet said, his boots pounding the rough, mud- and shit-stained puncheons as he continued down the hall, leaving the Chinaman scuffling around behind him.

He could hear a man and a woman laughing and splashing water behind one of the curtained rooms opening off the dim hall. Bright sunlight shone through cracks in the ceiling and unchinked walls. The air was steamy and rife with the smell of sweat and the horseshit crusted on the floorboards. He chose an empty ten-by-ten-foot room at the far rear of the place, with a simple bench, one plank shelf, a cracked mirror hanging from a bent nail, and a corrugated tin tub hanging from a square-hewn ceiling joist.

The tub was rusty and dented, and the curved rim was pulling away from the sides.

"Eight bits, my ass," Prophet grunted, dropping his gear on the bench, then hauling the tub off the post. He dropped it onto the floor with a loud clang that for a moment drowned out the sounds of carnal frolic emanating from up the hall.

He undressed slowly, peeling his grubby, sweaty clothes off his rawboned frame. The Chinaman, who'd obviously pegged Prophet for a troublemaker, came in grumbling with two steaming water buckets. He gave the bounty hunter the evil eye and dumped both buckets into the tub, then left to fetch cold. Showing his teeth like an angry cur, he returned and dumped some of the cold water into the basin then stood around as though awaiting a tip. Prophet threw him his dirty clothes instead.

"Wash those."

"Wash extra!"

"How much extra?"

"For this kind bad clothes, bad smelly clothes, one dollah!"

"Wash 'em. I'll be over at the Muleskinner's."

He kicked the chuffing, muttering Chinaman out of the room, then eased his bulk slowly into the steaming water, gritting his teeth as the near-boiling liquid inched up his ankles and locked its jaws around his balls.

He could do little more than sit down in the tub, knees raised nearly to his chin. Reflecting on the likely contrast between his bath and Louisa's, who was no doubt taking a leisurely, sudsy soak in one of those throne-like copper jobs you could virtually stretch out and take a nap in, he chuckled dryly. Grabbing his sliver of pale-yellow lye cake off the short stool that he'd positioned beside the tub, and onto which he'd dropped his hat and rawhide tobacco pouch, he went to work scrubbing the three weeks of grime from his hot, chafed hide.

When he was done scrubbing his body and his sandy hair that was curling over his ears and feathering down over his neck — soon he'd have to splurge for a trim — he called for a rinse. The Chinaman returned, no longer grumbling but grunting and shaking his head, and poured a bucket of warm water over Prophet's head, shoulders, and knees. Dismissing the fellow once again, Prophet sat back in the tub, grabbed his makings sack from the stool, and took his time building a smoke.

He fired the quirley with a stove match, and took even longer smoking it, sitting there in the tub, hearing faintly the water droplets falling from his body, the two groaners up the hall, and the sounds of the town beyond the squat bathhouse — the rumble of wagon wheels, occasional hoots and hollers, barking dogs, neighing horses.

Listening, he wondered what living in town would be like.

Likely anywhere he found a house to buy, he'd hear similar sounds. All day long, every day, the sounds of other people — their wagons, horses, and dogs. Their squabbling. Their industry. Could he get used to that?

Whenever he'd spent much time in a town before — Denver, Abilene, Dodge City, or Cheyenne — he couldn't wait to climb onto Mean and Ugly's back and salt the brush for the tall and uncut, for the silence of mountain and plain. There the only sounds were those of the birds, the river, the sound of the breeze in the cottonwood leaves. The rumble of thunder. The patter of rain off his hat.

Peaceful sounds.

Oh, there was the occasional screech of an angry bobcat, the snarls of hunting wolves or grizzlies, even the thundering train sounds of a distant cyclone. But somehow those sounds evoked less anxiousness in him than did the rattle of a wagon's trace chains or the sudden eruption of laughter from a nearby saloon.

Oh, give it a chance, for chrissakes, he silently scolded himself. *With any luck, Louisa'll fall for that young banker, Encina, and you won't have to worry about her anymore. He'll take care of her, likely put her up in a big house, and give her a passel of kids and the life you always wanted for her.*

She won't care if you stay or leave. Hell, she'd probably haze you out of town with a broom and a shotgun to keep from being reminded how far she'd once fallen, sharing the blankets of a beat-up old bounty hunter and former fighter for Jeff Davis's ill-fated, Confederate dream.

Prophet chuckled. There wasn't any humor in the laugh, and suddenly a dark, lonely mood was upon him. He drew deep on his half-smoked quirley, as if the pungent tobacco smoke would clear his head. He took the wet, tightly rolled cylinder between thumb and index finger and regarded it thoughtfully.

He liked Miguel Encina. The kid would make a good husband.

Yet, deep down inside the bounty hunter, where his fine-tuned instincts lay tightly coiled, apprehension beat a slight but insistent rhythm. . . .

As he stared at the burning cigarette, he spied movement out of the corner of his left eye, and he turned both eyes to the warped, dusty glass window four feet in front of him. It faced the scruffy yard of the bathhouse, a large stack of split wood, and several wheelbarrows and a long wash line sagging between aspens beyond. There was a shed there, too. Atop the shed's flat, corrugated tin roof, a man knelt, aiming a rifle at the bathhouse.

More specifically, he was aiming the rifle at Prophet sitting in a tub in the bathhouse's rear-most room.

Prophet jerked his head down, dropping the quirley, which sizzled out in the bathwater. At nearly the same time, the rifle's maw smoked and blossomed orange. There was a ping of breaking glass, a thwack in the wall behind Prophet, and a quarter second later, the flat report of the rifle reached the bounty hunter's ears.

Prophet felt an icy burn and touched his finger to the side of his head, just above his right jaw. He felt the oily blood that the bullet had drawn there before it had continued on over and past him and into the room's back wall.

His gaze flashed fire, and his face broke with an enraged snarl as he looked through the window again.

The man on the roof was quickly ejecting his spent cartridge casing from his Winchester's breech and racking fresh. The hammered silver discs of his hatband flashed in the afternoon sunlight.

"Why, you son of a bitch!" Prophet grunted, leaping up and out of the washtub, nearly upsetting the basin and causing a minor flood as he dashed to the wall on his right.

The rifle thundered again on the heels of the *thwack* of another slug slamming through the broken window and into the back wall but not before Prophet had felt the curl of air over his left shoulder.

Snarling a curse, Prophet grabbed his rifle from against the wall and racked a shell into the chamber. As he turned toward the window, another bullet slammed into the wall beside it, showing a round hole of yellow light. Prophet heard the Chinaman shouting angrily at the front of the place as he raised his Winchester to his right shoulder and aimed at the man who was racking a fresh round into his rifle breech atop the shed.

Prophet laid a bead on the man's chest

125

and fired. Apparently he missed — he didn't have a good angle, he was barefoot, and he was sopping wet. The man triggered another round himself, drilling another little sphere of yellow light in the wall right of the broken window.

Prophet ejected the spent brass and ran to the window's left side as the bushwhacker fired again. Then, hearing his own ejected cartridge casing rolling around on the wooden floor at his bare feet, Prophet stepped in front of the window, smashing the remaining shards from the frame, then drawing another quick bead on the shooter.

He fired four times quickly, gritting his teeth and squinting through his own powder smoke.

Two of his shots plunked into the corrugated tin roof on either side of the dry-gulcher. One blew the silver-banded, low-crowned hat from his head, exposing his bald pate around which thick, cinnamon hair hung straight to his shoulders. Another slug made him show his teeth below his straggly brown mustache and above his straggly brown goat beard.

The gunman jerked back slightly, then turned full around and scrambled to the back of the shed. As Prophet fired two more rounds, the man disappeared over the shed's far edge, seeming to half leap, half fall to the ground behind it.

Prophet snapped off another shot in anger, then leaned the rifle against the wall and rummaged through his saddlebags for a fresh pair of longhandles. The spares had collected some trail dust seeping in around the flap, but they were as clean as Prophet needed.

He struggled into them quickly, grunting and wheezing with exasperation, then stomped into his boots, donned his hat, wrapped his cartridge belt with its single holster and Colt Peacemaker around his waist, and grabbed his shotgun.

Holding the shotgun down by his side one-handed, the lanyard swinging slack, he clomped out the washroom door. The Chinaman stood several feet away, eyes wide and sparkling. He yelled in Chinese while a skinny gent stared at him from a near doorway. The man's grimy longhandles clung to his pale, wet skin, and a shabby brown bowler sat at a precarious angle on his head. A girl with curly brown hair stood behind him, staring wide-eyed over his shoulder.

"What the hell's goin' on, amigo?" the man said in a slow Texas drawl, his prominent Adam's apple bobbing in his leathery throat. He jerked a red thumb at the girl. "One o' them blue whistlers almost took Loretta's head off!"

"I do apologize, Loretta."

Prophet turned away from the trio and pushed out the door at the end of the hall. Just beyond the door, he paused, looking around, taking the shotgun in both hands, and thumbing back the rabbit-eared hammers.

"Where are you, you bushwhackin' son of a bitch?"

His deep voice echoed off the shed and woodpile. His heart hammering with red fury, he strode quickly across the rocky yard littered with wood shavings and stray logs amongst the rabbit brush and skunk cabbage and stopped at the front of the shed. It was missing both its front doors and the inside of it was cluttered with wagon wheels, rims, felloes, and sundry other junk. Prophet stopped at the far end and edged a cautious look around the corner.

There was nothing beside the shed but more junk, including moldering sluice boxes called Long Toms, dilapidated ore drays, and heavy rusting axles, all swallowed by brush. Prophet swung around the corner and strode straight back along the shed's west wall, holding the shotgun straight up in one hand, his right hand resting on the worn walnut handle of the his low-slung .45.

A man stumbled out from the back of the shed. The pin-striped shirt behind his black vest and tan duster glistened with fresh blood.

Prophet stopped.

The man moved shamble-footed toward Prophet, dropping the Sharps carbine he'd used to interrupt the bounty hunter's soak, and gritted his teeth as his cobalt blue eyes bored into Prophet angrily. "You killed me, you fuck!"

"Not yet," Prophet warned, dropping the double bores of his ten-gauge.

Foolishly, the bushwhacker clawed at the long-barreled Remington holstered on his right thigh. He continued stumbling toward Prophet and gritting his teeth. Prophet had no choice but to trip the shotgun's front eyelash trigger and blow the man ten feet into the brush and rocks behind him.

The man had no sooner hit the ground on his back and expelled a last, gurgling cry, when the sound of a boot snapping a thin branch rose behind him.

Prophet spun, saw the second man beside a gnarled cedar aiming a Spencer carbine at him, and tripped the barn blaster's second trigger. The boom sounded like a cannon blast echoing off the shed's near wall. The concussion blew Prophet's hat from his head.

The second bushwhacker rose nearly as high as the first one had, triggering the Spencer skyward as he went flying off into the brush before smacking the back of the dry-goods store west of the washhouse. He left a good-sized blood smear on the unpainted, clapboard-sided wall before slumping down into the rocks and sage at the wall's base.

"Oh," he said, kicking his silver-tipped black boots. His blond head was tipped at an odd angle against a rock, and he seemed to be staring at his bloody belly. "Oh . . . oh, shit. . . ."

Just beyond him, another figure stood aiming a rifle toward Prophet. The bounty hunter's heart thudded as he was about to drop the gut shredder and draw his Peacemaker.

A familiar voice said, "Lou!"

It was Louisa. She lowered her Winchester and came running. She was dressed in nothing more, it appeared, than a red poncho, hat, and boots. Her creamy legs were bare. Her wheat-colored curls bounced on her shoulders laid nearly bare by the poncho's wide neck. Others ran up behind her —

Hiram Severin and two other men wearing silver stars on their wool vests or coat lapels.

Louisa slowed to get a look at the dying blond bushwhacker slumped between the bathhouse and the dry-goods store. She glanced at the back of the bathhouse, where the Chinaman stood in the open doorway, yelling in his bizarre tongue while throwing his hands up toward the bullet holes peppering the bathhouse's back wall.

Swinging her head back to Prophet, Louisa sidled up to the big bounty hunter, who was only a little better clothed than she, and looked at the first gent he'd torn in half and flung off in the brush.

"You, too, huh?"

11

Prophet frowned at his comely younger partner.

Before he could ask her what she'd meant, Sheriff Severin jogged up, red-faced beneath his crisp bowler, breathing hard. "Lou, god-damnit — what's all the shootin' about?" The sheriff's tone was breathless and grieved as he looked down at the blond gent who lay blinking and kicking against the rock. "I told you, I run a peaceable town here!"

Prophet returned the sheriff's accusatory glare. "Sounds like empty boosterin' to me, Hiram. Both these gents tried to ventilate my hide as I washed it. At least one of 'em did. From the roof of this here shed. The other was skulkin' around out here, ready to finish off what the first gent left kickin'."

Sweating, Severin regarded Prophet skeptically. "You didn't start it?" He seemed surprised.

"I sure as hell did not!"

"No more than I could start a lead swap from the comfort of my own tub," Louisa expostulated saucily to the haggard-looking lawman, whose two younger deputies — one small and wiry, one tall and slender with cow-dumb eyes — moved up cautiously behind him.

Prophet swung his indignant gaze from the confused-looking sheriff to Louisa. "You, too?"

"No sooner had I dispatched my two than I heard the shooting over here. Had a feeling it wasn't someone putting down an old dog." She paused. "And I wasn't far from wrong."

"All right," Prophet said, cutting her off. "I ain't no old dog, but these snipes here are privy slop of the lowest grade. I don't recognize the first gent, but the blond one over yonder is Kentucky Earl Watson. Brother of Jed Watson, who I brought to Judge Parker in Fort Smith about three and a half years ago. He wasn't long out of the saddle before he was dangling about three feet off the ground. His little brother Earl there, who was in Parker's lockup at the time, though not for a hangin' offense, vowed he'd kick me out with a shovel, but that was so long ago, I'd forgotten about him."

Louisa kicked a rock and rested her rifle on her shoulder as she stared up at Prophet, who was having trouble not looking at her long, creamy legs even though he'd seen them plenty enough times before though perhaps not in such a favorable slant of sunlight. "I recognized both men who kicked my door in so rudely, Lou."

She tipped her glance up at Sheriff Severin, who, in turn, jerked his own appreciative glance from Louisa's legs, as did the two deputies flanking him. "They were Noah Calhoun and Big Dick Broadstreet. Broadstreet gave himself the favorable moniker, though I'd heard from a sporting girl in Dodge that Dick was big in name only."

"What was their beef with you . . . uh . . . little lady?"

"Did you notice the scar on Big Dick's right cheek? Came from a bullet of mine up near Little Box Elder Creek in southern Dakota Territory. I took down two of his partners for killing whores for fun in Bismarck, and he skinned out the back of the roadhouse that they were drinking in and jumped on a horse, but not before I triggered a forty-five round at him. I knew I'd hit him. I'd been hoping ever since he'd died miserably in some creek bottom. Noah Calhoun is his brother. Saw his likeness scratched on a handbill at Fort Griffin last year. It seems he had the same weakness for mistreating sporting girls as his brother."

"Well, I'll be damned."

"Maybe you don't run such a peaceable kingdom, after all, Hiram." Prophet couldn't resist getting the dig in.

"I said it was peaceable," the sheriff said as he walked over to the first man Prophet had shot. "Not Heaven."

The taller deputy had followed the sheriff while the short, wiry one had walked over to the blond bushwhacker. The sheriff shuttled his gaze between them. "You boys see either of these brigands around town before?"

"I seen 'em, Sheriff," said the tall deputy, who wore his curly hair long but whose scraggly beard couldn't hide his round, boyish face. "They drink over at the Mexican's place every now and then. They ain't in town all that much, though, so I never seen no reason to inquire about their business. You said to confront those who stay too long without any real purpose. Ain't that so?"

"Yeah, that's so."

"I figured these two must work for one of

the ranches," the tall deputy said and hiked a shoulder with a defensive air. "As for them that bushwhacked Miss Bonaventure — I wouldn't know either o' them from Adam's off-ox."

"This one here's still alive, Sheriff," said the short, blond badge toter standing over Kentucky Earl Watson, who seemed to be trying to lift his head. The bushwhacker's lips were moving as his chest rose and fell slightly.

As the short deputy prodded Kentucky Earl with his boot toe, Louisa strolled over, dropped her rifle down from her shoulder, spread her boots about shoulder-width apart, and aimed the Winchester at Kentucky Earl's head. The blond deputy looked at her, his eyes wide with shock. He opened his mouth, but before he could say anything, Louisa's Winchester barked.

Kentucky Earl's head jerked violently as the bullet went in one ear and out the other, blowing about half of Earl's brains out with it.

"Now he's not." Louisa shouldered her rifle once more and strode back off in the direction of the Golden Slipper, leaving all three lawmen staring incredulously after her.

Sheriff Severin looked at Prophet, who looked away, scratching the back of his head. "Can't blame her for wantin' to leave the profession in style."

After Hell-Bringin' Hiram Severin sent one of his deputies off to fetch the undertaker for the two dead men, the sheriff asked Prophet with a chagrined air if he'd join him and Jose Encina for supper at Avril Tweet's Cafe that evening, obviously feeling guilty that he'd been so quick to assume that Prophet had started the lead swap. Not one to hold a grudge, and since he had no one else to sup with, Prophet agreed to join the two men.

When the sheriff had given Prophet directions to the eatery, the bounty hunter clomped back into the bathhouse to finish dressing and endure more of the Chinaman's tirade.

When he'd dressed in relatively clean clothes from his saddlebags — faded denims, powder-blue denim shirt that had shrunk a couple sizes too small for his broad shoulders, and red neckerchief — he lugged his gear over to his second-floor room at the Muleskinner's Inn. The room was furnished with a lumpy iron bed wedged between the door and the right wall, a rickety wooden washstand, a backless wooden chair, and a few shelves and some

137

hooks for hanging clothes on.

It was little larger than a cookhouse broom closet. Not only was it sparsely and crudely furnished — the iron bed frame was speckled with chipped white enamel — but it had come with the threat that another lodger might be joining Prophet later that evening if the other twelve rooms filled up, unless Prophet paid an extra twenty-five cents for guaranteed privacy.

Prophet, who was almost broke and too proud to go on the take from Louisa, who was always flush, told the owner of the place, a shifty-eyed gent with dentures that didn't fit right, that if anyone disturbed him, the disturber would get a load of buckshot for his trouble. He wasn't promising the proprietor wouldn't get a load, as well.

The proprietor, Henricks, clicked his dentures, curled his nose, and snapped his newspaper as Prophet tramped up the stairs that were missing two entire steps, the whole shebang sloping dangerously to one side.

Now the bounty hunter dropped his gear on the bed, rearranged the possibles in his saddlebags, and rolled a smoke. He looked at his old Ingersol railroad watch and saw that he had some time before supper. Dropping the watch back into his jeans pocket, he dragged the backless chair up to the bed and, smoking, laid out all his guns — three pistols, shotgun, and Winchester '73 — side by side on the bed's stained quilt.

Always good to have clean weapons, and he hadn't cleaned his in over a week.

He hadn't used much of his arsenal in that time, outside of the rifle and shotgun, of course, but they might have collected just enough trail dust or plant seeds or moisture to hamper their actions.

No bounty man in his right mind — especially one who'd made as many enemies as Prophet had — carried guns with compromised actions. He never knew when said gun might come in handy, which his little run-in with Kentucky Earl Watson and his unknown compadre had so handily reminded him.

While Prophet worked, taking apart each weapon and carefully cleaning and oiling each part, he sipped from a bottle he'd picked up in a roadhouse along the trail up from Mexico. Nothing like a bottle to quell the frayed nerves on the lee side of a gun battle.

Nor for clarifying a man's thoughts.

While he cleaned the guns, smoked, and nursed the unlabeled hooch, he couldn't help wondering if any more of Kentucky

Earl Watson's gang was around. It seemed damn queer that several men from the same gang could have beefs with both Prophet and Louisa, from separate past dustups. But they had to all have been part of Kentucky Earl's bunch.

And if they were from the same bunch — and they *had* to have been — what had they been doing in Juniper? Obviously, they hadn't merely spotted Prophet and Louisa along the trail and followed them in. Hell-Bringin' Hiram's deputy had said he'd seen at least two of the men — Prophet's bush-whackers — around town.

What had they been doing here? Kentucky Earl Watson was many things, but a cow nurse was not one of them.

As Prophet put his rifle back together, caressing the forestock with an oily rag, he thought about Louisa.

A worry pang bit his belly, but the girl could take care of herself. He denied the urge to check on her before heading over to Avril Tweet's Cafe. Not only was it not necessary, but he didn't want to interfere with her evening with Miguel Encina. She'd look out for herself and the young banker tonight, and God help anyone who tried dry-gulching her. Unlike Prophet, the girl never took a drink of anything stronger than sarsaparilla — hell, she didn't even drink coffee! — so her mind was always as clear as Rocky Mountain snowmelt.

No, she could take care of herself. Prophet had no reason to worry about her. Of course, he had no reason to be jealous of young Miguel, either — since it had been his own idea for the young bounty hunting lass to settle down here in Juniper — but he was.

He puffed the quirley stub in his lips as he rubbed the rifle down, then tossed it onto the bed beside the others, the bluing of the entire arsenal shiny with fresh oil.

Christ, he thought. *Why don't I just pull out? I'm going to have to jerk my picket line sometime. I never should have taken the gold-guarding job. The only reason I did was because I wanted to get Louisa settled in here. I always knew I'd leave eventually. If she's already falling for the young banker, I have no business hanging around here, torturing myself and being a thorn in her side.*

He puffed the quirley and tossed it out the open window, then blew a long, ragged smoke plume after it.

12

Prophet rubbed water into his longish sandy hair and combed it.

He snugged his battered Stetson onto his head and, reluctantly leaving his ten-gauge in his room and armed with only his Peacemaker, tramped down the deathtrap stairs and out of the Muleskinner's Inn and over to Avril Tweet's Cafe. The eatery sat on a meandering side street on the town's north side near an open sage flat rolling up to distant, brown ridges. It was a wood-frame, two-story house with gingerbread siding and a simple but tastefully furnished interior, with two separate eating areas divided by a narrow, carpeted staircase.

The smell of fresh biscuits and gravy nearly flattened Prophet as he stepped through the door, but his enjoyment was tempered by a familiar voice raised in anger.

Doffing his hat, he followed the voice through a doorway and into the dining room on the house's left side. Jose Encina sat at a round, linen-covered table in the middle of the room. A cigar smoldered in his right hand as he draped his other arm over the back of his chair, craning his neck to look behind him, where Hell-Bringin' Hiram Severin stood before a small table against the far wall, under the head of a curly-horned mountain ram.

A young lady with long, brown braids and wearing a crisp white apron over a green, puffy-sleeved muslin dress stood a ways from the middle-aged sheriff, wringing her hands and looking worried. Two men dressed in ragged trail garb sat on either side of the table, looking up at Severin with much the same expression as that of the young lady. The two men's hats were hooked over their chair backs.

The man on the right had his hands on the table as though he'd been ordered to do so, while the sheriff, his left boot propped on the edge of the chair in which the other cowboy sat, crouched over the other cowboy, barking, ". . . And if you *ever* say anything like that to a young lady in my town again, you down-at-heel saddle trash, I'll haul you over to the hoosegow and lock you up for vagrancy!"

Striding slowly toward the table at which

Encina sat, Prophet saw the cowboy whom Severin was confronting staring up at the gray-headed, gray-mustached sheriff indignantly. When the cowboy only glowered, Severin jerked his right hand back behind his shoulder and swung it forward, his open palm connecting loudly with the cowboy's right cheek, jerking the young man's head around sharply.

The crack of the slap sounded like a pistol shot. The cowboy's cheek turned white as parchment, then quickly blazed as his jaws hardened in anger.

The girl, obviously a waitress, gasped with a start.

The slapped cowboy jerked his right arm.

"You sure you wanna do that, you scrawny little devil?" Severin had his coat flap peeled back behind the jutting grip of the ivory-handled Colt holstered butt forward on his right hip. "I say, you sure you wanna pull iron on me, slick?"

The cowboy's left eye twitched. He slid his gaze to his friend, who sat in his chair stone-faced, like a chastised schoolboy, then back and up to the menacing squint of the sheriff of Juniper. He said something too softly for Prophet to hear.

"That's right — you don't," the sheriff growled. "Now, I want you to apologize to

144

this young lady."

He glanced at the waitress who stood as though nailed to the polished wood floor, her eyes bright with fear. The cowboy swung his head to the girl then, too. He sniffed, cleared his throat, and said thickly, "Miss Dolly, I do apologize for sayin' you got nice ankles."

The girl's brows raveled and unraveled as she looked between the sheriff and the young cowboy, both regarding her expectantly. She didn't seem sure about how to respond. Finally, she pursed her lips, glanced at the floor, blushing brightly, and said, "I reckon that's all right, Mr. Fletcher," in a voice just barely audible.

"Th— thank you, ma'am," the cowboy said, returning his gaze to the sheriff.

The girl licked her lips nervously, then, still wringing her hands together, turned and fled through a door at the back of the room through which rose the occasional clatter of pots and pans.

"Now," Severin said, lifting his right fist from the cowboy's table and straightening, falling back on the heels of his polished, black, high-heeled boots, "I want you boys to leave them pistols and shell belts right there in your chairs, and I want you to get the hell out of here. I ain't sayin' you gotta leave town, but don't let me catch you over here at Mr. Tweet's place again — not until you've learned better manners."

The two looked at each other. Then, glowering, faces mottled with both chagrin and frustration, the two young drovers gained their feet, unbuckled their shell belts, and let them drop to their chairs with their holstered six-shooters. Casting indignant looks over their shoulders, they stomped out of the house and into the street where two dun cow ponies were tied at the hitchrail.

Prophet, who had slumped down in a chair across from Jose Encina, watched the still-glowering, red-faced lawman stride angrily over to the table and reclaim the chair he'd obviously been sitting in before. A nearly full glass of beer and a whiskey shot stood on the table in front of it.

"Damn, Hiram," the bounty hunter said, hooking his hat over his chair back, "I see you ain't softened any with age."

"Can't get soft, Proph," the sheriff said, easing into his chair. "Not when you got a town to keep on its leash, and one that's as far off the beaten path as Juniper. You know, they used to call it Helldorado."

"I seen the sign when we rode in."

"The name fit. We changed it about three

years ago, when it stopped fittin'. I don't ever want it to fit again. Leastways, not while I'm wearin' this sheriff's star. My actions might have seemed a little harsh with that younker. But 'the Kid,' as he likes to be called, stirs up trouble, or tries to. Starts by ogling the girls and making nasty comments, and the boot-stomping spreads to the other punchers, and before you know it you got a rowdy bunch tearing apart saloons or running wild in the streets, and the young ladies are afraid to show themselves after dark."

The old town tamer threw back half his whiskey shot and followed it up with a healthy pull from his beer glass. Smacking his lips and lowering the glass to the table, he added, "That ain't the kinda town I run, Lou."

"Si," said Jose Encina, regarding the sheriff sitting across from him with an admiring cast to his coffee-brown gaze. "Before Senor Hiram, my bank was robbed at least three times a year. I was ready to close up shop and move back to Mejico even with the revolutionarios running rampant over my rancho. I have the good sheriff to thank for my livelihood, as do most of the other business owners in town."

The young waitress, Dolly, approached

147

the table to take Prophet's drink order, and when she had it, she muttered her thanks to Hiram.

"Just doin' my job, Dolly. And I do apologize for the Kid's behavior."

She smiled nervously. "He don't really mean nothin' by it, Sheriff. He comes around, now and then, and says things. . . ."

"Well, from now on, he won't be comin' around," the sheriff said as he regarded the girl with gravity, turning his shot glass in his fingers. "And I suggest, young lady, you avoid that boy. He's trash."

"Yessir," Dolly said quickly and hurried back into the kitchen.

Prophet said, "I got me a feelin' the Kid's sparkin' that girl, Hiram. And I got me another feelin' she don't mind."

"Well, she should mind," the sheriff said gruffly. "I know the so-called Kid's family. His mother was a whore, his father a pig farmer who drank himself to death down New Mexico way. Knew some of his other kin in another town I tamed down there, and believe me, they weren't nothin' you'd want your daughter seen with, neither."

The men fell silent when Dolly returned with Prophet's beer and shot. She did not look at the sheriff and only raked her troubled gaze briefly across Prophet before

148

she said, "You gentlemen be eatin' tonight, will you?"

When they'd each ordered the night's special of pork roast with fried potatoes and green beans, Dolly again disappeared sullenly into the kitchen. Prophet sipped his beer and, feeling uneasy but not being able to put his finger on why, asked, "How was it you came up this way, Hiram? Last I knew, you was still bounty huntin', and that was after your hide-huntin' days."

The sheriff took a small sip from his whiskey, holding the glass almost daintily between his thumb and index finger, both of which were the red-brown of old, weathered brick, and chuckled. "Yessir, I hunted buffalo from up around Winnipeg, Canada, clear down to Mesilla, New Mexico. Them were the days, though they plum took some starch outta me, what with fightin' the Comanche every winter." The nostalgic smile left the man's face when, sliding across the table to Prophet, he said in a deep, serious tone, "Left bounty hunting when I killed the wrong man, Lou — or who I was told was the wrong man — and spent three years in the Kansas pen for it."

"Ah, hell, Hiram."

The sheriff nodded gravely. "I shot a young man I'd been tracking for nigh on

149

two months through the Indian Nations. He bushwhacked me, and I drilled him through his right eye. Hauled him back to Alva over his horse, and that's when I was told I'd killed the wrong man. Prominent rancher's son. No way the young man could have robbed that stagecoach and killed the shotgun guard, by god, because he just wasn't that kind of boy!"

"You catch him with the money?" Prophet asked, rolling a smoke while regarding the sheriff with mantled brows.

"Caught him with half of it. The other half was gone. Probably spent on whores in Clancyville or Ortega. The rancher claimed the money was from cattle the young fire-brand had sold in Fort Smith. Of course, I couldn't prove it wasn't, and the kid did have a receipt for sold cattle on him. And with most of the county, including the law-men, backing the rancher merely because he owned most of the town and half the county, the jury of twelve convicted me of manslaughter."

He chuckled ruefully and shook his head, staring down at the whiskey he continued to turn in his fingers. "I reckon I got off lucky. I was sentenced to five years but got out in two for good behavior. Reckoned the parole board figured I was gettin' too old to blast any more trails out of the limestone hills they had us workin', and they let me go. I figure they knew the kid I shot was bad seed and saw no reason I oughta be punished for doin' what his old man shoulda done a long time ago."

"Shit, Hiram," Prophet said. "I never heard about that."

"I never spread it around, Lou. Thing like that's hard on a man's reputation. Suffice it to say, my heart wasn't in bounty huntin' anymore. The only reason I pinned a badge on my coat was because I was asked to help a deputy U.S. marshal friend up in Montana file down the horns on Miles City. Hell, I had nothin' better to do than lug a shotgun up and down the street of that dusty cow town, and, after a few months, hell . . . the murderin' and robbin' had all but died off, and I found more folks from around the West wantin' me to come and help get their own towns on short leashes."

Sheriff Severin tossed back the last of his whiskey and ran the back of a hand across his mustache. "One o' them was Senor Encina here, and several other fine gentlemen from the Helldorado city council — all at their wits' end with bandits runnin' wild and claim jumpers and rustlers galore —

and here I sit, wearin' a county sheriff's star!"

"Well, hell," Prophet said, lifting his beer glass. "Here's to you, Hiram. Looks like you've done a real fine job."

"*Si, si!*" said Jose Encina, clinking his brandy goblet against Prophet's and the sheriff's beer schooners.

"And I do apologize for the foofaraw earlier." Prophet sipped his beer and, swallowing, shook his head. "And, Louisa . . . hell, sometimes I don't know what gets into that girl's head."

"Why?" Severin frowned at Prophet. "Because she merely shot a man even lower than a chicken-stealing coyote?"

"Well . . ." Prophet shrugged.

He sort of saw it the sheriff's way. But that wasn't necessarily the *right* way. As a bounty hunter, he'd always tried to keep the hunting and judging separate. If he didn't, he'd likely end up in a state pen, like Severin himself had.

"Speakin' of them," Prophet said, sitting back from the table as Dolly brought three steaming platters of roast pork, with rich brown, peppery gravy smothering the fried potatoes, and a liberal portion of garden beans. He made a conscious effort to keep from drooling as his stomach kicked like a stallion against his rib cage. "I got to thinkin', Hiram," he continued as the steam from the plate bathed his face, "it seems damn odd that four men gunnin' for both me and Louisa woulda showed up in town at the same time. Three of whom were known hard cases, the third probably known, too, though not by me."

Hiram ordered another round of drinks for the table then, tucking an oilcloth bib into the neck of his pin-striped, collarless shirt. He cleared his throat and scooted his chair toward his own heaping platter. "What're you sayin', Lou? You think I suddenly had the damn wool pulled over my eyes and become overrun with border toughs?"

Jose Encina chuckled as he gazed with delight at his plate and picked up fork and knife like a surgeon preparing for work.

Prophet hesitated, looking askance at his stubborn old friend. "All I'm sayin, Hiram, is that many bad boys at one time in one place could mean trouble. More than just one back-shot-old-bounty-hunter kinda trouble. Now, I realize you done scooped the shit out of what was once a privy pit here in Juniper. But there are regular gold runs from the mines to the bank here in town."

He glanced at Encina, who arched a brow at him as he cut into his gravy-covered pork slab.

"I know, cause I'm one of the guards now," the bounty hunter added wryly. "And not to consider the possibility that they're here for the gold would be just plum —"

"You're right." The sheriff was hunkered down over his plate, chewing a mouthful of potatoes and gravy. "You're damn right, like you always were, Proph." He swallowed, and as he buried his fork into his fried potatoes after forking a charred-edged chunk of meat, he added, "Sometimes I get cocky and muleheaded, and that ain't good. You're right, Lou. To not even consider that those gents might have been here for the gold would be right foolish. And to make sure there ain't any more skulkin' around, waiting for another team to head out on another run, maybe follow 'em and buschwack 'em somewhere in the mountains when they got a wagonload of ingots, I'm gonna turn my wolves loose."

"How's that?" Prophet said with a mouthful of the delicious food. He couldn't remember tasting gravy that good — but then, he never could remember the taste of good gravy after a long pull without a proper feed sack hooked over his ears.

"My deputies."

Encina chuckled and glanced cunningly at the sheriff as the banker sawed off another slab of the perfectly roasted pork.

"I'm gonna send 'em around to get careful looks at everyone in town. Scour the saloons. Anyone who don't belong here — and I mean anyone they ain't seen before and don't know or even heard of — they'll slap down and get acquainted with 'em real quick."

Prophet washed down his mouthful of potatoes and gravy with a healthy slug of beer. "You callin' them two badge toters I seen earlier *wolves?*"

"They're dumber'n a trainload of coal," the sheriff said, nodding. "But they're crack shots — both of 'em. And they're good deputies. Put the fear into folks, which is what a good lawman does. Cows 'em like whipped dogs." He shook his head and smiled grimly as he stared down at his plate, both hands working at the food. "I got three more where them two come from — Moffett, Horn, and Giuseppe Antero. They're out chasin' claim jumpers in the north part of the county. Them two you seen was Chase Appleyard — he was the tall one — and Frank Dryden. 'Dry,' as we call him, spent four years in Yuma. Only safe place for that scrappy son of a bitch is behind a badge!"

The sheriff looked at his friend Encina, and the two men shared a conspiratorial laugh.

As he ate, Prophet glanced at both men skeptically. "I'll be damned, Hiram," he said, trying to make it sound like a joke but unable to bring it off. "Don't sound like you got lawmen on your roll, but attack dogs."

"Out here, that's what ya nee—"

"Ah, look what we have here," Encina interrupted, lifting his head to stare, grinning with satisfaction, toward the front doorway.

Prophet followed the banker's gaze to where the young, handsome Miguel Encina was just entering the room behind Louisa Bonaventure, who parried Prophet's incredulous gaze with a coolly arched brow.

13

"Who let you in here?" Louisa asked Prophet in her snide, ironic way.

"I was invited in."

"Surprise, surprise."

Miguel Encina doffed his bowler hat as he walked up behind Louisa, who'd stopped before the table of Prophet, Hell-Bringin' Hiram Severin, and Jose Encina. "Good to see you again, Mr. Prophet. Father. Sheriff. We weren't wanting to interrupt your meal but didn't think it polite not to stop over and say hi."

"Oh, you mean you won't be joining us?" Severin said with mock surprise.

"Wouldn't want to interrupt, Sheriff."

Jose Encina held his fork beneath his chin, casting his admiring gaze across Louisa. "Miss Bonaventure, do you ever go anywhere without those fine-looking *pistolas*?"

"Not even to church, Senor Encina."

"Some would consider it unladylike." The

banker gave her a sidelong, mildly reproving glance.

"What's unladylike about letting yourself get back shot, Senor?"

Miguel Encina laughed nervously. The sheriff roared and shook his head. "She's got you there, Jose!"

The elder Encina smiled agreeably and hiked his shoulder. Prophet could see that Miguel wasn't the only man here smitten with Louisa.

"I don't suppose we could entice you into joining us?" Severin said with genuine beseeching.

"Sorry," Louisa said. "I'd feel outnumbered."

"And I'd feel ganged up on," the young man said with a laugh, tossing his head toward the door. "And, anyway, I've reserved a table in the other room. Shall we, Miss Louisa?"

"Certainly," the young bounty huntress said in her best civilized tongue, smiling up at the banker's son with obvious affection. It was a new expression for her. Prophet had never seen her look at anyone like that, including him.

When they'd gone into the other room and the bounty hunter was fighting a jealousy bout almost as severe as the hunger pang he'd felt before digging into the fine, half-devoured supper before him, the sheriff and the banker stared after the couple with wistful expressions.

"I think they make a nice pair," the banker said. "Of course, if they became serious, she'd have to hang up her guns. I couldn't have my son attached to a woman so prominently armed."

"I'd ask her real nice," Prophet advised.

"She might do that for young Miguel," the sheriff said, picking up his knife and fork and going at his plate once more. "I think she likes him. I know Miguel likes her. Then, there ain't much *not* to like about her, includin' the way she dispatches coyotes."

Snorting, Severin glanced at Prophet, who'd resumed eating with not quite as much vigor as before.

"How'd you two meet up, Lou?"

Prophet told the men, briefly, about how he'd run into Louisa during her vengeance quest for the men who'd killed her family in Nebraska. He himself had gone after the Handsome Dave Duvall bunch after the gang had shot up the town of Luther Falls, Minnesota, and he and Louisa had followed the wolf pack into the far northern reaches of Dakota Territory and taken down every one.

"She didn't know much about shootin' back then, but she's so damn purty and innocent-looking, no one believed she was on the blood trail. Most of the gang she lured away from the others, one by one or two by two, using her looks and girlish charm. Not to mention her guile. She kicked 'em out bloody. Even made one fella stretch his own neck." Prophet shook his head, remembering how absolutely merciless the girl had been.

"Good for her," the sheriff said, chewing slowly as he frowned across the table at Prophet, taking in every word. Then his eyes sparked ironically. "Sounds like she's bein' wasted as a gold guard. I oughta pin a deputy sheriff's star on her delightful little frame."

"I hope she ain't even gonna be gold guardin' long," Prophet said, swabbing the last of his gravy with a last chunk of pork. "I'm hopin' she'll settle down here, and that Senor Encina can talk her into hangin' up her guns." He grinned wryly at the banker, who was sipping from his goblet, one beringed pinky extended. "Uh . . . in a real nice way."

The men laughed.

As Encina set his tumbler down and pressed the end of a fist against his mouth to stifle a belch, the banker said, "That will be up to my son. He himself hung up a pair of guns that nearly got him killed, so he'll likely know how to convince Senorita Louisa to do the same."

Prophet slid his plate forward to make room for his elbows. "You tellin' me young Miguel was once in the cold-steel business, Don?"

Encina frowned, puzzled. "The what? The cold . . ."

"It's a gunfightin' expression, my dear friend," said the sheriff. "Proph means pistolero, and I can answer that one: no. Far from it. We got to him — Jose and I — before he got that far out of hand." He glanced at the banker. "But he was on his way, wasn't he, Jose?"

"Si, si," said the banker, shaking his head and pooching his lips distastefully. "He got in with a bad crowd here in Helldorado, before Sheriff Severin came and settled things down, including my son."

"I was glad to do it, Jose. But I didn't do it alone. The boy respects his father."

"Well, at least I believe he has learned to respect me," the elder Encina said. "As well as our livelihood."

161

Prophet shuttled his shocked gaze between both men. "That's right hard to believe. He don't look like the type."

"That's the thing, Lou," the sheriff said. "Miguel wasn't the type. He just got in with the wrong crowd. Lord knows there was enough of the wrong crowd here to get in with. When me and my deputies got the crowd whittled down to just one bad apple here and there every coupla weeks, me and Jose took Miguel in hand, as well. Let's just say we reminded him of his good upbringin' and sorta explained to him a life of rustlin' and pistol poppin' and carryin' on wasn't the life he really wanted for himself."

"He was a young man," the banker said, hiking his shoulders and lifting his hands. "No different from any other. Especially one who loses his mother early and is taken away from his home and all that he knows by a father he hardly knew at the time. I had so much to do on my hacienda, you see, back in Mejico, that I had little time for a child. But now my dear Miguel is a respected member of Juniper; I even made him president of the bank. I love him dearly, and we get along superbly. Now . . ." The banker smiled bemusedly. "Now, if he can only find the right woman to raise a family with, to fill our house with grandchildren . . ."

"Maybe he has," the sheriff said, glancing at Prophet and raising the corners of his mouth slightly.

"That's right," Prophet said. He wasn't overly troubled by what he'd learned about Miguel's early days. There were damn few young men who hadn't fancied themselves pistoleros before they grew old enough to learn better or were taken in hand by the right sorts. Still, something was troubling the bounty hunter, and he wasn't sure what it was exactly.

Louisa? Miguel? Louisa *and* Miguel?

The bushwhackers?

Or was it just being in a town — any town — that was already getting to him?

Whatever the cause, he tried to keep the unease from his tone when he said, raising his beer glass to drain it, "Yeah, maybe he has at that."

"Thank you for that wonderful meal, Miguel," Louisa said when she and the younger Encina were walking out the door of Avril Tweet's Cafe and into a sparkling, glowing Rocky Mountain sunset.

Miguel set his bowler hat on his thick mop of chestnut hair. "The pleasure was mine, Miss Louisa. Mr. Tweet does throw together a heckuva meal, doesn't he?"

"And a most welcome one after three weeks of trail food and Lou Prophet's coffee."

Miguel turned to the girl, who was staring westward at the fire-colored clouds stretching off over serrated, purple ridges. "Miss Louisa, would I be too forward to ask you to walk with me by the creek? I can tell you're a girl who appreciates a sunset, and the ones here in Juniper are best appreciated from there."

"I don't think that would be too forward at all."

"Even without a chaperone?"

In a blur of motion, Louisa pulled her matched, pearl-gripped Colts and twirled each on a finger. "What makes you think I don't have a chaperone?" She dropped the polished weapons smoothly back down into their holsters with a single snick of iron against oiled leather.

Miguel whistled. "My lord, where'd you learn to handle a brace of pistols like that?"

"Here and there," Louisa said, purposely cryptic.

She stepped off the boardwalk and angled across the side street. She pointed her chin at what appeared to be a deer path stretching off between a livery barn and a wheelwright's shop and curving into a rolling sage flat bathed in soft opal light. "Will that take us there?"

"It will."

Walking side by side, she and Miguel started up the path, stepping around trash littering the gap between the buildings. Ahead lay a row of cedars, aspens, and cottonwoods marking the meandering line of the creek, though Louisa could not yet see the water from here.

Neither she nor Miguel spoke for a time. It was the silence, a little awkward but laden with anticipation and expectation as well, of two people just getting to know each other.

The grass crunched beneath Louisa's worn boots and Miguel's polished brown half boots. Mourning doves cooed. An occasional blackbird caw rose from the creek just ahead.

"Miss Louisa," Miguel said finally, bending down to snag a bromegrass stalk when they were halfway to the trees, "about you and Mr. Prophet. You tell me if I'm getting fresh, but are you and him . . . ?"

He let his voice trail off. They both continued walking, meandering along the footpath worn through the sage and fescue, Louisa's eyes clouded with thought.

Finally, reaching down to pick a slender

Indian paintbrush stalk and caressing the tender, red blossom with her palm, she said, "We're partners." After a couple of more steps, she added, "Have been for several years now. I won't lie to you and say that we haven't been more than that. The bounty trail is a lonely, dangerous place."

She stopped suddenly, and then Miguel did, too. They stood facing each other under a green sky, mourning doves cooing and the sounds of the town — the clatter of a wagon, the thuds of an ax — hushed and far away. "Does that matter to you?"

"I reckon it does and it doesn't. I mean, I wouldn't want to get between you."

"There's already something between us, Miguel. There always has been." Louisa looked down at the Indian paintbrush blossom. "We're from different worlds, Lou and me. The only thing we've had in common these past years is man hunting. I don't mean that I don't love him, and I reckon he loves me, sure enough. We've been through a lot together. We've saved each other's lives more times than I like to think about, and he saved mine just a few weeks ago, down in Mexico."

She paused, feeling a knot in her throat. Prophet was a hard man to leave, but it was time to leave him. "With all that said . . . I realize now it is finally time for me to settle down. Lou — he'll never settle down. He'd never make a husband. . . ."

Miguel turned away and absently kicked a stone. "No, I reckon he wouldn't. Can't see a man like Prophet ever settling down." He turned to Louisa again, rolling the brome-grass stem between his lips and narrowing one eye. "Not with someone like you, anyways. But you . . ." He reached forward, took her hand in his. "I can see you settling down, appreciating all the good things a more settled life, with the right man, can bring you."

"You mean a house and a garden and all that?"

Miguel puckered his lips out, nodding. "Sure, all that. And the love of a good man . . . and a family."

Louisa jerked her hand back suddenly, and she felt as though she'd just been shot at. The reaction surprised even her, and she felt her face warm with embarrassment. Her eyes widened as she stepped back away from the handsome young man smiling down at her, a faint look of surprise in his soft brown gaze.

She slid a lock of blond hair back from her right eye and glanced at the town sprawled a hundred yards away, turning a darker shade of purple as the sun continued to sink lower behind the western mountains. She tried to see it as she might after she'd settled there a while, as a home. But for some reason it only looked foreign to her, like all the other towns she'd passed through on the hunting trail, and loneliness and desolation swept through her like a long drink of bad milk.

Why was that?

"I'm sorry, Louisa," Miguel said. "I didn't mean to be so forward. Good lord, we just met a few hours ago."

"That's all right." She continued to stare at the town where a few wagons and horseback riders were moving along the streets, glimpsed between the darkening buildings. "Love and a family . . . That's what I've been wanting. Just hearing them now, from you, suddenly gave me a shock. I'm sorry." She laughed but there was no humor in it, only confusion. "I don't know why. . . ."

"I do," Miguel said, apologetically. "I was moving too fast."

Louisa barely heard him. As she stared toward the sprawling settlement, the town faded. It was replaced by the sunblasted Mexican prison nestled in that stark desert valley, surrounded by rocks and cactus, smoke rising from the Rurales' cook fires.

She wasn't standing near the chuckling creek with a handsome young banker. She was tied to the bed of Major Montoya.

The major was laughing — roaring — as he threw back another shot of his sour-smelling liquor. He slammed the back of his hand against her face, his expression changing suddenly, and he was castigating her through chipped, gritted teeth: "If you do not perform well for me this evening, *puta rubia,* I will send you out to the stables for the amusement of my men!" He slapped her again. "How would you like that? *Huh?*"

The slap jerked Louisa's head back and sideways, and her knees hit the ground.

"Louisa!" Miguel dropped to a knee beside her, wrapped an arm around her shoulders.

Louisa steadied herself, head reeling from Montoya's assault. She automatically touched her hand to her cheek as though to prove to herself she'd only imagined it. As she turned to Miguel beside her, the young man's eyes turned dark with worry.

Her heart lightened. She glanced beyond him toward the town, relieved to see it really was the town there, the sage glowing a soft green around the dark purple buildings, smoke skeining from chimneys. "Willl-burrrr!" some mother called for her child.

"Come on home, now! Time for bed!"

Louisa had left the prison as well as Montoya back in Mexico.

Miguel stared at her, frowning, and as her eyes returned to his, he lifted his hand slowly, slid her hair back from her face, and smiled reassuringly. "It's all right. You're here now. That's all over."

She frowned. "You knew . . . ?"

"That you were back in Mexico?" His cheeks dimpled, and his eyes acquired a softer cast of deep understanding. "I've been there myself, a time or two."

Her brows furrowed still further.

"Come on." Wrapping an arm around her waist, he eased her gently to her feet. "Let's walk, and I'll tell you about it."

14

"Proph, I remember that look," said Sheriff Hell-Bringin' Hiram Severin. "What you need is your ashes hauled."

"Ah, hell."

Prophet, the sheriff, and Jose Encina had spent well over an hour chinning over post-supper whiskey and beer in Tweet's Cafe, with Prophet and the sheriff reminiscing about their bounty-hunting days. Now they stood outside the Hog's Head Saloon, bathed in the smoke of cheap tobacco, cheaper perfume, and surprisingly well-played piano music.

The sheriff said, "May I suggest Miss Maude Allen's place over yonder, behind the bank a couple of blocks? It's one of the few whorehouses I didn't close down, 'cause it's run by the fine, upstanding Miss Maude, whom you may remember from Hays, Kansas. She keeps only the cleanest, most polite girls in all the territory."

"Ah, shit," Prophet said, reaching behind his head to push the back of his hat up, the brim sliding down his forehead. "That usually means they're fat and ugly and missing enough teeth to matter even to me."

"Chubby is a better word," said Jose Encina, puffing a freshly lit cigar and hiking a shoulder. "Chubby and happy, with the man's best interest at heart. *Placer del hombre.* Senora Maude has taught them well."

"No, thanks," Prophet said. "The long ride and that good meal and hooch 'bout did me in. I think I'll mosey on back to the Muleskinner's Inn, maybe meet the boys I'll be ridin' with tomorrow, chew a little fat, and turn in."

"It's early yet, Proph," objected the sheriff. "If you don't want a girl, how 'bout a game of high-five? Jose and I usually play for an hour or so before we turn in of a night and I let my deputies take over." Severin hiked a brow enticingly. "I'll spot ya, if you're short."

"I appreciate that," Prophet said, nudging his old friend's shoulder with his own then pinching his hat brim at the banker. "And it has been a pleasure. But I'm pooped and tuckered as a coon hound with the Georgia sun on the rise. I'm gonna wander on over and tumble in."

He hiked his shell belt higher on his lean hips and moseyed on up the street, both the sheriff and the banker calling their "good-nights" and "sleep-tights" behind him. Soon the Hog's Head piano music was swallowed by the soft strumming of a guitar in a smaller, darker cantina from which also emanated soft, soulful lyrics sung by a husky-voiced Spanish woman. He stepped around several sets of subdued revelers clumped along the street — white men, half-breeds, blacks, and a few Mexicans dressed in the ragged garb of sheep men — near horses standing hang-headed at hitchracks.

Suddenly, he realized that several men were moving up around him from all sides, closing on him fast. Especially paranoid in light of recent events, Prophet slowed his pace and touched his pistol grips with the intention of swinging around, pulling the piece, and rocking the hammer back to forestall another dry-gulching.

But then a couple of the men brushed past him, and so did another and another — all heading away from him and angling off toward the big opera house in front of which two tall gas lamps burned like beacons. Prophet turned full around as he walked slowly, cautiously, in the same direction.

There were a dozen or so men — some in

173

ragged trail gear, others in cheap drummer's suits — behind him, and they were all talking loudly and smoking as they headed in the direction of the opera house. Others were angling into the street from the saloons and cantinas on the street's other side, seemingly headed in the same direction.

As he continued strolling, dropping his hand from his pistol grips, Prophet could make out above the crowd's din a man barking: "Come one, come all! Come one, come all! It's Miss Gleneanne O'Shay tonight, fellas, performing *Claudette: Portrait of a Chambermaid!* Come on over to the opera house tonight, gentlemen! Show starts in fifteen minutes! Only seventy-five lousy cents for a show that must not be missed!"

When Prophet was a couple of buildings away from the opera house that was lit up like a Dodge City whorehouse on the Fourth of July, he stopped and leaned against an awning support post, digging into his shirt pocket for his makings sack. The crowd rippled around him, smoking and talking, spurs ringing. The barker, the top-hat clad silhouette of whom Prophet could see standing in front of the gas lamps fronting the opera house, continued to hail the many and sundry away from the hitchracks and saloons.

They were heading for the ornate building's open doors like the doomed seeking sanctuary.

As he slowly, thoughtfully built a smoke, Prophet considered heading that way himself. He was feeling out of sorts about Louisa and young Miguel and vaguely, unconsciously testy about meeting up with his old town-taming pal and the banker who obviously felt the sun rose and set on the old hell bringer's shoulders. A good opera show might be just the distraction Prophet needed.

He'd just twisted the quirley closed and licked it sealed and was about to scrape a match to life on his shell belt when movement up the street caught his eye. He stayed his match hand and looked past the opera house's right side, from where several horseback riders clomped along the main street.

As the riders passed the opera house and came on along the street at a spanking trot, Prophet saw that they were all dressed in suits, one wearing a bowler hat, the other two wearing Stetsons. Five-pointed stars on their coat lapels flashed in the dusky light as they made their way toward Prophet, who could also see now that the third deputy, riding slightly behind the other two, was trailing four horses, tied tail to tail, by a single lead rope.

The third deputy, a black man with a short beard, held one arm out behind him, the tan-gloved hand of that arm clutching the rope. He glanced back occasionally at the four blanket-wrapped bundles tied across each horse's saddle.

Dead men, Prophet saw as the three deputies rode up even with him and continued on past before angling away down a southern side street. As the four packhorses made the turn, Prophet saw long, stringy red hair hanging down from the blanket-wrapped bundle of the last horse in the string, a high-stepping blue roan with one notched ear and a roached mane.

Flies buzzed around the dead man's hair that, even from Prophet's distance, appeared blood-matted.

Men along both sides of the street were gesturing at the deputies, one man near Prophet whistling and shaking his head and muttering, "Well, I reckon they run down them claim jumpers, eh?"

"Wonder what kind of a chance they give 'em?" asked a short, rangy, curly-haired Mexican standing with his back against the front wall of a cantina, smoking a brown paper cigarette, a shabby sombrero tipped back off his forehead. "Probably about as much as the ones they gave the Haskell boys, huh, amigos?"

"Shut up, ya damn pepperbelly," intoned a well-dressed man with an Irish accent as he passed the Mexican with another man, similarly attired. Both were heading toward the opera house. "Them Haskell boys got what they deserved." He glanced back at the Mex to add, "At least they didn't get any more than what they gave those poor freighters up from Alfred."

He turned forward and continued on to the opera house, where the barker was still loudly summoning one and all to the show.

The Mexican lifted a dirty middle finger at the man's retreating back.

"Don't be an idiot, Casol," said one of the other men standing outside the cantina who appeared uninterested in the opera house. He was hatless, with tangled pewter hair curling over his ears, dressed in ragged trail garb and shit-stained boots with Texas spurs. He slapped the back of his hand against the Mexican's chest as he nonchalantly lifted his beer schooner to his lips.

The Mex turned to him and stuck the finger with which he'd saluted the well-dressed man up his nose, regarding the pewter-haired drover flat-eyed. Then he removed his finger, turned a little unsteadily on his undershot, high-topped boots, and ambled through the louvered cantina doors behind him, grabbing the bare arm of a young Mexican girl who'd been standing there, looking bored.

Prophet heard the thumps of fast-moving feet and the raucous ringing of spurs moving up behind him on the hard-packed street. "Break it up, now, fellas," said an authoritative voice. "No lingerin' around outside after dark. Either go on over and enjoy the show at the opry house or get into a saloon. Better yet . . ."

The man's voice trailed off as Prophet turned to look at the deputy he'd met earlier after he'd blown Kentucky Earl Watson back to hell. Frank Dryden — at least, that's what he thought Hell-Bringin' Hiram had called this blond-headed fireplug of a man with a pinched-up face and narrow-set green eyes.

He was carrying a double-barreled shotgun like Prophet's from a lanyard around his neck, and he wore two pistols low on his black-clad thighs. On his head sat a small, crisp, black Stetson stitched with white leather.

His eyes met Prophet's, brightening with recognition, his thin lips forming a customarily belligerent, arrogant smile. Holding Prophet's gaze with his own, he continued, ". . . Better yet, get on to home or your favorite flophouse, get a good night's sleep. Nights are nice up here, real cool and starry. Man sleeps right good . . . when he ain't out shootin' up the town."

Keeping his expression bland, Prophet tipped his hat brim at the wiry blond. "Deputy Dryden is it?"

"Sure is, Prophet. I do apologize, but even gold guards ain't allowed to roam the streets directionless after dark." Dryden winked. "That's what you call a city ordinance."

"I call it horseshit."

The man who'd swatted the Mexican chuckled, then dropped his chin to his chest in chagrin. Dryden's right cheek twitched, and his eye narrowed at Prophet. "How's that?"

"A man can move around as he pleases, as long as he ain't breakin' any laws." Prophet stared at the belligerent little deputy, keeping an eye on the double bores of the deputy's shotgun, which the man held carelessly in his folded arms.

Prophet kept his voice affable but rimmed it with a slight, menacing edge. "And I'd just as soon them twin barrels didn't slide no farther in my direction. Me, I got an ordinance about havin' guns pointed at me. 'Specially since I know what a gut-shredder like that ten gauge of yours can do to a man."

Dryden's cheeks flushed, his jaws hard. He slid his gaze to the man standing with his back to the cantina, boots crossed, chin down as though he were sleeping. He and Prophet were the only two men on the street who were not striding for the opera house.

The deputy slid his stony green gaze back to Prophet but spoke out the side of his mouth to the pewter-haired man slumped against the cantina. "You goin' to the show, Sawrod?"

"Nah," came the almost inaudible reply.

"Then go on in and have a drink."

"You buyin', Frank?"

Dryden's cheek twitched again. Soundlessly, though Prophet sensed his silent amusement, the man called Sawrod leaned away from the cantina's front wall, turned lazily, and pushed through the batwings and into the low hum of conversations inside.

Dryden's lips barely moved as he told Prophet, "I'll let your friend Sheriff Severin know how you feel about his laws."

"You do that."

"You goin' inside?" Dryden canted his head toward the batwings that were still vibrating behind Sawrod.

"Nah." Prophet wanted to punch the ring-tailed varmint before him. But in deference to Hell-Bringin' Hiram, he merely slipped his quirley between his lips and drew deep. "I think I'll saunter over and take in the show."

"It's a good one." Dryden smiled. "If that lead actress filly is drunk enough, she might even show her titties."

"Good to hear." Prophet turned and began tramping toward the opera house whose gas lamps had grown brighter against the thickening darkness.

"One more thing."

Prophet glanced back at Dryden, whose nostrils flared. "I ain't afraid of you, big man."

Prophet grinned. "Ain't this a co-incidence? I ain't afraid of you, neither." He pinched his hat brim at the little man, turned, and walked away.

15

Prophet couldn't afford the seventy-five-cent ticket to see *Claudette: Portrait of a Chambermaid,* but he paid the money, anyway, leaving about two dimes in his pocket. He took the handbill a young usher gave him as he passed from the opera house's marble-floored lobby through an arched doorway of varnished wood and between two bronzed knights holding flambeaus and drifted with the crowd into the main auditorium.

He wasn't sure what had driven him into this castle-like construction filled with smoking, sweating, half-drunk townsmen and drovers. Maybe just a general unease and a feeling that if he tumbled into bed now he'd be in for some miserable tossing and turning before sleep got ahold of him. Or maybe he needed distraction, to let go of this crazy town that his old friend Hell-Bringin' Hiram Severin had in his crazy iron grip and forget that he'd brought Louisa to settle down here.

He'd never been in an opera house before, though he'd seen a few from the outside. But he'd heard that you could get lucky and, between actual operas that were exercises in mind-tearing, eye-gouging tedium, run into dance shows where feather-haired girls ran around in circles, taking their clothes off and kicking their legs.

That's what Prophet needed now — pretty girls showing their tits and high-stepping in red shoes.

He made his way down the center aisle in the main auditorium, tripping over his own boots as well as the spurs of the gent in front of him as he gaped at the massive vaulted ceiling and the plush, scroll-back chairs around him and at the stage with a burgundy, gold-trimmed velvet curtain at the back of the place. The stage was about five feet higher than the main floor, and there was a mural, too dim for Prophet to make out clearly, painted on the wall above the curtain.

Gas lamps at regular intervals along the walls and the cigarettes and cigars nearly every man in the place was puffing made the place as foggy as Chickamauga after four days of hard fighting. Through this haze

183

and from his plush seat, boot hiked on a knee, Prophet enjoyed the program just the same, though he couldn't make heads or tails out of the plot of what turned out to be, to his dismay, a theater play with a lot of serious chatter instead of dancing and titty-jiggling.

He might have been able to fathom a little of what was going on if nearly every man in the auditorium hadn't been hooting and hollering at the main actress, a stygian-haired, willow-limbed, big-breasted gal — Miss Gleneanne O'Shay, Prophet assumed — who frequently turned to the audience to shriek and cry and drop to her knees before slamming her head against the floor, quivering.

At one point, having been admonished by an old, gray-haired gal in a gray cape who didn't want the chambermaid making time with her rich young son any longer and kicked her out of the village, she tried to hang herself. She was about to put her head into the noose only to be saved by the tony-looking son with a waxed handlebar mustache, whom one of the cowboys threw a beer bottle at when he refused the chambermaid's kiss on account of his mother.

The play finally ended with the chambermaid, scorned by a rich old gent with curly silver hair, finally ending her miserable, heartbroken existence by downing poison from a small, green bottle. When she'd dropped into her bed after another long rambling cry complete with arm throwing and head wagging, her bed was lifted into a wool cloud by ropes and pulleys that Prophet could hear squawking even above the crowd's harangues.

"Jesus Christ, you mean we sat here for over an hour and she didn't even take her clothes off *once?*" thundered a resonant voice somewhere behind Prophet.

Prophet felt similarly disappointed though he added no catcalls and heckles to that of the others, some of whom were also throwing spitballs made from torn handbills at the curtain quickly closing on the cast taking hurried bows. He'd just risen from his chair and was about to make his way back to the lobby when someone tapped his shoulder.

He turned to see a skinny gent in a bowler hat and with longish, stringy red hair leaning toward him, an unctuous smile revealing two chipped front teeth. "Pardon me, Mr. Prophet?"

The bounty hunter frowned at him.

"Your presence has been requested backstage." In the man's English accent, "stage" sounded like "styge." His breath was rife with the smell of whiskey, and his eyes seemed to glow as though a bright candle burned behind them.

"I don't wanna go backstage."

This threw the gent off, and he frowned as the seats around him and Prophet cleared and both were jostled by the exiting horde. The Englishman looked around as though for help but, finding none, returned his befuddled gaze to Prophet. "But the lidy requests your presence, Mr. Prophet."

"Lidy."

"Yessir, the lidy," the gent repeated, jerking his head toward the closed, buffeting curtain to which spitballs clung like oversized lice.

"Oh, you mean lady," Prophet said.

"Yessir. The actress, sir. Miss O'Shay."

Prophet looked at the curtain and his inborn caution was etched deep in his eyes as he turned once more to the nervously bowing Englishman, who was wiping his grubby hands on his grubby, brown-and-yellow-checked trousers. "I wouldn't know her from Jehoshaphat's cat."

"Well, she must know you, sir, because she asked me to come fetch you." The little Englishman turned and beckoned. "Right this way."

"You better not be up to somethin'."

"I'm not up to anything, sir. I'm just the assistant stage manager, and I do what I'm told. The name's Pickwick. Llewellyn Pickwick. If the actors and actresses want me to fetch 'em a chimpanzee, I hop the train for the nearest zoo, if you know what I'm sayin', sir." The Englishman chuckled and glanced over his shoulder as he made his way toward the stage along the far right wall, making sure Prophet was behind him.

"If you got a bushwhack set up," Prophet warned, striding along behind the man as the rest of the crowd was heading in the opposite direction, "just because I don't have my gut shredder don't mean you won't go down screamin'."

As Pickwick climbed the steps along the stage's right side, he cast a troubled look over his left shoulder, then, muttering to himself, turned forward again and pushed through the curtains.

Prophet followed, bulling through the billowing curtains that smelled heavily of tobacco smoke, kerosene, and perfume. The heavy, smelly fabric wouldn't let him go until he gave them a hard swipe with both arms and stumbled into the backstage area, closing his right hand around his Peacemaker's grips and looking around carefully, half expecting to be facing grim-looking gents with pistols.

Instead, there were only a handful of men in overalls and cloth caps sliding set furniture around while smoking and, in the case of two men lounging on one of the couches, holding beer bottles. One saw Prophet standing there with his hand on his holstered six-shooter and looking owly and raised his bottle to the bounty hunter with a reassuring wink.

"Wasn't all *that* bad — was it?" he said, chuckling.

Chagrined, Prophet let his hand fall away from the revolver's handle and continued following the scruffy English gent across to the rear of the stage and down a set of stairs into a dingy, candlelit basement until Pickwick stopped at a curtained doorway and doffed his hat.

"Mr. Prophet to see you, Miss O'Shay!"

Someone made a slight choking sound behind the door, and a strangled female voice said impatiently, "Send him in, Llewellyn. Send him in, for cryin' in the king's crown!"

Pickwick stepped aside, throwing the curtain back with one hand, bowing, and gesturing Prophet through the door with a regal, exaggerated flourish of his free arm.

The bounty hunter wouldn't have been more befuddled if the queen of Timbuktu had summoned him across an ocean. There was something vaguely familiar about the woman's voice, so it was with less trepidation and more curiosity that he tramped slowly through the door and felt the English gent drop the curtain into place behind him.

As Pickwick's footsteps dwindled into the distance, Prophet looked around the small, tawdry-looking dressing room that was in sharp contrast to the immaculately appointed theater above ground. A creamy-skinned redhead sat bare-legged and all but nude at a crude table appointed with a mirror that leaned back against the rough, stone wall.

The woman smiled at him, rich, ruby lips spread wide. Her thick, red hair hung down over her shoulders and arms, and she sat with her bare knees facing Prophet, her heels lifted so that she leaned slightly forward on her tiptoes.

"Holy shit in a nun's privy," Prophet muttered, his eyes growing wide with recognition as he slowly doffed his ragged hat. *"Sivvy?* Sivvy *Hallenbach?"*

"Oh, Lou!" the girl fairly screamed, bolting up from her rickety chair and running across the cluttered room, her sheer black wrap billowing out like diaphanous wings, exposing her breasts.

The saloon girl whom Prophet had once spent a winter with in an isolated cabin near Devil's Lake, Dakota Territory, after their stage had been run to ground by rampaging Sioux, threw her arms around the bounty hunter's neck and pressed her delectable breasts against his chest, hugging him tightly.

"Oh, Lou!" she squealed, tucking her feet back against her thighs and hanging from his neck. "You don't know how happy I was to see you out there!"

Prophet held the girl tightly, genuinely thrilled to see her again. It had been three years since they'd parted in Bismarck after a winter that had nearly killed them but during which they'd made the best of things, not the least of which was sharing body warmth. He'd known a lot of women in his thirty-some-odd years, but none except Sivvy Hallenbach could he have spent a Dakota winter with in a two-room abandoned stage station cabin, and not killed her or been killed by her.

"That was you out there?" he said, looking down at her as he smoothed her red hair back from her temples. He looked across the room at a long, jet wig hanging from a nail on a square-hewn ceiling post.

"Sure was," Sivvy said, setting her feet back down on the floor and pulling her head back away from him, grinning up at him. "I come a ways in a few years, haven't I, Lou? How'd you like the performance?"

Prophet said haltingly, "Sure, sure . . . well, I liked it just fine. What I could hear above the caterwauling . . ."

"Ohh!" she cried, her face crumpling with irritation. "The men in these mountains wouldn't know a world-class performance if it ran up between their legs and bit 'em in the balls. All they want is to see a girl naked!"

Prophet chuckled. Sivvy might be donning wigs and performing in shows that he couldn't understand, but she hadn't lost the salty tongue that had kept him in stitches through that entire Dakota winter. He noticed also that she hadn't regained her inhibitions, if she'd ever had any, for he admired her naked, pale, pink-tipped orbs rubbing against his denim shirt as her sheer wrap hung back behind her nicely rounded hips.

"If you could have heard the words, Lou," Sivvy said, caressing his neck with the thumbs of her entwined hands, "you'd have been right proud of your old Sivvy. I studied

191

up with Mr. Simeon Nash Nye and Maude Granger over in Pueblo, and I traveled with them around the mountains putting on *The Brook* — that's by Lord Byron — and several Shakespeare plays, and I really cut my teeth on that stuff.

"Mr. Nash and Miss Granger told me last fall they thought I was ready to go off on my own, and I ain't seen neither since I took up with this show here, but I'm told by those who know about such things, that they can really see their influence in my work. I'm thinkin', Lou, after a few more performances in these parts, I might head on over to Denver and then gradually make my way back East. Oh, wouldn't you be so proud of your Sivvy if you heard she was performing in *New York City?*"

"If you performed that high in the golden clouds, I might just ride on over and take in the show myself. I bet I could even hear the words back there amongst the civilized folk. Bet they'd be hangin' on every word, silent as pack rats in the parson's closet!"

"We'd ride in hacks, and go out to all the finest restaurants, even the French ones." Sivvy pressed her cheek against his chest once more. "Oh, it's so good to see you again, you big saddle tramp, you! What're you doing here, anyway? Haven't heard from you or about you in so long, I figured you were nothin' but a pile of big old bones bleachin' out in the bottom of some deep canyon."

Prophet opened his mouth to speak, but the girl clamped her hands over his lips. "Let's catch up later. Let me throw some duds on, then let's you and me head on over to my first-class digs at the Golden Slipper and diddle like minks!"

16

"You never killed anyone?" Louisa asked Miguel Encina as they sat along the gurgling, drumming creek in the twilight outside Juniper.

"Nope." The young banker shook his head. He was perched on a tree branch just a few feet above the ground, his back against the trunk, one leg stretched out along the branch before him. "Thank god it never came to that. I have my father and Sheriff Severin to thank for it, too."

The young man stopped and stared toward the creek several yards away as it slid darkly over rocks between its cottonwood- and aspen-stippled banks.

"How so?" Louisa was perched on a broad cottonwood stump, one bootheel hooked over the stump's edge, one arm draped over her upraised knee. They'd been talking steadily for nearly two hours. It was almost dark, stars kindling brightly in the lilac sky over the canyon.

Miguel seemed to weigh his response before he turned to her. "After we'd held up the Laramie stage for the umpteenth time, the sheriff ran me and my gang down at an old miner's shack up amongst the rocky ridges just west of here. The rest of my gang got away, but I was drunk and I fell off my horse. The sheriff threw a rope around me, made me walk back to town and right on up to my father's front porch. The sheriff asked Pa what he wanted to do with me, and my father said, 'Keep him here. I'll saddle a horse.' "

Louisa frowned as Miguel stared at her, an oblique smile on his lips, the last light showing dully in his warm eyes.

"What do you think happened next?"

"They threw you in jail, which is right where you belonged."

Miguel chuckled and shook his head. "They half dragged, half walked me up to an old mine claim on that ridge up there." He pointed toward the peak rising on the far side of the creek, toward a jumble of boulders near the top. "They lowered me into the mine shaft and left me one canteen and a small burlap sack with jerky in it. My father told me he was going to leave me there for four days, and during that time I was to think about what I wanted to do with the rest of my life — whether I wanted to remain a fiddle-footed firebrand who'd likely end up in jail or hanged if I kept on the way I was going, or the respected son of a banker with a nice income and a bright future. Then they went away and, true to his word, Pa rode back to the hole four days later."

"A tough way to come to a decision," Louisa said. "But it looks as though you made the right one."

"I reckon I did. It led right on up to now, with you and me sittin' here beside Pine Creek and," he added with a smile, "not shooting it out in some canyon." His eyes dropped to the pearl grips of Louisa's Colts that shone brightly in the last light. "I got a feeling my trail would have ended in that canyon."

"I got a feeling it would have, too." Louisa looked off, and they were silent for a time. "Miguel?"

"Yes, Miss Louisa?"

"I just got to Juniper and all, but I have no idea if I'll stay here or not. You see, I've been through what Lou would call — if you'll pardon the expression — knee-deep shit. I'd like to tell you about it someday. But for now, I don't really trust myself to think too clearly."

"All right."

"So, what I'm saying is — I like you and all, and even though we just met a few hours ago, I think it's very possible I might get to like you even more."

"My past hasn't soured you on me?"

"Your honesty's made you right sweet. We've all got trouble behind us."

"So what you're saying, Miss Louisa, is that you want to take things slow."

"That's right."

Miguel fidgeted around on the branch for a time before turning to her again with that disarming smile of his. "Does that mean I can't come over there and steal a quick kiss?"

Louisa felt herself blushing and was glad the growing darkness hid it. "You wouldn't have to steal one."

He slid off the branch, walked over to her, and stooped down. She remained on the tree stump, one arm still hooked around her knee, as he set his hands on her shoulders and closed his lips over her mouth.

When he straightened, he said, "That was nice."

Louisa smiled. Her heart was swelling, and it felt good to just go ahead and let it swell. She suddenly felt a tingle of excitement and hope for the future. She hadn't felt hopeful about her future in a long, long time.

Miguel Encina offered his arm to her. "Can I interest you in a cup of coffee before turning in?"

"Do they serve sarsaparilla in Juniper?"

"A bounty hunter who drinks sarsaparilla . . ." Miguel laughed as they strolled off toward the town together, arm in arm. "As a matter of fact, they do."

Lou Prophet wasn't all that taken with the idea of heading over to the Golden Slipper hotel to diddle like proverbial minks with Sivvy Hallenbach, aka Miss Gleneanne O'Shay, because Louisa was holed up over there. His comely partner, or former partner, was well versed in Prophet's roguish behavior and seemed to have acquired a philosophical attitude about it, but he was just enough embarrassed by it himself that he didn't want her to actually *see* him at it.

On the other hand, he wasn't strong enough to deny a pretty girl's request for carnal pleasure, especially one standing right in front of him clothed in a dark silk wrap so insignificant that he could have stuffed the entire garment inside his right cheek and still had room in his mouth to chew a full meal.

And he couldn't very well expect Miss Gleneanne O'Shay to follow him over to the Muleskinner's when she had her own private suite at the Golden Slipper.

So it was to the latter, better-appointed flophouse that he followed Sivvy. The girl — Prophet still considered her a girl though she had to be twenty-six or so — was dressed in a sparkling gold gown, pearls, and mink stole fit for a queen, all of which set off her dark red hair to stupefying effect. It also showed a goodly portion of her pillowy, pale cleavage, nearly causing more than a few heads to swing her way on the route between the opera house and the hotel.

As Prophet followed her across the lobby and up the broad, carpeted stairs, he felt humbled by his own wash-worn though relatively clean trail garb in sharp contrast to Sivvy's queenlike elegance. She said she had to soak in a hot tub before any horsing around.

"I'd invite you to join me, you handsome ape," she whispered as two men dressed like wealthy cattle buyers passed them in the hall, giving the actress a cordial nod before glancing at Prophet and looking vaguely befuddled. "But the tub isn't big enough,

199

and you'd likely crush the daylights out of me. I have to be careful not to damage my lungs."

"And that's a right fine set you got there, too, Miss O'Shay," Prophet quipped as they stopped outside her door, marked by the gilded number 9.

"Oh, Lou," she squealed, giving him her key and rubbing her shoulder coquettishly against his arm. "I don't think you're talking about my lungs!"

Prophet unlocked the door and threw it open, stepping aside to let her pass ahead of him, grinning. "I don't think I am, either."

She rubbed against him alluringly as she strode into the cavern-like room with a massive canopied bed and four tall windows bedecked in pleated red-and-gold drapes with bloodred roses stitched into them. There was a thick gold carpet on the floor, several beveled mirrors on the walls, and big chests and marble-topped washstands. Clothes of every shape, color, and size were strewn everywhere.

Sivvy stepped behind a massive privacy screen adorned with more roses, denying Prophet's request to watch her undress and bathe because: "All women worth their salt know that letting a man watch them bathe diminishes their mystery. And I'm not some harlot, you know, Lou!" As she chided him, she tossed the gold dress over the privacy screen and batted her false eyelashes.

"No, ma'am," Prophet said, kicking out of his boots.

"At least, I'm not anymore, though I reckon when we first ran into each other I was plying the lesser trade."

"Never held it against you, Miss O'Shay. A girl's gotta do what she can in this old world, same as a man."

"Don't call me that, big man," she said, as sounds of water emanated from behind the screen. "Miss O'Shay sounds funny coming from you, Lou. I want you to always call me Sivvy, so I'll always remember the time we had in that frigid cabin. The good times, anyway — not the Injuns that kicked in our door in that cold, cold night and you had to blast 'em both to smithereens with that big shotgun of yours."

"Ah, yes," Prophet said. "Those were simpler times."

Behind the screen, Sivvy splashed and laughed.

"We were lucky to get through them, but you're right — things were simpler back then. I was just starting out, heading for Fort Totten to perform at the officer's theater there. Never made it, but I got an

201

even better job in Bismarck. You know, the territorial governor even watched me perform in *Forty Thieves*. Didn't visit me backstage or anything, though. He had his wife with him."

"That's a damn shame."

"What're you doing here, Lou? Still in the bounty-hunting business or you give it up? That and your pact with Ole Scratch?" Sivvy clucked with disapproval.

Prophet poured some liquor from an unlabeled, cut-glass bottle into a thick red goblet, threw back the shot, and poured out another one. It wasn't rye, but it would do after a long day. "Once you make a pact with Scratch, Sivvy, there's no goin' back. No, sir, I'm still high-steppin' with my tail up, havin' as much fun as I can find, and in return I'll likely be shoveling coal for as long as the Devil needs my services."

"You shouldn't talk so," Sivvy counseled. "He might just hear you and hold you to it." More splashing, and then her voice deepened as though she were scrubbing her neck. "So, what brought you here? Don't tell me the fork-tailed one had a hand in this, too — our meeting again!"

Prophet sipped his drink, then set the glass on a varnished oak table beside the massive bed and began unbuttoning his shirt. "Nah, a girl brought me here. It ain't what you might think. I'm tryin' to get her to settle down. She's had a tough time. A bounty hunter. A damn purty one. And a young one. She's got no business in the business, and I figured this was as good a place as any to drop her, hope she sends down a taproot. So far, so good," he added, hearing the sadness in his own voice.

Sad? What the hell was he sad about, for chrissakes?

"What's this girl's name?" Sivvy asked.

"Louisa."

"Really?"

"A crazy coincidence."

"You learn this girl to hunt men, did you, Lou?"

Prophet chuckled as he shucked out of his denims. "I reckon Louisa learned me as much about the owlhoot hunt as I learned her and probably a little more."

Water splashed loudly, and then Sivvy's red head appeared above the privacy screen, her delectable tresses pinned into a comely but careless French braid. "What in the world made you decide to bring her here?" Her head moved as she dried herself, frowning over the screen at Prophet, who'd sat in a chair in the middle of the room, dressed in only his socks and longhandles, holding

203

his drink in one hand on a thigh. His shell belt hung over the back of the chair.

"My friend Hell-Bringin' Hiram said it was quiet here. And the folks were law-abidin'. I figured Louisa wouldn't be tempted so to strap her guns on once I finally got 'em off her."

"Yeah, the folks are law-abidin'," Sivvy said, tossing a white towel over the privacy screen and bending down out of sight. "Them that's still alive, that is."

She said this last so softly that Prophet had barely heard her.

He frowned at her as she straightened, then walked out from behind the privacy screen, wearing nothing but a single strand of pearls jostling across her jiggling, cherry-tipped, flour-white orbs. Prophet was about to ask her what she'd meant by that last comment, but the vision of her there, moving toward him slowly, gracefully, shaking her head so that her hair tumbled deliciously across her shoulders and down her breasts caused his throat to swell almost painfully and his tongue to stick to the roof of his mouth.

And then as Sivvy got down on her knees and began peeling his longhandles down his legs, he just got too distracted.

■ ■ ■ ■

A long while later, after he and Sivvy had fallen asleep, something woke him.

He opened his eyes to see the hall door close. It latched with a faint click. In the room's dense darkness he'd seen a pale figure slip out in front of the door. Now, lying with his eyes open, fully awake, Prophet stared at the door's black rectangle from behind which he could hear Sivvy say in a harsh whisper, "What the hell are you doing here?"

A man spoke in a slightly hushed tone: "We came to tell ya . . ."

Sivvy must have shushed him, because his voice trailed off.

More softly, but loudly enough for Prophet's keen hearing, he said, "Came to tell ya he's here. They're both here."

"I know," Sivvy hissed.

She must have said something else or made a gesture, because the man in the hall chuckled and said even more softly than previously, "You do work fast — I'll give you that, Miss O'Shay."

"Get outta here. I'll talk to you later."

"You gonna . . . ?"

"Go!"

205

There was the soft tread of boots. The door clicked, and a vertical strip of light shone in the wall where the door was, and Prophet closed his eyes. He heard the soft tap of bare feet on the carpet. The door clicked again.

Sivvy moved across the room, around the end of the bed, and then he felt the bed sag slightly as she crawled back into it.

Prophet rolled onto his back and said abruptly, "Visitor, Miss O'Shay?" He couldn't keep the irony out of his voice.

The girl gasped then covered it with a laugh. "You know how it is — bein' famous and all."

"I reckon."

"And it ain't all that late . . . for an actress."

Sivvy rolled against him, kissed his shoulder, and ran her hand down his belly. Her warm, soft hand slid down even farther. But even the former saloon girl's beguiling fingers couldn't keep Prophet from wondering who her visitor had been.

And what they were up to.

17

Louisa awakened the next morning in love.

Or at least in the expectation of love. She hadn't known Miguel Encina long enough to really be in love with him, and she was far too guarded a young lady to let herself be carted off on gilded emotions by dimpled cheeks, warm brown eyes, and a rich mop of curly chestnut hair. Not to mention money and a stable life.

But she felt downright airy. Buoyant. Light as a dancer.

As she sat up in her canopied bed in her room at the Golden Slipper and raised her arms for a good, long stretch, her silky honey-blond hair falling back away from her face, she felt as though stardust were dancing off her eyeballs.

What had ratcheted up her emotions a notch was Miguel telling her all about his jagged back trail — a trail that might have led to a wasted life if his father and Sheriff

Severin hadn't come to his rescue — if you could call tossing him into a deep, dark mine pit rescuing him. But it had done the trick, though Louisa doubted that Miguel's harrowing four days in the mine shaft had been his only savior.

The young man must have wanted to be saved from his life of crime. Otherwise, his "salvation" would probably have only turned him further away from the straight and narrow. Like a whipped and beaten dog, it would have made him even wilder, meaner. Untamable.

Deep down, he was good. And like Louisa and strong steel, he'd been tempered by hot fires. He was a good young man, with a tested soul, and he'd likely make some deserving young woman a good husband.

Maybe a woman like Louisa herself.

She lowered her arms. Her skin tingled with a subtle craving. The feeling amazed her because no man had ever had that effect on her besides Lou. But she felt it now, and as she did she tossed her covers back and stared down the length of her long, creamy, delicately curved body.

Lou had remarked that she had the body of a debutante, though he'd pronounced it "deb-ya-tent," with accents on the first and last syllables. She was glad to see now that her debutante's body showed only light patches of purple where Montoya had abused her. Even the cigar burns were healing, the former round scabs on her hips and thighs and belly showing only round patches of pink.

The ride up from Mexico in the clean, dry air, and all the spring water she and Prophet had drunk, and the wild food they'd shot and grubbed themselves had worked miracles.

After Mexico, she hadn't given her body to Lou. She hadn't been ready to give it to any man. But as she cupped her firm, pale breasts in her hands now, squeezing gently, feeling a response in her loins, she knew she was ready to give herself to Miguel. To have his hands on her, to feel his lips on hers, his body on hers, making her feel like a woman.

She wouldn't rush it, though. And she wouldn't let him rush it, either. She'd been raised to lay with a man only after she'd married him, and while her wild life on the bounty trail had rearranged her values as well as her priorities and given her appreciation for the satisfaction of her natural carnal desires when they were often all she had, the values she'd been raised with in Nebraska were still inside her, dormant but waiting for her to return to them and the life they were meant for.

A life with a good man and a family in a civilized town. A garden and a chicken coop. Wash days. Prayers before meals. Church on Sunday. Picnics along the river.

A rich life gentling into a seasoned, sweet old age.

Cupping one breast, she ran her other hand across her flat belly, groaning with the pleasure of lying naked in silk sheets. She'd scoffed at such luxury when she'd been on the hunting trail, unable to fathom a life not directed at hunting down killers, but now she found herself wanting to remain here.

Unfortunately, she had a job to do. Wishing she'd not been so eager to take the gold-guarding job — that was one time her knee-jerk defiance of Prophet's often too-patronizing wishes had backfired — she swung her feet to the floor and walked naked over to one of the room's two windows and threw the curtain back. She stared out the fine, unwarped glass into the blue-misty dawn of a clear mountain morning.

Birds chirped as they flitted over the rooftops of Juniper, which were limned in soft pale light while the southern ridge leaned away, its rocks and pines bathed in purple. Someone had been sweeping, but now the snicks of the broom stopped. Louisa looked down into the street to see a man standing outside the opera house straight ahead, holding a broom and grinning up at her.

She frowned, puzzled. Then, with a gasp and crossing her arms on her breasts, she stumbled straight back away from the window.

"Pervert," she groused, feeling her face warm with anger.

There was one bad thing about living in town. She had to mind how she was attired when peering out her own window to see how the day was shaping up.

Hearing the snicks of the broom across the boardwalk fronting the opera house once more, Louisa went to the washstand, filled the marble basin with water, ducked her face in it, then straightened quickly, tossing her head from side to side and using her hands to rub the cold water up through her hair.

When she'd finished giving herself a quick sponge bath, she dressed in her freshly laundered clothes — cotton camisole, knee-length pantaloons, cotton socks, calico blouse, wool riding skirt, red neckerchief, and tan felt hat. She strapped her matched Colts around her waist, quick drew each to make sure there were no impediments, then grabbed her saddlebags and rifle and headed out.

As she made her way to the cafe on the first floor, she pondered her situation.

She shouldn't have taken the gold-guarding job. She'd come here to settle down, and it probably looked odd for a girl being courted by the banker's son to be guarding his gold shipments. She'd make this run today then resign her position and look into the job being offered at the haberdashery.

She wasn't sure she really wanted to wait on persnickety old ladies in feathered hats and gauntleted gloves buying buttons, piping, bolt goods, and such, but she could manage it until something else came along. Maybe she'd rent a house — unlike Prophet, she had a rather large nest egg stashed away in her saddlebags — and raise chickens to sell to the Juniper eateries.

It was only five thirty, but the Golden Slipper's cafe was open. Louisa was the day's first customer. She had her usual pancakes, bacon, and tall glass of goat's milk. She ordered two pancakes instead of her usual one. Normally, when on the trail — and she was always on the trail — she ate a minimal breakfast to keep her edge up. Sometimes just a handful of beans washed down with creek water.

Nothing like an overfilled belly to slow a bounty huntress down.

But since she was trying to settle down and become civilized again, she could do with more grub in her belly and even a little extra tallow on her bones. It wasn't the fashion in town to be too thin. Besides, a civilized girl needed curves and the extra sustenance for the hard work it took to make a home.

When she finished her breakfast, she headed over to the livery barn behind the hotel to saddle her horse, then headed over to the Muleskinner's Inn on the other side of the opera house that occupied much the same place in Juniper that churches did in Mexican pueblos — the center.

She saw Prophet as she approached his dingy hotel that looked as though the first strong wind would scatter it like stove sticks. He was sitting on the porch in a wicker chair, kicked back against the front wall, spurred boots crossed on the railing. His hat was tipped back, a quirley smoldered between his lips, and a stone coffee mug smoked in his right hand.

The bounty hunter's despicable horse stood saddled at the hitchrack fronting the shabby place, twitching its ears that were frayed from many fights. Louisa's brown-and-white pinto whinnied anxiously as it approached the hammer-headed dun, and Mean and Ugly swished his tail and gave a customarily belligerent snort.

Prophet sipped his piping-hot belly wash and watched Louisa draw her horse up just out of biting distance of his dun. The blond looked up at the building, gave her head a condescending little wag, and crossed her gloved hands on the saddle horn. "Sleep well?"

Prophet merely grunted. Louisa didn't need to know he'd spent most of the night at the same hotel she had, in the company of the actress known as Gleneanne O'Shay, though he hadn't slept a wink after the actress's mysterious caller had left. After Sivvy, as he preferred to call her, had gone back to sleep, Prophet had dressed quietly and tramped over to the Muleskinner's where he'd had a big breakfast in the shabby, makeshift kitchen before fetching his horse.

He'd considered asking Sivvy outright who the man in the hall had been, but his manhunter's sixth sense had told him he wouldn't get any straighter answer than the one he'd already gotten. And he didn't want to tip his hand about his suspicions.

Damn perplexing, though. And disappointing, too. He liked Sivvy and had figured she liked him. She'd certainly *acted* like she'd liked him, judging by all the racket she'd made, writhing beneath him. Had she only been playing him? If so, for what reason?

The gold he'd be guarding was the only thing he could think of.

"How was Mr. Fancy-Pants?"

"You mean Miguel?"

"Is that his name? I forget."

Louisa spread her pretty lips slightly as she stared over her horse's head at Prophet. "He's handsome."

"Too much hair, you ask me. But I reckon girls like hair." Prophet sucked his quirley, blew the smoke out over his boots. "He steal a kiss?"

"Wouldn't you like to know."

"Not really. I was just makin' conversation."

Louisa glanced at Mean and Ugly, who was eyeing her horse owlishly, the pinto looking away as it tensed its withers. "You're up early. I figured I was going to have to bang pots over your head."

"You know that ice-cold witch's finger that pokes the back of my neck from time to time?"

"What about it?"

Prophet sipped the hot mud again and winced at the burn in his throat. "It's pokin' again."

Louisa frowned. She knew not to take Prophet's premonitions lightly, however superstitious they seemed. He was a hillbilly from the Georgia mountains, birthed by witches and raised with talismans on his crib, and he'd grown up with weird Appalachian legends and evil hexes.

His dark presentiments had proven real more than a time or two in the past. They'd saved both their lives, in fact.

"What's it about, do you think?" Louisa asked him.

Prophet hiked a shoulder. It wouldn't do her any good to know what had spawned his unease. "We'd best just keep our eyes open today."

"You think those men who ambushed us were here for the gold, and they might have friends who are still after it."

"Like I said . . ."

Prophet let his voice trail off as the door on his right flank opened, scraping across the veranda's warped floor, the window curtains jostling. A man stepped out, followed by three more.

They were a ragged-looking but well-armed crew, three holding either Henry or Winchester rifles, the last one holding a long-barreled, double-bore shotgun on his shoulder, two bandoliers filled with shells crossed on his chest.

As the men filed out, their eyes found Prophet, who'd instinctively dropped his hand to his holstered revolver. Louisa kept her hands on her saddle horn, leaning forward slightly, but her pistols were in easy reach. The newcomers stopped on the porch, making no sudden moves with their guns.

The first man rolled a stove match from one side of his mouth to the other. He was tall, with thick red hair hanging over his forehead, beneath his gray, flat-brimmed hat, and his gray eyes had an insolent air. He wore a gold ring a little larger than a wedding band in his right ear. "You Prophet?"

"All depends," Prophet said mildly.

"It's him," said the man with the shotgun, whom Prophet suddenly remembered from outside the cantina last night. He was the pewter-haired man wearing large Texas spurs, called Sawrod. "He almost got tangled up with Dryden last night."

The man beside Sawrod was the Mex, Casol, who'd also been outside the cantina last night and had made disparaging comments about the procedures of the local law. He grinned under his low-crowned straw sombrero, black eyes flashing. Under them were heavy purple bags. The whites of his eyes were a deep bloodred. Obviously, he'd drunk his share in the cantina last night.

"I'd like to see that," he said, staring at Prophet. "A big man like him against Dryden."

"Dryden'd pull a knife."

"Hell, he's got a knife," the Mex said, pointing at the tip of the hide-wrapped knife handle barely visible above the collar of Prophet's shirt.

The red-haired man with the earring, with Indian-flat facial features, changed the subject in a sharply sarcastic tone. "You're our new boss."

Prophet glanced at Louisa as he eased his grip on his .45. "You're Encina's gold guards?"

"*Si,*" said Casol. He wore a bull-hide charro jacket and baggy sheepskin leggings tucked inside his worn, brown, copper-tipped boots.

The man standing beside the red-haired, gold-earringed gent was the oldest of the crew — a large, potbellied man with bulg-

218

ing blue eyes and a large belly shoving his double shell belts down nearly to his crotch. His face was haggard but friendly, as was the light in his eyes.

"You'll have to forgive Bronco here," he said, canting his head toward the red-haired gent to his right. "When the old ramrod Chisos Owens pulled out, Bronco thought he'd get the job. In fact, he was throwing money around at the blackjack tables like he already had it."

The older gent laughed, stepped forward, and extended his right hand to Prophet. "I'm Hitt. Orrie Hitt." With another glance at the red-haired man, he said, "This here's Bronco Brewster. These two are Juventino Casol and Royal Sawrod. Or Saw for short. Fittin' if you ever heard him snore, which you'll likely do since we're often on the trail a few days at a time, holin' up together in old mine shacks an' such."

Prophet rose from his chair and shook Hitt's hand, then that of the other men, saying, "I reckon Casol and Saw here I did meet last night, though not so formal-like."

Bronco Brewster chomped down on his stove match as he gave Prophet's hand a fishy, insolent squeeze before shunting his lustily brightening gaze to Louisa. "And who might this golden-haired little filly be?"

"This here is Miss Louisa Bonnyventure," Prophet said. "She's throwin' in with us fellas."

"That's Bonaventure," Louisa corrected. "There's no 'y' in it."

Brewster clouded up as he slid his gaze back to Prophet. "You mean, this sprite in a skirt's gonna help us men guard a gold shipment? A useless *girl?*"

Ah, shit.

The thought hadn't finished passing through Prophet's mind before a gun popped. In the corner of Prophet's vision, he saw Brewster's sweat-stained cream Stetson fly off his head and tumble into the dirt behind him.

Prophet looked at Louisa. She'd returned her empty hands to her saddle horn, over which she was slightly leaning. The only evidence that she'd fired one of her pearl-gripped pistols was the blue smoke wafting in front of her expressionless face.

Brewster had ducked down and was looking around as though for the source of the bullet that had removed his hat. The other two had seen it, though Prophet knew they hadn't seen much. Probably just a blur and a flash of silver-plated .45 steel.

Louisa was that fast.

Orrie Hitt threw his head back, guffawing.

Casol chuckled through his teeth, bloodshot eyes twinkling as he stared at Louisa. "*Christos,* I think she'll do, amigos. And the scenery won't be bad, either!"

18

"So, tell me, Miss Louisa — how'd you get started in the man-hunting trade?" asked the earring-wearing redhead, Bronco Brewster.

"You mean, besides a general hatred for the whole male race?" Prophet said with a snort.

Louisa glanced back over a shoulder at him, wearing her customary look of strained but cool tolerance.

She and Bronco were riding ahead of the empty gold wagon, which was used by the bank for hauling the gold back down from the mines. The wagon was nothing more than a buckboard with a large steel, chained, and padlocked strongbox riding in the back. The guards' camping gear and foodstuffs rode back there as well, along with two extra rifles, a shotgun, ammunition, and a cream tarp for putting up when it rained.

"I don't like most men — that's true."

Louisa turned her head forward as her pinto stepped smartly to the right of Bronco's buckskin. "I have no tolerance for brigands of any stripe but especially those who kill women and children."

Bronco turned to her, arching a brow. He had a long, black cheroot wedged between his teeth. "You sorta specialize, do ya?"

"You might say that."

"Plenty o' men out here of that stripe."

"There certainly are, Brewster."

Prophet was riding up close to the wagon's driver's box, leaning out from his saddle to light his freshly rolled cigarette from Orrie Hitt's cigar stub. Hitt was driving the wagon and leading a saddle horse. The oldest member of the gold-guarding crew looked at Prophet and then at Louisa's back as she rode about twenty feet ahead of the two mules pulling the wagon.

Hitt's fleshy, craggy face acquired a troubled, thoughtful expression as he leaned forward, elbows on his knees, holding the mules' ribbons lightly in his gloved hands. "Say, you know, my cousins Burt and Jimmy DePaul were taken down by a young girl. 'Bout two, two and a half years ago. Outside a little farming town in Kansas."

Hitt glanced at Prophet, his shaggy, gray-brown eyebrows knitted. "Sure, I remember now. My other cousin, Rex, wrote and said they was taken down by a pretty little blond-headed girl who wore two Colt pistols. Just rode right into that town, found Burt and Jimmy diggin' worms behind their shack for fishin', and she said, 'It's right fittin' you both got shovels so you can dig your own graves.' And then that's what she did — she made 'em dig their own graves while Rex watched, frightened out of his boots. He watched her shoot both Burt and Jimmy through their hearts, bid Rex a good day, and rode off, never to be seen or heard from again."

"Oh, I was seen or heard from again," Louisa said, riding with her back straight, blond hair bouncing on her shoulders. "By quite a few more men like your cousins, in fact, Mr. Hitt. Men who raped children, like your cousins raped the girls they took from that country schoolyard near the Colorado border and abused terribly before leaving them to wander naked and dehydrated back to their ranches."

"That was you?"

Louisa turned her horse off the trail and arched a blond brow at the wagon driver. "You weren't close to your cousins — were you, Mr. Hitt?"

The driver stopped the wagon and regarded the girl seriously, his dust catching up to him, sweeping over the wagon. Prophet halted his own horse near the buckboard, drawing on his quirley with a speculative, bemused air as he shuttled his gaze between his partner and the wagon driver.

Hitt squinted at the girl. Louisa stared back at him. She could have been inspecting a stone wall.

The other three riders, who'd also halted their horses, looked between Hitt and Louisa. The Mexican, Casol, chuckled softly while Bronco and Sawrod curled their upper lips, eager to see who'd show his hand first.

Hitt's face opened, his eyes brightened, and he laughed heartily. "Ah, hell!" His blue eyes dropped to the Colts jutting on Louisa's slender waist. "I oughta thank you for beefing them two depraved little bastards. Both of 'em was nothin' but black eyes on the Hitt and DePaul clans." He turned his head and gave Louisa a wink. "You shoulda taken ole Rex down, too — that's how I see it, sure enough!"

"I thought about it," Louisa said. "He looked squirrely enough. But only Jimmy and Burt had taken the girls."

"Yeah, Rex was probably too drunk, layin'

up with a twelve-year-old whore some-where." Hitt laughed again loudly. "You coulda killed him, though. No skin off my teeth. And there's a few more in my family that need beefin'. Me — I'm the only up-standin' one o' the bunch!"

He slapped his thigh and laughed some more and then he shook the lines over the mules' backs, and the wagon clattered forward. As the others continued ahead with the wagon, Louisa rode back to where Prophet sat his horse, one boot hooked over his saddle horn. He eyed the girl with mild reproach.

"Don't you know that ain't no way to act?"

"No."

"I reckon you don't. Couldn't you see he was just froggin' ya, to see how you'd react? Probably wanted to see your purty tits heave when you got mad at him."

"Were they heaving prettily?"

"Your tits always heave prettily." Prophet spat to one side. "We gotta get you a differ-ent job. You're settlin' down, now. You don't need to be off with no passel of men who probably don't get their ashes hauled more than once, twice a month, and when they do get 'em hauled they're hauled by fat, toothless whores."

"I've already decided that myself," Louisa

said defiantly.

"Well, ain't you special." Prophet eyed her askance. "When'd you decide that?"

"Just this morning."

"Why?"

"None of your business."

"The young banker, huh? Well, good. Maybe he is the right one, after all." Prophet dropped his right boot into his right stirrup and kneed Mean and Ugly forward. "Come on. Let's get this job out of the way."

"Hold on."

Prophet stopped in front of Louisa's pinto.

Louisa was looking around cautiously at the ridges humping on both sides of the gulch they were following into the higher reaches of the Rawhide Range. "I've seen the way you've been looking around as we've been riding. Any particular reason?"

"Just seein' shadows of shadows, is all." Prophet puffed the quirley wedged in one corner of his mouth. "Still got that icy finger pokin' the back of my neck, just under my collar. Damndest thing."

He hipped around in his saddle, sliding his gaze from the western ridge, across the narrow gulch through which Sanderson Creek snaked through wolf willows and boulders, to the eastern ridge that was slightly higher than the other and was cloaked in the fuzzy, spruce-green shadows of midmorning.

"Maybe this one is just that — a shadow," Louisa opined. "I mean, Lou, why would anyone fog an empty gold wagon? It's after we have the gold they'll shadow us — if anyone's planning to shadow us, that is."

"You got a short memory, Miss Bonnyventure."

"The bushwhackers?"

"We weren't guarding any gold yesterday afternoon, were we?"

"For once, you have a point." Louisa gigged her pinto along the trail, looking around cautiously. "I declare, Lou — if it's not the Devil tickling your feet, it's witches poking their cold fingers against your neck."

"Yeah, I know — one damn thing after another." Prophet booted his horse after the girl, field stripping his quirley one-handed and letting the midmorning breeze take the bits of paper and tobacco.

The Sweet Loretta Gold Mine sat in a broad horseshoe of Sanderson Gulch, at the base of a boulder-strewn ridge that was humped with tailings that had been wrenched from the mountain's bowels. The stamping mill sat on a plateau just above the mine office, foundry, bunkhouses, and corrals, and the steel pistons that crushed the ore sounded like God laying into the earth every second with a massive hammer. The ground vibrated with the constant pounding, causing the mules to bray and the horses to twitch their ears apprehensively.

Higher along the ridge, the tramcars hauling the ore out of the shafts clattered and clanged.

Picking up the gold was a simple procedure. While Prophet, Louisa, and the other guards watched for possible robbers, the mine manager and two other men hauled the gold ingots out of a barred foundry room in a steel lockbox that had a stout rawhide handle on each end.

When the lockbox was set in the back of Orrie Hitt's wagon, the manager unlocked the padlock that secured it while Hitt opened the steel box in the wagon bed. The manager transferred the ingots — there were six, Prophet saw as he stole a glance over his shoulder — into the box in the wagon, and then Hitt promptly closed the lid and locked it before slipping the key back under his shirt, where it hung around his neck by a leather thong.

Hitt scribbled out a receipt for the gold, and with a pinch of his hat brim to the mining supervisor, kicked off the wagon's brake and shook the ribbons over the mules' backs.

The caravan was off once more to snake farther up the canyon, deeper into the Rawhide Mountains.

Prophet wasn't surprised that after the gold had been loaded onto the transfer wagon the witch didn't poke the back of his neck harder with her cold finger. Even after they'd taken on three more ingots from the smaller and less productive Holy Ghost Mine in Squaw Canyon, the witch held steady with that chilly finger of hers.

She pressed neither harder or lighter but held that finger steadily against the back of his neck, strumming his nerves just enough that he kept his eyes on his back trail or flicking cautiously across the trail ahead.

He wasn't sure why he wasn't surprised. Maybe it had something to do with the fact his unease had started last night even before he'd run into Sivvy Hallenbach, and he figured he wasn't in any more danger out here than he had been in town.

Late in the day they circled back toward Juniper via the west fork of Elk Creek and approached an abandoned prospector's shack where they intended to spend the night before finishing the trip the next day.

Louisa put her pinto around behind the wagon to where Prophet was riding off the left rear wheel and kept pace beside him.

"Did you see that?" she asked.

"See what?"

"Reflection off a rock, maybe." Louisa was peering up the low ridge on the other side of the creek and towering spruce and tamaracks on her left. "Maybe off gun iron."

Prophet's eyes had been sweeping the right side of the trail, where he'd spied a doe and a fawn running into the brush. Now he followed Louisa's stare up the eastern ridge, the rock of which was bathed in the salmon light of the late-day sun.

He rode along for a time, sweeping the ridge with his gaze. There was a dull flash between two boulders about halfway up the bluff. As the flash died, Prophet thought he also spied a man-shaped shadow, maybe just an elbow and a rifle stock, a quarter second before there were just the two boulders again.

His belly tightened. Shucking his Winchester from its saddle boot and keeping his gaze on the spot where he'd seen the flash, he said calmly, "Stay with the wagon." He told the other riders to keep moving toward the shack and he'd catch up to them later. He reined Mean and Ugly off the trail and through the trees, ducking under evergreen boughs.

The dun splashed across the fast-moving creek, slipping on the mossy stones. As the horse gained the other bank, lunging with its front hooves, Prophet cocked the Winchester one-handed, then lowered the hammer to half cock. He stopped just beneath an overhang of the ridge and stared up along the boulder-strewn wall. The two boulders around which he'd seen the gun flash were a hundred yards up and to his right, and he could see only one of them from this angle.

If a man was hunkered down up there, he was good at blending with the rock. And patient.

Prophet considered heading straight up the slope, which wasn't too steep for Mean and Ugly. He raked a thumb along his unshaven jaw and chewed his lower lip. No good. A gunman would have a clean shot at him.

He glanced through the trees, saw the wagon and the other riders including Louisa dwindling into the distance. Looking back the way he'd come through the dense spruces, aspens, and tamaracks, he decided there was a good chance he hadn't been seen leaving the trail. His inclinations honed from years of man tracking told him he should maybe hunker down right here, let a would-be bushwhacker come to him.

If there was indeed a man up there, and Prophet and Louisa weren't merely seeing natural lights and shadows . . .

He drew the dun's reins back and squeezed the saddle with his knees. "Back, boy."

Mean backed up, lifting his snoot in the air and blowing incredulously.

"Just do what I tell you without arguin' for once," Prophet grumbled, looking up the ridge until his view was blocked by a giant mantle of weather-polished, brick-red sandstone.

He lifted his right boot over the saddle horn and dropped to the ground. Holding his Winchester in one hand, he slipped Mean's bit from his mouth, so the dun could forage, and loosened his latigo strap, letting him blow. As the horse snorted and ambled a ways off through the brush, grinding grass and switching his tail at flies, Prophet hunkered down beneath the rock mantle.

He waited.

The sun angled low. Shadows dropped out of the trees like silent, massive birds. The only sound was the quiet rush and chugging of the stream.

After a half hour or so, a rock clattered down the ridge and dropped into the grass a hundred feet ahead of Prophet. It was followed by one more that barked off a deadfall aspen log.

Prophet tensed slightly. He drew the Winchester's hammer back to full cock.

Hold on, he told himself. Just stay put. *Give 'im time to make it down the ridge. . . .*

19

From somewhere ahead, Prophet heard a horse blow. It was followed by the squawk of tack and heavy clomp of hooves. Then there were the crackling thuds of a horse coming down the ridge into brush.

The hoof thuds dwindled slowly into the distance.

Prophet jogged over and tightened Mean's latigo strap, slipped the horse's bit into his mouth, and swung into the saddle. He rode ahead until he saw the back of the rider about twenty yards ahead of him. The tail of the bay horse the man was riding fluttered in the breeze.

The man was following the ridge wall, keeping the stream and the trees to his right. He carried a rifle across his saddlebows but he seemed in no hurry. He wore a black coat and a low-crowned black hat, with high-topped black boots shoved into his stirrups.

Prophet closed the distance between them

to fifteen yards.

"Hold it."

The man jerked back on his reins and whipped around in his saddle, swinging his carbine around as he did, gritting his teeth. He fought the reins as he tried to level his rifle barrel.

Prophet already had his Winchester raised in both hands. The rifle roared, causing Mean to tighten his back muscles and lift his head with a start. The hammer-headed dun was of questionable breeding and irksome disposition, but Prophet had trained him not to sunfish as he fired from his back.

His slug hit its mark, plunking through his shadower's right shoulder. The man screamed and dropped his rifle. The bay, not as well trained as Mean and Ugly, pitched and whinnied, and the shadower lunged for the saddle horn and missed. He fell back off the bucking horse's left hip, then gave another scream as his left boot got caught in its stirrup and his head and shoulders bounced off the brushy turf.

The man grunted and groaned and tried desperately to kick himself free, but his boot toe was wedged tight. And then the horse was galloping full-out, angling through the trees.

"Shit!" Prophet groused, sliding his Winchester into its saddle boot.

He gigged Mean into a lope after the runaway bay and its rider flopping and bouncing along the ground behind it, flattening brush and throwing up small branches in his wake. His yells rose above the snapping sounds and the thuds of the bay's hooves.

Prophet bulled through the trees, raising a shielding arm and ducking his head. When he came out of the trees, he reined Mean to a sudden halt at the water's edge.

The bay stood ahead a ways, several yards out from shore but facing back toward it, its reins caught around a rock. Its left side faced Prophet, and the bounty hunter could see the bay's rider flopping around in the water beside the horse like a fish on a hook, desperately trying to reach up and free his boot from its stirrup. As he flopped, throwing his hands toward the stirrup, then falling back in the knee-deep water, Prophet saw the red blood in the water washing off the man's left shoulder.

Prophet stepped down from his saddle and waded into the stream, taking long steps and throwing his arms out to keep his balance in the fast current. He walked up to the horse and lifted the stirrup so that it angled toward the stream. The rider's boot toe slipped free, and his leg splashed down in the water.

As the horse nickered and sidestepped away from the men, Prophet grabbed the wounded, half-drowned man by the back of his shirt and coat and dragged him through the current and onto the rocky shore, the man flapping his arms and loudly hacking up water all the way.

The man coughed and choked and threw himself onto his belly, violently heaving the stream from his lungs. Prophet glared down at him.

"Who are you, you son of a bitch?"

The man convulsed violently as he coughed up more water.

"Wait a minute."

Prophet reached down and turned the man over onto his back and stared into his flat, fair-skinned face that was covered with a neatly trimmed, wheat-colored beard. He'd only glanced at the manager of the Holy Ghost Mine, but he'd be damned if this gent wasn't him.

The man convulsed once more, water dribbling down over his chin. His eyes were fear-wild, panicked. The blood gushing from the hole in his chest was frothy, which meant Prophet had nicked a lung. More blood from a good-sized gash on the side of the man's head dribbled down over his ear.

He coughed, cleared his throat and said between deep, ragged breaths, "I figured you was after me. You an' her . . ."

"Why?"

The man stared at him, a pained befuddlement adding to the misery already there. His pain-racked face acquired a fleeting, forlorn look, and then he raised his arms and let them fall. "Ah, hell. You wasn't after me, after all. I'll . . . be goddamned. . . ."

"Why would I be after you, hoss?"

"The bank in Joplin?"

When Prophet only frowned down at him, he said, "Figured . . . when I seen ya today . . . ole Lou Prophet was out for me, sure enough. But . . . but I was wrong, wasn't I?" He gave a wet sigh. "Damn."

He laughed and coughed up more water. Then his breathing shallowed. He winced, and his eyes gradually lost their light as his head sank back against the ground and he turned his face slightly away from Prophet. A gurgle sounded from deep in the man's chest, and he became very still.

"Well, shit."

Prophet straightened and looked around, his mantled eyes dark and haunted. He grabbed his folding shovel off his saddle, dug a shallow grave, and rolled the outlaw-

239

turned-mine manager inside and covered him up quickly, covering the eyes first because they wouldn't stay closed and they seemed to stare accusingly at the bounty hunter from all angles.

Prophet scowled down at the mounded grave. Even if he'd known about Joplin, he wouldn't have bothered the gent. The man had an honest job, was walking the straight and narrow.

"Ah, shit," Prophet said.

It was one of those times he hated his job.

He returned the shovel to Mean's back, mounted up, grabbed the bay's reins, and, trailing the dead man's horse, headed off after the gold wagon.

He rode up to the prospector's cabin at twilight. Smoke curled from the squat, gray shack's tin chimney pipe. The wagon sat near the shack's open front door from which emanated the sound of men's voices. The male guards were playing poker.

Louisa was leaning against the corral in which the horses and mules milled, some still with feed sacks draped over their ears. She held a smoking cup in her hand.

"What happened?" she asked Prophet.

He stepped down from his saddle and tossed the reins of the bay to her.

"The Holy Ghost gave up its manager."

■ ■ ■ ■

"Kind of late for a lady to be goin' for a horseback ride, ain't it, Miss O'Shay?" asked Llewellyn Pickwick, holding the reins of a copper-bottom mare behind the opera house.

Miss Gleneanne O'Shay grabbed the reins out of the Englishman's hand then adjusted her split riding skirt and held her other hand out for assistance. "You know how wound up I get after a performance, Llewellyn. Taking a good long ride is what the doctor ordered."

"I knew you to ride in the mornings and afternoons, but not this late. Why, it's pret' near dark in this canyon!" Frowning, Pickwick helped Miss O'Shay, as Sivvy Hallenback preferred to think of herself these days, into the saddle.

"Llewellyn?" The actress stared down at him. She'd taken off her wig but had left her face paint on and donned a frilly-fronted white blouse, short leather jacket, and the spruce-green riding skirt.

"Yes, ma'am."

"No one likes an assistant stage manager who can't keep his nose out of other people's business."

241

"Yes, ma'am," Pickwick said, the corners of his mouth drooping with chagrin.

Miss O'Shay reined the copper-bottom mare around tightly and said over her shoulder, "I'll be back in a couple hours. Wait for me so you can tend the horse!"

"You know how Sheriff Severin don't like folks loitering about the streets and back alleys, Miss O'Shay!"

"Tell the sheriff to go diddle himself!"

Gleneanne O'Shay ground her bootheels into the mare's flanks, and as the horse lunged off its rear legs, spraying dirt and manure over Pickwick's brogans, the assistant stage manager gave a grumbling curse and said, "Easy for you to say!" There was no danger of the actress hearing above the mare's thudding hooves.

Muttering to himself in disgust, Pickwick stared after the actress's retreating back as she and the horse headed south past the Muleskinner's Inn and then into the thickening darkness at the outskirts of town.

"Damn easy for you to say, and a prime bitch is what you are . . . !"

Pickwick sat down on a stack of lumber used for stage construction, plucked a small, leather-covered flask from the breast pocket of his checked, clawhammer coat, and took a long, stress-relieving pull.

Meanwhile, Gleneanne urged the mare over a rise at the southern end of town and then turned onto an old, switchbacking mine trail, heading southeast along the canyon's southern ridge. She came to a canyon a few minutes later and, after following the twisting crevice deep into the stony ridge, crossed a spring-fed creek and put the mare into the mouth of another box canyon.

The bright stars lit the trail, but Gleneanne had followed the trail so many times in the past that she could have followed the thin trace, likely carved by prospectors following color, in total darkness. She halted the horse near the box canyon's dark back wall, saw a small pinprick of orange light, smelled the cigarette smoke, and heeled the mare ahead slowly.

Off in the shadows beneath fluttering aspens, a horse whinnied sharply. The copper-bottom mare replied in kind.

"Be quiet, 'Pache," a man said.

The cigarette coal glowed again. Gray smoke wafted in the darkness.

Gleneanne stopped the mare in front of the silhouetted figure in a bowler hat and foulard tie.

"I told you, Gleneanne — we can't meet like this anymore."

"Goddamnit, Miguel," the actress said, sliding lithely out of the saddle and walking up to the young banker, who stood smoking against a large, pale boulder. "I had to see you, and since you won't see me in town —"

"I told you that's nothin' personal, honey," Miguel Encina said, his voice taut with admonishing. "I just don't want to blow this thing sky high. And you sending a note to the bank is just the way to undo two miserable years of careful planning."

"The girl I sent to the bank handles our costumes. If anyone saw her delivering a note, they'd probably think the poor girl had eyes for you." Gleneanne grabbed Miguel's wrist and squeezed, looking up into his cold, brown eyes that appeared all the colder for the icy starlight reflected in them. "Miguel, let's light a shuck out of this place! Let's leave together. Tomorrow morning. Oh, please, Miguel — tell me you will!"

He shook his head and opened his mouth to speak, but before he could get a word out, Gleneanne leaned toward him, pressing her breasts against his chest and throwing her arms around his neck. "Oh, please, honey! Won't you please consider it! This whole thing is wrong, and it's going to be the end of both of us. It's a downright dastardly thing, and it's not only crazy — I've never heard of anything so crazy in my life! — but it's *impossible!* It'll never *work!*"

Miguel peeled her hands from around his neck and lowered them to her sides, squeezing them firmly in his own.

The cigarette bobbed in a corner of his mouth as he said evenly, in a voice pitched low with menace, "It would have had a better chance if you'd done your job last night, Gleneanne. I mean, you had that bounty hunter in your bed, and you so easily could have slipped a stiletto between his ribs." He paused. "Why didn't you do it? Perhaps you were enjoying yourself a little more than you thought you would?"

Gleneanne shook her head. "It wasn't like that, damnit. I —"

"How do I know, Gleneanne? Maybe you like them kind of big and rough, with broken noses. Did you have fun in your well-appointed room with that bounty hunter grunting around between your legs like some — ?"

Crack!

Gleneanne dropped her hand back down to her side. "You got no right to talk to me like that, Miguel."

Miguel's own hand made a chopping motion in the darkness. The smack of it against

245

Gleneanne's right cheek was louder than hers had been against his, and she gave a shriek as it whipped her head to one side, causing her red hair to tumble over a shoulder. She placed her hand on her burning jaw and looked up at him, hardening her face and pinching her eyes with anger.

"I'm just trying to talk sense!"

"Bullshit! You had a job to do last night and you didn't do it. We won't linger over the question of why. You're a tramp. You were a tramp when I found you in that little mining dump in the San Juans, singing at night and letting yourself be bent over rain barrels when the suds shops closed. That little urchin you birthed running around and squealing his damn head off . . . You've always been a tramp and you'll always be a tramp."

"Goddamn you to hell!" Gleneanne clenched both hands at her sides, gritting her teeth. "I'm no worse than you! Why, you're nothing but a goddamn penny-ante stage and saloon robber. Why, when I found you, you were rolling drunks in alleys because your father had cut you off from your monthly allowance!"

She jutted her chin like a hammer. "And I won't have you talk about my boy that way! If you talk about him again, Miguel — if you ever mention Sam again, so help me God you'll regret it. The men I know are bigger and meaner and *tougher* than the ones you know!"

Miguel drew deep on his quirley and blew the smoke toward the stars, laughing. "Well, I guess we're about to find that out, aren't we?"

Gleneanne glared up at him. Slowly, her eyes softened, and she opened her hands. "Please, Miguel. Don't you see, honey, this can never work. We're gonna get ourselves killed. If not killed, then hunted till the end of our days."

"It would have helped if you'd killed one of the two hunters that came to town."

"It would have helped if you'd convinced your father not to hire them."

"I had no say in that, just as I have no say in anything around the bank in spite of the fact I'm supposed to be the president of the goddamn thing! The old man didn't consult me on the topic — neither Severin nor my father did! — and I only found out about it when they mentioned it among themselves in passing. . . ."

"Okay, we've covered that," Gleneanne said, reaching up again and placing her hands on his jaws. "The fact is they're here. The ambush didn't work and I made a mistake. I hesitated, didn't do my job. But truth to tell, it wouldn't have mattered, anyway. Because even with Lou and that girl out of the way, this plan is just rotten to the core. If we continue, we'll get nothing out of it but blood. Our own blood spilled in the streets of Juniper!"

Miguel laughed again. "You're sounding like you do on stage!"

Gleneanne chuffed and folded her arms across her breasts. Now he'd offended her work. She knew that, in spite of all the work she'd put into learning how to act on stage, she was no Lillie Langtry. But he didn't have to throw that up in her face as well. First her fallen ways, then her bastard son — a son who had Prophet's features, which was why she'd had so much trouble sliding that stiletto into the bounty hunter's heart the previous night — and now her thespian aspirations.

Aspirations that, like her son, she'd given up on. The son she'd adopted out.

Her aspirations had turned to dust inside her while she'd stacked all her chips, every one, on this handsome, evil jasper before her. This handsome, evil man who had a father and a sheriff to wreak vengeance on . . . and likely get her and himself killed in the bargain.

Miguel gave a sheepish sigh and placed his hands on Gleneanne's shoulders. "Ah, I was just joshin', honey. I'm a little nervous, I reckon, with what we got comin' tomorrow."

"That's what I'm sayin', Miguel," Gleneanne said, biting back her anger. "I'm nervous, too. Let's forget this thing. It's too big, too crazy. Let's leave here tomorrow, first thing!"

If she was going to get out of here, and away from this ghastly thing they'd been planning together for the past two years, getting all their men and themselves in place in Juniper, she'd have to leave with him. He had money. She had only the few dollars she was paid each week by the theater company she traveled with.

That didn't mean, however, she wouldn't get shed of the revenge-happy firebrand as quickly as she could, once she had a sizeable grubstake and could make another go of it somewhere else on her own. If there was one thing Gleneanne O'Shay knew how to do, that was how to make the best of a bad situation.

"That's out of the question." Miguel's voice turned hard once more. He squeezed her shoulders and looked down at her seriously. "We're going through with this, and when we're richer than you've ever dreamed and sitting pretty in San Francisco, you'll be glad you didn't pull out on me."

"It's not gonna work, Miguel. I got a bad feelin'."

"Because of Prophet?" Miguel scowled down at her. "He and Miss Bonaventure will be taken out of the equation soon. Before the last gold shipment pulls into town. We've seen the last of them."

Gleneanne's stomach turned to ice, thinking about Prophet being gunned down like a rabid dog. The father of the boy she'd never see again. But if her and Miguel's plan had any chance of working at all, Lou had to be taken down.

She didn't like it. She didn't like it at all. Prophet was a much better man than Miguel Encina could ever hope of becoming. The best man she'd ever known. But it was too late to change that part of the plan. It was all set. It was a dog-eat-dog world, and poor Lou would have to be sacrificed.

Gleneanne realized now that she could beg Miguel until sunrise tomorrow, but there was no changing their part in it, either. Seeing something in the young banker's eyes, she narrowed one of her own and canted her head slightly as a pang of jealousy nipped at her consciousness.

"What's the matter? You sorta wishin' things were different with that blond-headed pistoleer?"

Miguel dropped his hands from Gleneanne's shoulders.

A chill rippled through the former Sivvy Hallenback. Was Miguel considering double-crossing her, as she was considering doing to him?

She stepped back as she said tightly, "You sorta wishin' you hadn't given the order to gun them both? Maybe just Lou? Spare the blond . . . maybe let her take my place in your crazy plan?"

It was so dark that she didn't see the hand snapping toward her until it was too late. A more vicious blow than before, it spun her around and sent her sprawling in the pine needles and gravel, her head reeling.

"Maybe, maybe not," Miguel said, standing over her and balling his fists at his sides. "You best remember whose plan it is and who has the power to change it. In the light of that, you might want to take care how you talk to me in the future, Miss Gleneanne O'Shay."

With that he flicked his cigarette stub at her, spun, and walked away in the darkness.

Pushing up on her hands and knees, Gleneanne shook her head to clear the cobwebs.

She heard the squawk of tack as Miguel mounted his horse. Thuds sounded as he cantered past her, heading back toward town.

"If you're still a part of this," he said over his shoulder, "I'll see you in town tomorrow. If not, I'll see you in hell!"

The thuds of his galloping horse dwindled to silence.

Gleneanne heaved herself to her feet, sobbing quietly, utterly confused and frightened, and staggered back to the copper-bottom mare.

20

"Hey, Prophet!" Orrie Hitt called. "Casol's comin' like his hoss's tail's on fire!"

Prophet, who was riding ahead of the wagon the next day, with Louisa riding on his right, turned his horse off the trail and hipped around to see Juventino Casol bounding down the rise behind the caravan. The Mexican rode crouched over his saddle horn, sombrero flopping in the wind behind him, dust rising in the wake of his galloping white-socked black. Hitt stopped the wagon, hauling back sharply on the mules' ribbons and bellowing.

The other two guards, Sawrod and Brewster, halted their own mounts behind the wagon and turned, shucking rifles from saddle scabbards and levering shells into chambers.

"What do you think's his problem?" Brewster said, spitting a cigar stub into the dust beneath his horse.

"Looks like he seen a ghost," said Hitt.

Prophet glanced at Louisa, who returned it warily. The Mexican had been watching their back trail from a half-mile out, and he'd obviously spied something out of whack. Prophet gigged Mean and Ugly back along the side of the trail, skirting the wagon, while Louisa remained ahead of it, her rifle in her hands and her gaze directed up trail in case they were about to be ambushed from the front.

Prophet was ten yards behind Sawrod and Brewster when the Mexican checked his sweat-silvered black down, breathing hard. He jerked a thumb over his shoulder. "Three riders. Been shadowing us a while. Whenever I ride back to get a better look, they disappear, like phantoms. When I ride ahead I look back and there they are again, keeping pace with the wagon but neither speeding up nor slowing down."

Casol sleeved sweat from his black brows. "I don't like it."

Prophet didn't like it, either. It had all the ear notches of a bushwhack.

"You fellas keep movin'," he ordered. "Me an' Louisa'll hang back and check out Casol's shadows. Keep your eyes skinned."

Nodding, Hitt shook the ribbons over the mules' backs, bellowing, "Giddyup there, ya

254

dunderheaded cusses!"

"We'll wait for you just beyond the canyon yonder," Brewster yelled behind him as he, Casol, and Sawrod cantered their mounts after the wagon while Louisa turned her pinto off the trail and held back.

When the wagon was gone, she turned to Prophet. "Wait here?"

"Why not?"

"How's your neck?"

Prophet raked his gloved left hand under his shirt collar and winced. "That bitch is really pokin' me. But it ain't just recent. She started proddin' me hard in the middle of the night. Didn't sleep much after three a.m."

Louisa stepped down from her saddle and led her pinto into boulders and brush along the trail's west side. "You could hang up your guns and start telling fortunes for a living, Lou."

"Maybe I'm just gettin' rattled."

Louisa shook her head. "It's starting to add up." She glanced back at Prophet, who was leading Mean and Ugly up behind her while peering north along their back trail. "The bushwhackings in Juniper. Now Casol's three riders. Must mean a holdup's on the way."

"I don't know." Prophet scowled as he led

Mean around behind a boulder snag and looped the horse's reins around a cedar branch. "My tail's up, girl. Somethin' don't feel right in my belly, so I got that to go with the cold finger against my neck."

"You keep on, you're gonna need a sawbones soon."

"You don't feel nothin' unusual?"

"Maybe I've been relying on you too long."

"Or maybe you're just feelin' all fuzzy and gooey over that banker's boy." Prophet set his rifle on his shoulder and stole slowly around the boulder, heading toward the trail but keeping his head down.

Following close on his heels, Louisa said, "If any man could ever do it . . ."

Prophet gave a caustic snort. He hunkered down behind a boulder, edging a look over the top. The trail snaking through pinyon pines was quiet, only a jackrabbit nibbling fescue in the shade of a gnarled cottonwood.

"Let's hole up here." Prophet sank to his butt and raised his knees. "Should be able to hear 'em when they pass by. When they're just beyond us, we'll haul down on 'em, get 'em off their hosses fast, find out what they're up to."

Louisa sank down beside him, rested her

back against the boulder. "You think they're just gonna come right out and say, 'Oh, darn, you caught us. Yes, we're after the gold, all right. Badmen's what we are.'"

Prophet gave her a sidelong look as he dug his makings out of his shirt pocket. "I been in the business long enough to know a gold thief when I see one. If they're drovers, they'll have shit on their boots. You can tell a prospector from a couple miles out. They smell like enclosed places and bacon grease. Most gotta wild look in their eyes."

"And what do gold thieves look like?"

"Greedy sons o' bitches," Prophet chuckled, dribbling chopped tobacco onto a leaf of brown paper troughed in his fingers. "And they'll be sweatin' it."

"You're not gonna smoke that?"

"What do you think I'm rollin' it for?"

"You know how I hate the smell of tobacco smoke."

"So get downwind of me." Prophet chuckled again, this time wryly. "Lordy, I hope that young Encina boy knows how easy it is to twist your panties."

"It's only easy for you," Louisa said, getting up and moving to his other side, upwind of him, before sitting back down against the rock once more. "No one could ever twist 'em like you could."

257

Prophet lit the quirley.

"You don't think they'll smell it?"

"I ain't no fool, girl. I know which direction's the wind's from. That's why I'm sittin' over here and not on the other side of the trail. I can smell them from here — them and their hosses."

Louisa looked at him, her eyes crossing slightly with skepticism. "You can really smell a man and a horse from thirty yards?"

"Thirty yards, hell!" Prophet drew deep on the cigarette, blew it toward the ground, and watched the wind carry it straight out away from him. "I can smell a miner from a hundred."

He felt Louisa's eyes on him. He turned to her. She stared at him, smiling obliquely. She reached over, tugged the brim of his battered hat down a little, and said with the thickness of emotion in her voice, "I'm gonna miss you."

"You think so?"

She nodded. Leaning toward him, she pecked his cheek, then rubbed her own cheek on his shoulder.

Prophet draped his arms over his knees and stared into the brush and rocks beyond him. "I raise a stink for fun, but that Miguel kid's a good young man. I got a sense about folks."

"I hope you're right."

"You got a good sense about him?"

Louisa hiked a shoulder. "I did have a good sense. Last night. But after I slept on it — I don't know — maybe he just seems a little too much like the young buck from every girl's dream. Too much of a shine on him."

"You're just nervous," Prophet told her, filing ashes off his quirley with his thumbnail. "You tried settlin' down before and it didn't work out. You don't think it will this time, neither. But he is only the first younker you met here, so if he ain't the one, there's plenty more where he came from." He chuckled. "But maybe not with as much money."

"Money's nothing, Lou."

"To some, it sure as hell is." Prophet frowned and craned his neck to look around the boulder toward the trail. "Where the hell are them two, anyways? Were we chinnin' so hard we let 'em get around us?"

"I would have heard." Louisa pushed off her hands, climbed to her feet, and stared through the brush toward the trail.

As she stepped around one side of the rock, Prophet stepped around the other, holding his quirley down low by his side. They met in the trail, glancing back in the direction from which they'd come.

"Nothin'." Prophet puffed the quirley absently, sending his glance into the brush off both sides of the trail.

"Maybe they smelled your quirley and chose a different trail."

"Maybe they smelled you, you burr-tailed filly, and decided they wasn't up to it." Prophet strode back off the path, heading for Mean and Ugly. "I reckon we'd best check it out."

When they'd mounted their horses, they trotted back over the rise, both holding their rifles over their saddle horns and looking around cautiously. They rode a mile back along the twisting trail, with broken, rugged terrain showing on both sides, but no extra sets of tracks overlying their own and the twin furrows that had been ground by the wagon's steel-shod wheels.

"Damn peculiar," Prophet said, scouring the ground.

Louisa was looking toward a bluff whose crown had been eroded down to bare rock, spying nothing untoward. "They must have left the trail farther back. They gotta be circling around, Lou, meeting up with others farther ahead."

"I reckon you're right, Miss Bonnyventure. We'd best catch up to Hitt and the boys, and we'd best catch up to 'em fast. That witch ain't only pokin' me now — she's snarlin' in my ear!"

With that, he neck-reined Mean around and touched spurs to the horse's flanks. He didn't stop galloping until nearly a half hour later, at the mouth of a narrow canyon, the trail of which rose steeply ahead of him, between craggy gray walls. Pines stood atop the walls, offering good cover. The lips of both ridges were a couple of hundred yards away, but a good rifleman could make the shot.

"What is it?" Louisa was looking around, holding her carbine up high across her chest, her lips parted with a worried look.

"Never liked canyons." Prophet clucked Mean ahead. "Let's go easy."

They rode single file, Prophet in the lead. Their hooves clacked on the canyon's pitted stone floor.

Ten yards, twenty. Up the canyon floor they climbed, Prophet's heart beating in his ears.

One good thing was that the cold finger had been removed from the back of his neck. Why that made a difference, he didn't know, with his heart beating a powwow rhythm. But then, ever since the war, he'd had a fluttery heart. You couldn't see that many kith and kin killed horribly before your eyes and not come out of that bloody fandango with something fluttering oddly.

Prophet's eyes raked the ridges around him. On the ridge on his right, a dark shadow moved between two trees.

"Hold it!" Prophet jerked back on Mean's reins and narrowed his eyes at the shadow.

"What?"

Prophet pointed. "There."

The shadow crouched down behind a rock, and Prophet expected to see a rifle barrel snake out from behind the same rock. He raised his Winchester, pressing the stock firmly against his shoulder, but before he could thumb the hammer back, the rock suddenly leaned out away from the ridge, exposing the man-shaped figure standing behind it.

Prophet caught a fleeting glimpse of a short, bandy-legged man in a short-crowned straw sombrero — Juventino Casol — before his attention returned to the rock that seemed to float in the air for an instant just beneath the ridge's lip. Then it slammed into a nest of similar-sized boulders about thirty yards below the ridge, the shotgun-like blast of the concussion reaching Prophet's ears a second later as the first boulder and several more began rolling and plunging down the side of the ridge.

Each rock loosed several others. In turn, the others loosed several more, and in a matter of seconds Prophet was staring up the ridge at a hundred boulders crashing, leaping, bounding, and rolling toward him, some cracking in half, others in thirds, the dust of the plunging rocks boiling like steam from a teakettle.

"Let's go!" both Louisa and Prophet shouted at nearly the same time, wheeling their pitching horses in tight circles and spurring them back down the canyon.

Prophet glanced over his shoulder, his loins turning to ice.

The rocks hit the canyon floor fifty yards behind him and plunged toward him brutally, mercilessly — roaring, causing the ground to leap beneath Mean's plundering hooves. The rocks doubled, tripled in size in Prophet's eyes, the rising din turning to merging thunderclaps in his ears.

Prophet turned forward in his saddle, and crouched low, whipping Mean's flanks with his rein ends. He flung a hand up to snatch his hat from the wind.

"Haul ass, you ugly cayuse!" The shout was drowned by the rockslide's raging fury. He could no longer hear the hammering of the horses' hooves, either.

Prophet glanced at Louisa. She rode as one with her horse, stirrups up and back, her head nearly hidden behind the pinto's extended neck and buffeting cream mane. She held her carbine in one hand over the pinto's left wither.

Prophet jerked his gaze forward, willing the canyon mouth closer. Unlike the rocks plunging toward him with the dumb fury of gravity hazing them on, the daylight-filled gap seemed to be standing still.

The bounty hunter gritted his teeth, feeling the hot, dusty wind of the rocks gaining on him — leaping and lunging and seeming to try to overtake each other as they hammered straight down the pitched canyon floor — snarling, fire-breathing demon hounds hell-bent on overtaking the furiously galloping riders and turning the canyon into a sarcophagus.

Prophet whipped his head from side to side and cursed.

Nope . . . they weren't going to make it.

21

Prophet's heart lightened slightly as though to an unexpected, strangely affecting piano chord. He glanced over his shoulder to see that the rockslide had slowed just enough that he and Louisa were staying ahead of it, with the slide's front rocks bouncing and tumbling about ten yards behind Mean and the pinto's hammering hooves.

The gap yawned like the sunlit door to heaven, birds flicking this way and that.

Prophet and Louisa careened through it, each turning their horses off opposite sides of the trail and behind the canyon's jagged front walls. Pointing Mean toward some spindly aspens, Prophet checked the dun down and curveted to see a few gray rocks spilling from the canyon mouth to settle in the trail just beyond it.

Dust rose. The rumbling inside the canyon sounded like a distant thunderstorm. The rocks shifted as they settled, clattering over one another, a few smaller ones spilling farther out along the trail beyond the canyon.

A silence settled. It was like the silence after a plains twister, heavy and complete. There weren't even any birdcalls, and the wind had died as though in awe of the recent calamity.

Prophet looked over the pile of smoking rubble to see Louisa riding toward him. They met in the trail in front of the rubble, peering over it toward the canyon mouth. The rocks and boulders, with here and there a cedar or pine branch, had sealed the mouth up tighter than a cork in a whiskey bottle.

Louisa could face five pistoleers and look cool as a stone statue. But almost being hammered to pulp and shredded saddle leather under the rockslide had even her rattled. Her eyes were glassy, and strands of blond hair stuck to her sweaty, dusty face.

"How in the hell did that get started?" she asked Prophet.

"You didn't see?"

"I saw the first rock fall."

"Casol pushed it off the ridge."

Louisa looked at him, skeptical lines digging into her tanned forehead. "The Mex?"

"I think I glimpsed Hitt behind him."

Prophet looked around for an alternate route, seeing none. His heart was still hammering and his shirt was sweat-plastered against his back. Mean and Ugly coughed, blew, and rippled his withers as he studied the rocks in front of him, lowering his snout to give the rubble a delicate sniff.

"I do believe, Miss Louisa," Prophet said with a fateful sigh, shifting around in his saddle, "we done been hornswoggled." He sleeved sweat from his brow. "Yessir, hornswoggled like a whiskey drummer at a church social where nothin' stronger than sarsaparilly is a served."

Hell-Bringin' Hiram Severin stood on the front porch of the sheriff's office, smoking a cigar and enjoying the quiet commotion of a controlled but industrious day in Juniper, when he heard the clomp of hooves in the street to his right.

He turned to see his chief deputy, Frank Dryden, angle toward him while holding a Henry rifle on his shoulder. Dryden's eyes, hardened by his years in Yuma pen, and shaded by the brim of his brown bowler, looked official.

"The gold's on the way, Sheriff," the deputy said, halting his blue roan at the hitchrack fronting the office, where two

267

more saddled horses stood tied. "Horn gave me the signal from Ute Ridge. Wagon should be pullin' into town in a half hour or so."

"All right," Severin said with a nod, removing the wet cigar from his mouth with a puff of blue smoke and inspecting the gray coal with a bored, quiet air. "Gather the other deputies and take up your positions. I'll grab my pistol and head on over to the bank."

Dryden pinched his hat brim to the old town tamer, then nudged the roan ahead with his spurs, heading off to summon the other deputies, Brink Moffett and Giuseppe Antero, who would be patrolling the western side streets this time of the day — two in the afternoon. Severin watched Dryden recede into the slow, midweek traffic, heading toward the main drag, then turned and went into his office.

He liked not wearing a gun most of the time, when he could remember not to put it on. To him, walking around unarmed, wearing only his sheriff's badge to show he was the law, was a sign of success. Sort of the way a successful businessman wore a pot-belly to signify his prosperity. Only a sheriff who had tamed his town could walk around unarmed in it, letting his deputies do whatever minor bits of dirty work needed cleaning up with six-shooters or carbines.

When he'd strapped his old but clean and well-oiled Peacemaker onto his hip, he adjusted his brown bowler at its customary angle on his head and headed out of the office and into the street. The jail office was on a side street southwest of the bank, and Hell-Bringin' Hiram, knowing he had ample time — it usually took the wagon at least a half hour to arrive at the bank after being spotted from Ute Ridge — took a leisurely stroll.

Severin was a proud, taciturn man, and an entire team of Prussian plow horses couldn't have dragged it out of the old lawdog that he enjoyed his reputation as a whang-tough law bringer and that he enjoyed a frequent, slow stroll through town, tipping his hat to the ladies, ruffling the hair of the towheaded boys, for the sole purpose of basking in the glow of their admiring eyes.

Usually, he got the opportunity to order a couple of out-of-work saddle tramps, or those lingering too long in town from one of the ranches, to move along or saddle up and to see them nod and quicken their paces, maybe favor the aging sheriff with a glance of wary caution. He did so now outside of the Rawhide Saloon, where a couple of men from the Chain Link were drinking beer and sparking a little, red-headed whore in plain sight of any passing womenfolk or younguns.

"Yessir, Mr. Severin," the Chain Link fore-man, Case Reeve, said, flushing and clear-ing his throat as he unwrapped his arms from the little redhead and tipped his beer at Severin. "We was just havin' one and fixin' to head on back."

"Finish the one and head back now, Case," Severin ordered in passing, keeping his voice affable but with that uncompro-mising steel edge.

He didn't look back to make sure his orders were being followed. He knew they'd be followed, and looking back would only be a show of weakness. To a lawdog, confi-dence was almost as handy a weapon as a finely tuned six-shooter or a Winchester rifle that had been used so often the owner's cheek had worn a pale wedge in the stock.

At the bank, Severin pinched his hat brim to one of the lady tellers, despite his not ap-proving of women working out of the home, and opened the gate in the low, varnished rail that separated the small lobby from the bankers' offices. He paused when he saw young, impeccably attired Miguel Encina speaking with the loan officer, Herman

Mayville, near Mayville's desk by the solemnly ticking grandfather clock with its big, gold pendulums.

"Your father in, Miguel?" the sheriff asked.

"Pa's in his office," Miguel said with his customarily friendly smile. "Anything I can help you with, Sheriff?"

"Gold wagon's on the way." The sheriff continued straight back toward the senior Encina's office, on the opposite side of the large, open, carpeted area from his son's. "I'm gonna let him know."

"You could let me know, Sheriff."

Severin paused to turn back to young Encina, who had turned to face him beside Mayville. The smile on the young banker's face had become rigid, his brown eyes wide and brash. The dimples in his cheeks looked counterfeit. The loan officer, Mayville, turned toward the sheriff with a vaguely puzzled frown.

"I am the bank president, Sheriff," young Miguel said, an edge in his voice, the wooden smile frozen in place. "In spite of the sign on my office door. You need only let me know that the gold is on the way. If I think my father needs to know, I'll inform him."

Severin held the young banker's gaze. He knew that beneath the surface affability, Miguel hated his guts. The young man had never really gotten over his four days at the bottom of that mineshaft. Oh, he pretended he had, and he'd straightened out and made a good life for himself in Juniper under his father's tutelage, but he really hadn't forgiven the sheriff.

Which had always made Severin wonder if young Miguel had ever really forgiven his father.

"Well, now I reckon you know," Severin said with a wink. "And I'll just go make sure your pa knows about it, too . . . seein' as how you seem busy with Mr. Mayville an' all."

Severin turned, leaving young Encina staring after him, the smile fading from the young banker's face like fresh paint in a sandstorm, and knocked on the older Encina's office door.

"Come, *por favor!*" came the friendly command from inside.

Severin shoved the door open and peered into the small but well-appointed office filled here and there with trinkets and mementos of Jose Encina's home country, including a puma-hide couch trimmed with black-and-red-striped cloth and a statuette of Our Mother of Guadalupe hanging on the wall behind his leather-covered desk.

"Ah, mi amigo," the banker said, returning an ink pen to its holder and removing his steel-framed spectacles as he sank bank in his cowhide chair. "The gold must have made an appearance."

Severin moved into the room and closed the door behind him. "I'd say we got time for one cigar." He plucked two cigars from the breast pocket of his black, clawhammer coat and held them up with a cunning grin.

The banker, whose thinnning, pomaded hair was liberally touched with gray, returned the expression. "And a brandy?"

"Got some of that fine Spanish brandy?"

"Of course, mi amigo. Would I serve you anything less?"

"Well, then," Severin said, sinking into a leather-upholstered, walnut-armed visitor chair angled in front of the desk, "why the hell not?"

Chuckling, Jose Encina rose from his own chair and walked over to a table under a framed map of Chihuahua, Mexico, and poured out two brandies from a cut-glass container. He brought the snifters back to his desk, set one in front of the sheriff, the other in front of his own chair where Severin had laid one of his cigars.

Sinking back into the chair, the banker said with a weary sigh, "How do you do this

273

fine day, my friend?"

"I reckon I'm old and gettin' older." Severin slid a match across the desk to Encina, who'd picked up the cigar to sniff one of the Cubans that the town tamer regularly ordered in from Denver. "Ain't no stoppin' that."

"No, there is no stopping it. I, too, grow old. Older than you by ten years, and I have to tell you, I think it is time for me to turn the bank over to my son."

"I thought you had done that, Jose." Severin was holding the match flame to his cigar, puffing smoke out his lips and nostrils as the flame danced in front of his washed-out blue eyes.

"Miguel is the president, *si*. But I still keep an eye on the books and do most of the hiring and firing. It is time now, though, to turn it all over to him. He has learned well these past two years, and my shoulders and hips make it hard for me to come into the bank every day."

"Got the chilblains, do you? Or *burseritas*? Me, too." Severin blew out the match with a puff of smoke and cast it into a glass ashtray beside the banker's pen-and-ink holder. "Sitting around too many cold cow camps on them frigid New Mexico winters up high in the mountains is what I'm

274

reminded of every time I try to heave myself out of a chair. Damn feet bark like dogs of a mornin', soon as I set 'em on the floor."

"You, as I, Hiram, need a woman to warm them."

Severin thew back half his brandy and sighed, his eyes watering from the burn. Chuckling, he sank back in his chair, crossed his legs, and puffed the stogie, sucking half of each puff into his lungs and letting it slither out his broad, pitted nostrils. "I ran the last one off the year before I came here. A Ute girl with the biggest tits you ever saw. Couldn't keep the house for shit, though, and took to drink."

Encina drew deep on his cigar, blew a little smoke into his brandy snifter, then sipped the liquor and threw his head back with a sigh of satisfaction as he swallowed the amalgam of smoke and brandy. "I ran my last one off, as you say, a long, long time ago. She ran off on me, rather. Leaving me to raise Miguel alone in Mejico. The daughter of an American cavalry captain."

Encina formed a bitter expression and shook his head, taking another sip from the snifter in which a couple of small snakes of smoke still slithered. "She got restless and tired of the ranch. It was a hard life down there, the Apaches always a threat and running off my horses. She wanted to take Miguel, but I wouldn't let her. She wrote a few times from Fort Worth, but then I heard she married again, and the letters stopped." He wrinkled his nose, and his brown eyes darkened. "She was a harlot. Once, I caught her visiting my *segundo*'s sleeping quarters."

"You fix that?" Severin wanted to know.

"The bullwhip for them both. I had the *segundo* dragged off the hacienda with his own horse and rope. I made Alexandra watch, and I thought that would put an end to it. A few months later, she told me she would either leave or kill herself. I had my suspicions about her possibly continuing to visit the bunkhouse, so I told her to leave without the boy, and I'd see her in hell!"

Red-faced, Encina threw the rest of his brandy back and puffed the cigar.

Severin shook his head and let the story sink in. He'd known Encina had married a gringa, but he'd never gotten the details. "About the boy, Jose," he said after a time, haltingly. He wasn't sure how to say what was on his mind. "Are you sure he's ready to take over the bank? Run it completely on his own, without the benefit of your supervision?"

Encina frowned across the desk. "As you always say, mi amigo, chew that up a little finer for me, will you?"

Severin grunted and squirmed in his chair, turning the cigar in his fingers. He wasn't sure how to tell the man that, when he got down to brass tacks, he wasn't sure that he trusted his son. Not with as much gold as passed through the bank via the gold mines in any given year. And the town was growing, the bank acquiring more and more depositors. It needed to be run by a trustworthy, professional man like Jose himself. A man with years of experience.

But if Jose couldn't see that his son may not be quite as good as he seemed, there was little Severin could do to make him see it. After all, the sheriff had no firm evidence to support his suspicions that Miguel might possibly be every bit the ringtail he'd always been. He wasn't sure he entirely believed it himself. After all, people can change for the better. Maybe he was just too damn cynical.

Nervously, frustratedly puffing his stogie, Severin shook his head and threw out a dismissive hand. "Never mind, Jose. You know how it is with an old mossyhorn like me. Just hard to see times change. I'm sure Miguel'll handle things just fine around here."

Severin himself would make sure he did,

277

and he'd have his deputies keep an extra-close eye on the younker. Maybe he'd even get a spy in the bank somehow, working one of the teller cages.

The sheriff killed his brandy and rose creakily from his chair. "I reckon we best go see about that gold, eh?"

"*Si, si,*" said Encina, sticking the cigar in a corner of his mouth and gaining his feet with a wince, his old bones popping like distant pistol shots. "Let's see about the gold!"

22

Hell-Bringin' Hiram walked out of the bank into the crisp, damp air of a coming storm. The sun was still shining, but a purple, wedge-shaped thunderhead was building in the southwest, capping the southern ridge. Distant thunder rumbled.

The sheriff was still puffing the Cuban stogie and casually rolling it between his lips with his fingers. Jose Encina walked out behind him, also puffing a cigar while dipping his free hand in the pocket of his fawn wool vest. The two men stood appraising Severin's deputies, four of whom were positioned at various points around the street fronting the bank, all holding rifles either in the crooks of their arms or resting on their shoulders, ready.

Frank Dryden stood in the middle of the street directly in front of the bank. There was no traffic because he and the other men had cleared it for two blocks in all directions. There was no one on the boardwalks, either; those, too, had been cleared by the deputies.

Chase Appleyard stood over by the back of the opera house, sucking on a matchstick, his hat pulled low over his eyes. The black man, Brink Moffett, who had once worked for the Pinkertons, had taken up position to Severin's right, fifty yards away on the boardwalk fronting a harness shop.

Giuseppe Antero stood across the street from Moffett, in front of the bathhouse, leaning slightly back against one of the posts that held up the bathhouse's porch roof, his boots casually crossed. Smoke dribbled from the brown paper cigarette wedged in a corner of the Mexican's mouth that was capped and framed by a long, drooping mustache.

According to Sheriff Severin's dress code, all five deputies were as well attired as most prominent businessmen. Well-groomed, too: hair, beards, and mustaches neatly trimmed. Even to Severin the tailored garb stood out in sharp contrast to the men's hatchet, cold-eyed faces. But to the sheriff's way of thinking, lawmen dressed in rags were given little respect and deserved even less.

"Here it comes," Encina said as the wagon came into view from the east, rolling along the main street behind the two beefy mules.

Orrie Hitt rode slumped in the driver's seat, on his red velvet pillow, his boots on the dashboard, elbows on his knees. The big man clucked to the mules, hoorawed them toward the bank. Three other riders rode along behind — Brewster, Casol, and Sawrod. Flanking them at thirty or forty yards, rode Severin's fifth deputy, Jim Horn, who'd scouted the wagon from Ute Ridge. Horn, a thickset man with a high-crowned cream Stetson and sand-colored handlebar mustache, stopped his horse in the middle of the street, east of the bank, and cradled his rifle in his arms.

Behind Severin and Encina, the bank door rattled open, and Miguel Encina stepped out, positioning his crisp brown bowler hat with both hands. "We get any more gold out of the mines this month, we're going to have to rent out a room for it at the Golden Slipper."

The elder banker chuckled as he puffed his stogie and eagerly watched the wagon angle toward him. "There's always room for gold, son. Always room for gold."

"When's the next shipment leave for Denver?" the sheriff asked, his spooked eyes roaming the eastern edge of town for Prophet and Bonaventure.

"Not till next week," Miguel said. "But, like Pa says, we always got room for gold." He wrapped an arm around his father's shoulders, dimples deep and shadowed. "Ain't that right, Pa?"

The elder Encina's shoulders jerked slightly as he laughed, envisioning spending next winter, the first one of his retirement, in Monterrey. "You're learning, my boy. You're learning. . . ."

All three men stepped forward as Hitt swung the wagon in front of the bank, about ten feet from the boardwalk. A gun roared. Severin's hand dropped to his Peacemaker's ivory grips as he looked over the mules' backs to see a burr-laden collie dog turn on a dime with a startled yip and run back toward the alley mouth it had slunk out of, tail between its legs.

Laughing, Giuseppe Antero triggered another shot at the dog, blowing up dust behind it. The dog yelped louder, kicked its back legs, and disappeared into the alley. Frank Dryden laughed, as did Severin's other men around the bank.

Severin gritted his teeth, slowly lowered his hand from his Peacemaker, glanced at the startled Encina, and shook his head as if to say, "Sometimes, you gotta take the horns with the hide. . . ."

Orrie Hitt, too, was chuckling as he kicked the wagon's brake. Severin said, "Where's Prophet and Miss Bonaventure?"

"Ah, Jesus," Hitt said, running a gloved paw across his bristled, pudgy cheek. The other guards sat about ten feet from the wagon, their dusty, trail-weary horses hanging their heads. "Bad news about them," Hitt reported. "You know Lost Canyon about ten miles north?"

Encina frowned, nodding, absently puffing the stogie. His son's eyes were expressionless. Severin just waited, his craggy face implacable.

Hitt had wrapped the reins around the brake handle. Now he crawled over the back of the driver's seat into the wagon box, and was fishing the lockbox key out from under his sweat-soaked shirt. "Well, they was both ridin' our back trail, keepin' an eye out for bushwhackers, don't ya know. There was a rock slide. You know how easy them slides get started in there, with all that talus. They got caught in the middle of it, nowhere to run to. They tried hightailin' back but the rocks overtook 'em, buried 'em under enough rock for one o' them big Egyptian temple things."

Hitt poked the key in the lock.

"That's impossible," Severin said, scowling at the big, sweating, dust-caked gold guard. "I don't believe that for a minute."

"Why not?" Hitt asked amiably.

"That does sound odd, Hitt," Encina growled. He poked his cigar at the big guard, who was now removing the padlock and unwrapping the chains from around the box. "You men didn't have something to do with that slide, now, did you?"

"Maybe because you resented Prophet being hired as ramrod?" Severin added, dropping his right hand once more over his Peacemaker's grips.

Hitt looked up at the sheriff and ground his jaws angrily. He glanced over his shoulder at the three other guards, who stared insolently across the wagon at Severin. As Hitt turned back to the sheriff, the wagon driver allowed a humorous light to reclaim his eyes, and his lips spread away from his large, square teeth.

"Hell," he chuckled with a menacing edge, "I'd never kill a man over a tinhorn job like that." He laughed again, then lifted the lockbox's lid.

Severin glanced uneasily at Encina, who'd moved up closer to the side of the wagon, his eyes bright and waiting. "How much did you bring back?" the banker asked, a thickness in his voice.

"Not as much as some trips," Hitt said, reaching into the box and lifting out a gold ingot about a foot and a half long. "More than others. Lookee there, Mr. Encina. How do you like the way that shines?"

Encina's chest rose and fell heavily, and his eyes glowed as though he were having a vision of the Mother Mary. He stuck his stogie between his teeth, and while Severin continued to glower at Hitt and the other three riders, the banker reached over the side of the wagon for the ingot.

He took it in both hands, wincing a little under the weight and letting quick little smoke puffs leech out from between his smiling lips. He fairly groaned, his eyes riveted on the ingot. "I have been in this business for a long time now, have seen much gold, but it never ceases to grab hold of my heart and twist. Like the most beautiful of Spanish women."

Severin sensed danger in the eyes of the gold guards and the very air around him, but he hadn't quite gotten his right hand over the ivory grips of his Peacemaker again before there was the snick of steel against leather and he felt the weight on his hip suddenly lighten.

There was the ratcheting click of a gun hammer.

Something cold and round jabbed against his lower back, and as he began to swing around, Miguel Encina said, "Uh-uh." He jabbed Severin's own pistol harder against the sheriff's kidney. "One more quick move like that and I'll drill you."

Encina swung around, lowering the ingot in his hands, and frowned at his son, his lower jaw loosening so that the stogie almost dropped from between his lips. His eyes dropped to the two guns in Miguel's hands, one pressed against Severin, the other cocked and aimed at the elder banker's own belly, just up from his polished black belt.

"What is the meaning of this, Miguel?" It was more of an exclamation than a question.

"You'll see in a moment, Pa." Miguel glanced beyond his father and Severin at Hitt, and, grinning devilishly, nodded.

As Hitt removed his shabby hat, Severin looked at Frank Dryden, who stood staring toward the wagon, canting his head to one side and narrowing one eye, vaguely puzzled. Neither he nor any of the other deputies could see the two guns that Miguel Encina was holding on the sheriff and elder banker.

Grinning at Severin, Orrie Hitt waved his hat above his head and then calmly put it

286

back on.

"What's goin' on over there?" Dryden called, taking one step toward the wagon.

Severin looked at the wiry, blond deputy just as Dryden's hat flew off his head. The whip-crack of a rifle echoed around the street.

Dryden's head jerked forward. He stumbled, lowered his Winchester, and triggered it into the ground a few inches from his right boot, blowing up dust. Dryden dropped to his knees, his forehead looking as though it had been smashed with a large, ripe tomato.

Severin's gut tightened. He saw the man who'd shot Dryden lying atop the roof of the drugstore directly across the street. The shooter lifted his rifle slightly as he cocked it.

Whipping his gaze around, Severin picked out a dozen other men stepping calmly out of alley mouths or lifting their heads over stock tanks and rain barrels, holding rifles to their shoulders and canting their heads to aim down.

Severin's mouth grew dry.

His heart lurched, and his gut tightened. He was about to yell to his deputies but only gave a pained grunt when Miguel Encina rammed Severin's own pistol hard against

287

his kidney. By then it was too late, anyway.

There was a short burst of staccato gunfire from various points around the street, and all four of Severin's remaining deputies, all taken by surprise, grunted or screamed as bullets tore through them.

The black deputy, Moffett, hit in the chest, flew straight back off his heels and slammed into the wall of the store behind him, giving a clipped scream and triggering his rifle skyward. The rifle flew out of his hands, and by the time it clattered down to the boardwalk beside him, Moffett was lying with his head propped against the store, violently convulsing as his life puddled out across his chest.

At nearly the same time as Moffett had been hit, two slugs had thrown Jim Horn from his saddle. As Horn's bay bucked and pitched, screaming, another bullet took Horn through his belly, and the thickset deputy lay with his forehead in the dirt, moving his knees as though trying to stand but only grinding his forehead deeper into the dirt and horseshit of the street.

Chase Appleyard was shot in the back twice by a bushwhacker who'd stepped casually out of the cantina behind him. As the bushwhacker finished the writhing Appleyard, Giuseppe Antero, wounded in his left arm, fired two quick rounds, yelling Spanish epithets, at the man who'd shot him from an alley mouth.

Both his bullets only tore wooden doggets from the store flanking the bushwhacker. Firing from his hip, the bushwhacker drilled Antero twice more, direct hits in the chest and right arm.

Screaming louder, Antero spun.

Two more shots from elsewhere around the streets sent him flying and tumbling into the dust. He groaned, sobbed, feebly pushed onto his hands and knees. The bushwhacker who'd first winged him stepped out from the alley mouth — a big, red-bearded man with a large green bandanna billowing around his neck — and walked up to Antero. The big man casually aimed his Henry rifle one handed at the Mexican's head and tripped the trigger.

The whip-crack resounded. The Mexican's head jerked in the same direction in which blood and brains spewed from the bullet's exit hole to paint a long, grisly stain in the street.

Antero dropped and lay still.

"Jesus Christ!" Severin bellowed, lunging forward and angrily closing his hands over the side of the wagon box.

From Frank's Dryden's death to Antero's,

the shooting hadn't lasted over fifteen seconds. The sheriff's mind had been slow to catch up to what had just happened, but it was catching up fast now as he saw all his deputies lying in bloody piles around him.

23

The gold guards glared at Sheriff Severin like hungry wolves, each now casually aiming his rifle across the wagon at him. Behind them, the bushwhackers — hell, executioners! — were disarming the dead deputies. Severin thought he recognized a couple of their faces from wanted posters.

There were at least a dozen of them. Cutthroats, all . . .

He heard a sharp slap and turned to see Jose Encina snarling at his son as he lowered the hand that had left a crimson welt on the side of Miguel's handsome face. The banker had dropped the gold in the street, near his polished half boots.

Miguel stared at his father, menace in the upward curve of his mouth corners.

"Why?" asked Encina through gritted teeth.

"Why not?" Miguel said. "The past two and a half years I been waitin' for this.

Waitin' to rob you blind, steal all your precious gold and" — he slowly turned his head to Severin, keeping a cocked pistol aimed at each man — "take over your civilized, law-abiding town. Turn it back over to the kinda men that started it."

Severin clenched his fists and narrowed his eyes. "I knew you were still as rotten as the day you dropped from your mother's womb!"

Too fast for the sheriff's age-slowed reactions, Miguel raised the pistol high and swept the barrel across Severin's right temple, raking it savagely down across the man's nose and opposite cheek. Severin gave a pained grunt and fell back against the wagon, throwing his arms at the side panel but missing and falling in a heap on his butt.

A red welt blossomed on his temple. The pistol's front sight had carved a bloody notch over the bridge of his nose and another on his lower left cheek. He grabbed his temple as he sat in the dirt and glared up at the young outlaw, a few strands of gray-brown hair hanging loose across his forehead.

Miguel's nostrils expanded and contracted, and he was breathing as though he'd run a mile. "You leave my mother out of it, you old bastard."

"Miguel!" ordered Encina, brown eyes bright with exasperation. "Put those guns down! Tell these men to throw theirs down! Or everything I've done for you will have meant nothing!"

Miguel broke into crazy laughter as he staggered backward and squeezed his eyes closed. "Ah, don't sell yourself short, Pa. What you did for me meant a helluva lot. Shit, it meant the whole world to me."

Suddenly, his laughter died without a trace, and his jaws had turned hard as twin anvils. He lurched forward. His father had just started to raise his arms defensively and turn his head away when the same pistol Miguel had used on Severin crashed down across the top of the elder Encina's head.

Jose screamed and staggered sideways before he fell at the base of the wagon's right front wheel, groaning and clamping a ringed hand over the top of his head. Blood shone between his fingers.

"That's how much it meant to me, you hog-wallopin' son of a bitch!"

A gasp sounded in the bank door behind Miguel. He turned to see a young, plain-faced female teller staring out, hands over her mouth, eyes bright with terror. Another, older woman stood to her right, partly hid-

293

den by the door frame, steel-framed spectacles hanging low on her pale, upturned nose. The loan officer, Mayville, stood behind both women, his eyes wide, lower jaw hanging.

"You three are fired," Miguel said, waving a pistol toward the bank. "I want no one on my payroll who's worked for this chicken-livered son of a bitch, kissing his ass and licking his boots. From now on, only my friends here'll be workin' for me . . . though I don't 'spect the bank'll be open for business much longer" — he turned to cast a jeering gaze at his father — "seein' as how there won't be any gold or much of anything else left in the vault. Fact, I might just turn the vault into a whore's crib . . . once me an' the boys have divvied up the gold!"

Miguel laughed.

"Go on — git!" he shouted at the three bank employees looking nearly ready to pass out in the doorway.

They jumped as one. The youngest teller bolted out of the building first, sobbing and holding her skirts above her ankles as she ran stiffly up the street. The older woman followed, her face bleached, her glasses hanging off her nose. Mayville shoved her quickly along in front of him, a hand on her back.

Miguel fired two shots into the street a foot behind them, blowing up dirt and grit. The youngest woman screamed while the other tripped and nearly fell. Mayville jumped nearly a foot straight up in the air before breaking into an all-out run, leaving the older woman behind him.

In the wagon, Orrie Hitt roared.

The other outlaws followed suit, including the bushwhackers who'd now walked up to form a shaggy semicircle around the three horseback riders and the wagon, holding pistols or rifles with casual menace. They pointed and laughed, and the big man who'd shot Antero slapped his thigh as he doubled over with deep guffaws.

When all three bank employees had disappeared around a bend in the crooked street, Miguel, chuckling and swinging around loose-limbed with his new-found defiance and sudden freedom, saw his father glowering up at him from the dirt.

"You'll never get away with this, boy. You can desecrate everything I've built here, steal my gold, turn the bank into a brothel . . ." He swallowed, overcome with emotion, then continued growling through gritted teeth. "I'll have you hunted down and hanged like the mangy cur you really are! A cur from a worthless bitch!"

Jose Encina had barely gotten that last out before Miguel buried his right half boot in his father's belly. The elder banker gave a shriek and bent forward, clasping his hands across his stomach.

"You little bastard!" shouted Severin, still in the dirt to the banker's right. Orrie Hitt and Bronco Brewster, who'd stepped into the wagon, both covered him with rifles. "I'll hunt you down myself, and I'll see no judge wastes his time on you. No judge and no jury, neither!"

"You think so, town tamer?" Smiling savagely, Miguel raised the pistols in his hands. He fired them both at the same time, the twin slugs punching through each of the sheriff's upper arms.

Severin jerked back against the wagon, throwing his chin high and showing his teeth through an enraged, agonized grimace. His mouth drew wide, but no sound emanated as he clutched both bullet-torn arms with his hands, the blood welling up between his fingers.

"You miserable savage," he grated out, his eyes tearing up from pain, his cheeks looking suddenly blue and hollow.

"Miguel!"

The female voice lifted the blood-hungry Miguel's head and turned it slightly. Gleneanne O'Shay was running toward him from the Golden Slipper, a silk cape fluttering about her shoulders in the freshening breeze that smelled of rain. Her red hair danced across her shoulders. Her eyes were wide, horrified.

She stopped and looked down at the sheriff and Jose Encina, both breathing sharply, lips stretched with misery. "Oh, my god!"

The actress looked at Miguel. "What have you done?"

"What have I done?"

Miguel ran a sleeve across his sweaty forehead, set his pistols on the jockey box attached to the wagon, and picked up the gold bar that his father had dropped at the edge of the street. He ran a hand across the ingot, removing the horseshit and dust, and held it up for Gleneanne's inspection.

"This is what I've done, my sweet."

The actress's eyes found the gold and fairly glowed. "Oh, my . . ." Color rose in her cheeks. "Holy shit," she breathed. "I don't believe I . . . I don't believe I . . ."

"Believe it," Miguel said, pressing the bar against her breasts. She looked at him in disbelief as she wrapped her arms around the ingot and held it taut against her chest, staring down at it as though at a beautiful, newborn babe.

"Stop him," pleaded Jose, staring through watery, bloodshot eyes at Gleneanne, who ignored the old man.

Miguel chuckled and gave his father another kick. He kicked the elder Encina again and again, until he'd kicked him out into the street in front of the wagon.

"No, Miguel!" the old man shrieked, dust- and shit-caked from the crown of his thin, silver-haired head to the toes of his twelve-dollar shoes. "Please, I beg you . . . stop this savagery! You're going to *kill* me!"

"Intend to."

Miguel kicked Jose in the ribs, rolling him over with a horrific shriek. Gritting his teeth, Miguel buried his boot again and again in the old man's body, a grisly smile returning to his gaze as he felt and heard his father's ribs pop and splinter, saw the anguish and terror build in the old man's darkening eyes.

He heard a shout and turned to his left. Hitt and Brewster were giving Severin the same punishment twenty feet away, between the bank and washhouse. The two outlaws took turns ramming their boots into the sheriff's dusty, battered body, rolling him gradually toward the bathhouse on the other side of the street.

The other outlaws, Casol and Sawrod on horseback, the others standing, were yelling and hoorawing, a couple firing shots of revelry into the air.

Severin and Encina's shrieks dwindled to gasps and then groans barely audible above the growing rumble of thunder issuing from the storm clouds piling up over the canyon's southern ridge.

When he could no longer get even a sigh out of his father, Miguel wheeled toward Hitt and Brewster.

"Hold it!"

The men stopped and looked at Miguel.

"Hell-Bringin' Hiram ain't dead, is he?"

Orrie Hitt grinned. "Not yet!"

Miguel turned to one of the horseback riders — Sawrod, a killer and rustler whose acquaintance Gleneanne had made after a performance in Ouray — and waved an arm. "Get over here, Royal. Bring your rope. I do believe it's time for a Dutch ride through prickly pear!"

Both riders whooped and peeled their throw ropes off their saddles. Sawrod rode over to Miguel, swinging out a head-sized loop and tossing it down on Jose Encina's bloody, rumpled chest. Miguel crouched to work the loop over his father's shoulders and arms.

Jose looked up at him through the narrowed lids of his swollen eyes. His voice was a raspy whisper as he said, "You will burn in hell for this. . . ."

"Maybe." Miguel winked. "Maybe ole St. Pete's got a special place just waitin' for me, Pa."

Miguel stepped back and slapped the rear of Sawrod's horse. The blaze-faced roan shot forward with a whinny, heading west. When the rope snapped taut behind it, Jose Encina's ragged body lurched violently forward, more bones snapping audibly.

The elder banker wailed shrilly as he dashed like a human missile westward along the street behind the galloping roan, angling past the opera house and heading toward the open country beyond the town.

Severin wasn't far behind, fishtailing and bouncing along in the dust of Juventino Casol, who whooped and fired his pistol into the air. As the sheriff shot past Miguel, his arms pinned to his sides by the noose, Severin cast a fleeting, dark gaze toward the young banker.

Former young banker.

Miguel waved. As Hell-Bringin' Hiram lurched and jerked up the empty street, he cupped his hands around his mouth to shout, "Didn't much care for that old mine shaft, Sheriff!"

He chuckled and lowered his hands to watch Casol and Severin thunder out of sight as the first of the pellet-sized raindrops began ticking off Miguel's bowler hat.

"Nope. Didn't care for that one damn bit. . . ."

He turned to the men behind him and raised both arms high in the air. "It's a wide-open town, boys. Drinks are on me, but you gotta pay for the whores your own damn selves!"

His dimples cut into his cheeks as he roared.

Then he walked over to where Gleneanne O'Shay was still admiring the gold.

24

At the same time, and about six miles as the crow flies from Juniper, Lou Prophet put Mean and Ugly into a side canyon that forked off the main canyon that he and Louisa had been following since nearly being hammered finer than a breakfast serving of Georgia grits by the rock slide loosed by the gold guards.

"Hell, I'm not sure if this is the way back to Juniper or not," he grouched, off his feed and feeling dumber than a lightning-struck steer for having let himself be hornswoggled like that.

Louisa rode along beside him, feeling no better than he did. "Then why are we taking it?"

"Because the sign in the other one said Copper Gulch, four miles straight ahead, and I know from lookin' at a map before we rode out here that Copper Gulch is west of Juniper, and there's a tall ridge between the two towns."

"What sign?"

"You didn't see the sign?"

"I saw no goddamn sign."

"Jesus, you're startin' to curse bad as me. We gotta get you back to town quicker than I thought."

They rode up the canyon a ways, both sitting their saddles sullenly. When they reached a broad open park threaded by a chuckling creek sheathed in wolf willows, Prophet reined Mean in again and looked ahead at several piney ridges, blue-green in the distance, dropping into the same canyon another four or five miles away.

The vista looked like a bunch of green paint on some novice landscape painter's canvas, mountain ridges obscured by other mountain ridges, but Prophet knew there was another canyon there, angling off in the direction of Juniper, so he kneed the dun ahead once more. The land would sort itself out in due time, and maybe he'd find another sign. The trail they were on had been traveled recently, judging by a couple of sets of overlaid wagon tracks, so maybe they'd run into a camp or at least another sign soon.

As they let their horses drink in the middle of the broad park, whose grass rose to their horses' knees, Louisa broke the silence. "How do you figure it, Lou?"

"What's to figure? A couple of the other guards, or all of 'em, maybe, hightailed it with the gold."

"You think they're the ones who sicced the bushwhackers on us in Juniper?"

"That's how the cards look to me. Why they weren't waiting for a bigger truck of gold, I got no idea. Maybe they'd just made up their minds this was the day they was gonna become outlaws and followed through."

Louisa leaned forward as the pinto drank from the crystal-clear creek gurgling over polished stones. "I think we oughta run 'em down. Work our way around the canyon they tried to kill us in, and track 'em from there."

"You know how to get there, you take the lead."

"Don't get owly. I'm not the one who double-crossed us."

Prophet sighed with chagrin, leaned back in his saddle as Mean slurped at the creek, and hooked a leg over his saddle horn. "Since we're lost, we'd best head back to Juniper, tell the Encinas and Hell-Bringin' Hiram what happened, then head out from there and pick up the wagon's trail. Hitt an' them won't get far if they stay with the wagon. If they transfer the gold to their horses, they'll make a little better time, but not much. Unless they've got pack mules cached somewhere along their getaway trail."

"Then they could mosey down any little trail between any two ridges, cover their tracks, and be gone before we even reach town."

Prophet glanced at her, one eye narrowed. "Got a better idea?"

Louisa sighed wearily and looked around. "Let's build a camp. Our mounts are blown, and I'm blown, too. We'll think on it overnight, after a meal and a cup of tea, and start fresh in the morning."

Prophet dropped his boot back into its stirrup. "Sometimes you make sense, girl."

"One of us has to."

"Believe I'll have coffee and rye whiskey."

"I figured you would."

Prophet grunted and put Mean across the creek, through the willows, and angled him toward the southeast corner of the park, where a stone scarp jutted from the side of the pine- and fir-carpeted ridge and appeared to offer adequate cover for a night camp.

There was another creek — a freshet,

mostly — that tumbled out from beneath the scarp and along the base of the ridge. Along the trickling watercourse, in the thickening shade of the ridge, they unsaddled their horses then took their time rubbing both sweaty mounts down with scraps of burlap. After they'd fed the horses and tied them to short picket lines where they could forage and drink, they set about wordlessly setting up camp.

As Prophet gathered wood for a fire, something didn't feel right to him and it didn't seem to have anything to do with the chill finger poking the back of his neck. He wasn't sure what caused this additional ill feeling until he'd gotten the fire going and had filled a coffeepot at the spring-fed creek.

As he swung away from the stream, he stopped in his tracks, the tin pot made cold by the icy water fresh from the earth's stony bowels dripping in his hand.

No, it wasn't that something didn't feel right. It was that something did feel right — him and Louisa out here, hunting owlhoots like they'd done before they'd split up in Mexico, him going to Monterrey and her getting herself caught in the Rurales' trap and ending up in Montoya's prison.

He watched her kneeling by the fire, setting her tin teacup on a rock in the flames, then, turning away from the fire, and reaching behind her to toss her hair out from under her shirt collar. She began untying the leather thongs securing her blanket roll. Her clothes rustled, and her boots crunched pine needles and fine gravel, her pistols moving in their holsters as she worked, one of her spurs reflecting a stray ray of saffron-colored light angling between pines at the peak of the western ridge.

He could smell the nearby horses, the leather tack, the smoke of burning pine, hear the snapping fire, the horses cropping bunchgrass and ferns along the creek. Louisa's teacup begin to purr as it heated, the water swirling gently in the cup on which a single white ash floated.

Prophet felt a soothing hand wash over him, knowing suddenly that what bothered him was that nothing was bothering him except the stolen gold. But even that felt right. At the moment all felt perfectly as it should be, and deep inside he wished it could remain this way — him and Louisa together, building a camp, her teacup smoking on the fire and the horses stomping and snorting nearby — forever and always.

Why did things have to change? The notion was no less poignant for being so childishly maudlin.

They ate beans and jerky washed down with tea and coffee, sitting back against their saddles on opposite sides of the fire. They each washed their own plates at the creek, then Louisa made more tea and Prophet brewed another pot of coffee. Setting his smoking cup on a rock beside him, he leaned back against his saddle to watch the stars kindle brightly in the black velvet sky over the silent park before him and slowly, thoughtfully built a quirley from his makings sack.

On the other side of the fire, Louisa sipped her tea, then picked up her rifle, running an oiled cloth along its clean lines.

When she'd finished with the rifle, she did the same to her pistols, unloading them to clean the cylinders with a small brush, then filling the cylinders again — five pills in each wheel, then giving each a spin before replacing both pearl-gripped hoglegs in their oiled holsters, which she wrapped over her saddle horn, both guns close at hand.

"I think you're right, Lou."

It was the first either of them had said anything in over an hour; her voice sounded fresh and new to him, and imminently welcome and somehow reassuring.

"When have I not been right, Miss Bonnyventure?" he said with a wan, contented smile as he shaped the quirley in his big, brown fingers.

"We'd best go on back to Juniper, let Miguel and his father know what happened. I bet those scurvy dogs are headin' for Durango. It's the easiest route south, and from there they'd have a clear shot at Arizona and then Mexico. With that much gold, they'd have to head for Mexico."

"I hear you."

Louisa finished her tea and wandered into the brush to answer the call of nature. When she came back, she said, "I'm going to turn in."

"I reckon it's about that time." Prophet took the last puff off his quirley and flipped it into the fire. On the other side of the dancing flames, Louisa kicked out of her boots, unbuttoned her skirt, and let it fall to the ground. "I wonder how cold it's going to get up here."

Prophet shrugged and glanced at the sky before returning his gaze to Louisa, who lifted her poncho up over her head and tossed it onto her skirt.

"I'd reckon pretty chilly, this high up."

"How high up, do you think?" With customary immodesty — they'd been on the trail together too long, shared each other's blankets too many times, for modesty —

309

she unbuttoned her blouse and dropped it down with her other garments.

Prophet's voice thickened as she crossed her arms and lifted her cotton camisole. "Oh . . . nine, ten thousand feet maybe. The air feels a might thin to me."

The camisole caught on her nipples for a second, jostling her breasts, as she lifted it up and over her head and tossed it away. Her hair fell back across her shoulders and breasts in a disheveled mess that gripped Prophet hard by the loins.

"I haven't been up this high many times before," Louisa said, bending over to pull her socks off. Her breasts sloped down, dancing this way and that, just visible behind the rustling screen of her honey-blond hair that the firelight caught and turned several different shades of gold. "I reckon that's why I'm so sleepy all of a sudden."

When she'd removed both socks, she reached down again to gather her clothes and lay them in an orderly pile beside her saddle. She shivered as a chill night breeze caught her, and she crossed a slender arm over her lovely breasts as she dropped to her knees, then, sitting sideways to Prophet, opened her saddlebags and rummaged around inside.

"You sleepy, Lou?" She'd found her nightshirt — a heavy flannel man's work shirt that was several sizes too big for her and that hung almost to her knees — and held it out in front of her as she turned to him. Her hair looked like a tumbleweed, all mussed and spiking about her head and dangling off her shoulders. The firelight glowed in her hazel eyes, caressed her smooth, tanned cheeks.

"I was."

She made a face, then, turning toward him as if to punish him, held the shirt out for a moment, adjusting it, before swinging it back behind her, thrusting her shoulders back, breasts forward, and shrugging into the shirt and closing it over her chest and buttoning it.

"No need for that," Prophet grunted. "Come over here, Miss Bonnyventure, and whisper a sweet-nothing in ole Lou's ear."

She looked up between the mussed wings of her hair. She'd only buttoned the shirt's bottom two buttons, and it exposed her alluringly. She left it like that as she stared across the fire at Prophet, then rose and walked around it to him and dropped to her knees. She leaned forward, ran her hands through his hair, pulling it gently, then closed her hands on his ears and kissed

311

his forehead.

Prophet reached up and peeled the shirt down off her shoulders. She sat before him, her chest beginning to rise and fall heavily, her nipples pebbling. He could hear her breathing, feel the heat rise in her hands still clamped on his ears, as his own breaths grew labored.

Prophet feasted his eyes on her delectable form, from her flat belly down across her well-turned thighs to her little pink feet curled beneath her and then up across her heavenly, welcoming breasts to her lips that seemed to swell with need for his own.

Prophet lifted his head, kissed each of her breasts, the tender budlike nipples, then drew her down to him and closed his mouth over hers.

He kissed her for a long, long time, eating her slowly, like a well-ripened Georgia peach. When he'd undressed, he finished undressing her, then spread her out before him, and buried his face in her belly. She ground her hands in his hair, pulling his head taut against her.

"Oh, Lou," she cried, writhing, spreading her knees. "I miss you already!"

25

Two days later, after a hard, meandering trek through and around the mountains, Prophet said, "Girl, if I told you once, I told you a thousand times — doesn't matter how well you think you know a town. You always scout it before you mosey on into it."

"Shut up, Lou."

"You can think you know a town, but a town's like a woman — fickle as hell. Like this goddamn wet mountain weather."

"I'm scouting it," Louisa said.

She was on the ridge above and behind him, while he sat on the ground, leaning back against a sun-bleached log, smoking a quirley and lost in his own banter. Their horses grazed, ground-tied, a little farther down the hill. A drizzle had fallen all day though there was now a break in the heavy, purple-bellied clouds.

"I ever tell you about the time I rode into Dog Bone, Wyoming, and ran smack into

313

the Lyle Cretin Bunch. Hadn't scouted it first, of course. Too much in a hurry. Well, shit, there they were — all four of 'em — sittin' around outside a saloon, and who do they see ridin' into town on his trail-blown dun?"

Louisa stared down the ridge, facing away from Prophet, through her spyglass. "You?"

"You guessed it. Wasn't prepared at all. Not at all." Prophet chuckled ruefully, drew deep on his quirley, and shook his head gravely. "I paid for it, too. Them boys had me dancin' in the street, and you know how I can't dance. Well, I was dancin'! Pow, pow, pow, and I was doin' two-steps and three-steps and several steps you never seen before. Fortunate that the Cretin fellas was so drunk they didn't realize I was dancin' over to ole Mean and Ugly and somehow got my barn blaster off my saddle and managed to fill the whole gang with buckshot while I only took one of their ricochets in my kneecap. Just a glancing shot, but damn, it hurt like hell! A bullet to the kneecap. But my point is —"

"I know — scout a town before you ride into it. You never know who's there." Louisa lowered the spyglass and looked down the hill behind her at Prophet. "And if you wouldn't blow so hard, you'd realize that's what I've been doing. And you'd realize, you big ape, that you'd better come up here and take a look at this."

"Look at what?"

"Juniper."

"What about it? It's still there, isn't it?"

Prophet chuckled, a little trail-addled, and stuck his quirley in a corner of his mouth as he climbed to his feet with a grunt. He tramped heavily up to the top of the hill where Louisa stood, her hair blowing in the wind, in a notch between two monolithic boulders. She stepped back from the narrow notch, handing Prophet the spyglass.

The bounty hunter took another drag off his cigarette, rubbed it out with his boot, and raised the spyglass to his right eye, adjusting the telescopic focus. The notch offered a clear view of Juniper nestled in the broad, bowl-shaped valley with the creek running along the town's north edge, through brush and trees.

What caught Prophet's immediate attention, however, were the large, shaggy birds circling the town from about twenty or thirty feet in the air. What also got his attention was a distance-muffled gunshot carried by the damp, westerly breeze.

"What the hell?" he growled, again adjusting the focus for a better view of the town.

315

"Do you hear the shooting?"

"I hear it." Prophet stared through the glass. "Might just be ole Hell-Bringin' Hiram makin' some vagrants dance. . . ."

He let his voice trail off as he focused on a gap between two false-fronted Main Street buildings, from their right flank because that was pretty much his angle on the town. What he saw in that gap were two or three men milling around, one swinging something high in the air. He couldn't see what the man was throwing, but he could hear the muffled pistol report, sort of whipped and torn on the breeze.

"You see the buzzards?"

Prophet raised the spyglass to the birds winging in a shaggy circle over the main street, in the vicinity of the large, ornate opera house that sat like the jewel in the crown of the frontier town. Again adjusting the focus, Prophet picked out one bird, saw the broad black wings and ratty, streamer-like feathers, and the ugly bald head with the long, hooked beak.

"Buzzard, all right."

"How's that witch's finger?"

"Been proddin' me so regular I've sorta got used to the old bitch." Prophet collapsed the spyglass and gave it back to Louisa. "You stay here. I'm gonna ride down

316

and take a look."

"Maybe you best wait till dark, Lou."

"I'd best, but I'm ridin' in." Prophet strode quickly down the hill toward Mean and Ugly grazing a safe distance from the pinto. "Somethin's damn peculiar."

"Lou?"

He turned back to her standing with the cleft in the rocks behind her. "Miguel told me something about the sheriff and his father. He'd started out bad, and they threw him down a mine shaft to reconsider his evil ways."

Prophet canted his head and narrowed an eye at her. "So I heard."

"Don't look like that, Lou. People can change."

"Miss Bonnyventure, if you're not careful, I'm gonna start to think you see me as a narrow-minded son of a bitch."

He turned and continued down to Mean and Ugly, grabbed the reins, and swung into the saddle. His trail weariness was gone. Now he was anxious. Something told him he was about to find out why that witch had been rawhiding him.

"You stay here, now, hear?" he told the girl, slinging his shotgun over his shoulder so that the double-bore hung barrel up behind his back, the lanyard stretched taut across his broad chest.

"I don't like taking orders."

"You wouldn't like being taken across my knee, neither, and I can still do that." Prophet gigged Mean and Ugly toward the canyon's south wall, where he'd be less conspicuous from town. "I'm just gonna take a quick peek, drift over to Hiram's office, have a chat with the old hell bringer. If all's well, I'll be back for you inside an hour, say."

"You come back if all's *not* well, damn you."

"Watch your mouth, girl." Prophet put Mean into a lope, slanting across the hill a good ways down from the rocky crest. "I swear your tongue's gettin' as blue as mine."

A ravine ran along the base of the southern ridge, shallower in some places than others. At the shallow spots, Prophet stepped down from the saddle and walked the horse, keeping his own head down and keeping a careful eye on the town, the southernmost shacks and corrals shifting around in the sage and cedars to his right.

Some came right down to the ravine — mostly the town's first mining shacks, an old stamping mill, and several sets of Long Toms that had been abandoned when their

318

owners pulled out or went looking for richer color farther downstream.

At one point he'd been so busy watching the town's southern backside that he'd run into an old trash pile, his boots and Mean's hooves raising a ruckus with the discarded food tins. He gritted his teeth, stopped, drove Mean to his knees, and took an extra-long gander at the town, spying nothing but one shapeless woman in a bright red scarf, hanging wash along the side of a small, tin-roofed cabin, a washtub in the yard nearby.

She was too busy with a heavy pair of men's dungarees to notice Prophet. Likely she was trying to take advantage of a break in the weather to get some work in, but the way the clouds looked, low and brooding, her clothes were about to get a second soak.

Prophet pulled Mean back to his feet and continued along the draw, then followed a well-tramped cleft up out of it. He was taking a chance at being spotted here; he just hoped he wouldn't be spotted by anyone not happy to see him.

Fifteen minutes later, having been seen by no one, because no one had been out and about but a few chickens and a free-roaming, claybank colt, he tied Mean to an old freight wagon grown up with sage and bromegrass between a small, silent, white-

frame house and a lumberyard. The lumberyard was just as quiet as the house, which
was strange for it being a weekday. You'd
think someone would be backed up to the
loading dock, buying boards or nails or roof-
ing shingles.

Hell-Bringin' Hiram's office sat just beyond the lumberyard. Patting Mean's butt,
slinging the ten-gauge out in front of him,
and taking a slow, cautious gander around
this southern side street, Prophet stepped
out of the alley mouth and, staying close to
the lumberyard and keeping his hat brim
low, began striding for the jailhouse.

There was a side shed attached to the
lumberyard — an adobe-brick shack with a
corrugated tin roof and a tin chimney pipe
from which smoke lifted. The door of the
shack opened as Prophet walked past.

He stopped, turned to see a stoop-
shouldered old man in torn coveralls, red
stocking cap, and with a pipe clamped in
his teeth step outside. He lifted his head,
and his eyes found Prophet.

He gave a startled grunt, gray eyes snapping wide, and, pulling the pipe from his
teeth, stepped back inside the shack.

"Wait a minute," Prophet rasped.

The plank door closed, the flour-sack
curtains jostling in the rough-cut window

that had a diagonal crack across it.

"What in holy hell is goin' on around here?" Prophet grumbled, continuing forward, holding the barn blaster in his left hand and keeping his right hand clamped over the walnut grips of his low-slung Peacemaker.

He stepped down off a boardwalk, started across a narrow side street that was not much more than a wheelbarrow path, and stopped. He looked straight ahead, at the jailhouse on the corner about twenty feet in front of him. The old stone, shake-shingled office building had a front gallery, and on the gallery, a ragged figure slumped against the office's front door.

A drunk.

Prophet started across the gap.

He stopped again when he saw the dark red blood and clothes hanging in swatches from the man's twisted, battered limbs. He moved forward once more, leaping up onto the gallery and dropping to a knee over the man slumped back against the jailhouse door.

The gent was so beaten up, cut up, bruised, and bleeding, that it probably would have taken Prophet a while to figure out who he was if it hadn't been for the six-pointed sheriff's star dangling from Hell-

Bringin' Hiram Severin's torn coat lapel.

"Good Christ, man," Prophet said, lowering his head to stare into the man's slack, downcast face. "What the hell happened to you?"

The swollen eyes remained shut. The lips were cracked and bleeding. There wasn't a square inch of Severin's rugged, mustached face that wasn't gouged or scratched. Sand and cactus thorns clung to the dried blood.

That he'd been dragged belly down behind a horse was also evident by the fact of his brutally torn clothes, so that Prophet could see as much of the man's torn longhandles and skin as his twenty-dollar suit.

Severin's thin, sandy-gray hair hung like a screen over his forehead, obscuring his eyes.

Prophet placed a hand on the man's chest. If there was a heartbeat, Prophet couldn't detect it. Keeping his hand on the man's chest, he leaned down to listen for a breath.

Suddenly, the body writhed, and an icy hand closed around Prophet's wrist.

Prophet jerked with a start, pulling his head back and looking into Severin's brown eyes set deep in purple sockets. The crazed eyes glared at Prophet with a killing fury, a rage that set the man's entire near-dead body to quivering.

"Miguel!" he rasped, just loudly for

Prophet to hear.

Prophet frowned.

Severin squeezed Prophet's wrist tighter. It was like a death grip. The sheriff leaned up away from the door slightly, winced as a wave of agony swept through him, and swallowed.

"Kill him!"

"Miguel did this to you?"

"The whole town's . . . gone back . . . to the hell . . . it came from!"

Prophet saw that the killing fire was fast leaving the sheriff's eyes. He was dying. Prophet pulled his wrist free of the old law bringer's dwindling grip and gripped Severin's own. "Where, Hiram? Where will I find Miguel?"

Severin's eyes closed. His chest fell still once more.

Prophet thought the man was truly dead now, but then his bloody lips moved, and a whisper sounded little louder than the flutter of a small bird's wing. "Find . . . that actress. You'll find him with her." Severin nodded slightly, took a deep breath, and his eyelids fluttered though he didn't seem able to open them.

Still, Prophet sensed the killing fury in the man's words when he said even more softly, "Send him to hell, Proph. No . . . no questions asked. . . ."

All the muscles in his body slackened, and his head tipped to one side. His chin rolled off his shoulder, and then his shoulder slid sideways to the spur-scarred gallery floor.

Prophet stared down at the old law bringer's slumped corpse. He rubbed the twelve-gauge and looked around at the empty side street on which the jailhouse sat. A fine mist slanted from a gunmetal sky, cloaking the pines on the steep southern ridge.

Faintly, Prophet heard wild laughter emanating from the main drag northeast of the sheriff's office. The gunfire he'd heard from the ridge had died, but now there were two quick gunshots fired as though in anger.

A man screamed a ripping curse. More laughter. A final shot.

Someone clapped and shouted something Prophet couldn't make out.

He was only half listening. His mind was elsehwere.

He stood slowly, caressing his shotgun and muttering, "Sivvy . . . ?"

26

Prophet hunkered down behind a rain barrel at the corner of the side street and Main. Diagonally right across from him was the opera house. It stood dark and silent, tombstone gray under the low clouds and in the slanting drizzle.

Up the main drag to Prophet's sharp right were several saloons and cantinas from which emanated men's laughter, occasional gunfire, and the screech of shattering glass. Occasionally, a girl gave a shrill scream.

There were many men on the boardwalks, spilling into the street. All were drinking. Most were smoking. They were having a good, rowdy time. The hitchracks were stirrup to stirrup with saddle horses.

The town was as open as Dodge City before Wyatt Earp had moved in. Wide open.

Prophet rubbed his jaw as he appraised the setup. He hoped all those men were not Miguel's. He didn't know what Miguel had going, but he certainly hadn't needed many cutthroats to hornswaggle Prophet and Louisa and abscond with the gold. Four had worked just fine. The wagon that had carried the gold now sat in front of the bank, which Prophet could only glimpse from this angle, with the opera house obscuring his view.

He could see a couple of figures humped in the street. Dead men. Maybe Severin's deputies. If there were more, they were obscured by the men milling off the boardwalks.

Prophet glanced at the birds circling in the gauzy sky a couple of hundred feet above the bank. Doubtless, the birds were waiting for night to fall, so they could come down under cover of darkness and finish what they'd started — clearing the street of carrion — a couple of days ago. They'd probably started smelling death here just after the gold wagon had pulled into town and Miguel had pulled his double cross.

If Severin was right about Miguel, that was.

It was hard for Prophet to work his mind around what he was seeing here. He'd thought he'd seen it all in the burned-out town of Seven Devils last year. That had been a nasty piece of business, but this right here — whatever it was — rivaled it for depravity.

Prophet rose from behind the rain barrel, strode half a block back the way he'd come, then tramped through an alley, making his way west, away from the brunt of the hub-bub just east of the opera house and the bank. He circled back north and jogged across Main Street, unseen as far as he could tell by the bawdy revelers, and continued heading for the Golden Slipper.

That's where he'd likely find Sivvy. If Severin had been right and not just addled by the severe beating and dragging, he'd also find Miguel there. Thinking about that, fury set Prophet's blood to sizzling like acid. He could see letting himself get buffaloed by the banker's son. Deep down inside himself, and despite his hope that Miguel and Louisa would end up together, he'd never fully trusted the lad anyway. Like Louisa had said, there was something too good about him.

But Sivvy?

He just couldn't wrap his mind around such a sweet soul being part of whatever in hell was happening here. Somehow, Miguel had to have coerced her, though he couldn't see the earthy, bawdy Sivvy falling for someone who wore expensive suits and bowler hats and shoes that cost as much as Prophet spent on ammunition over any given year.

There were no more people out and about on the north side of town than there'd been on the south. The shops and shacks were silent, windows shuttered. There were people in some of the frame houses and in the older hovels that hailed from the days of Helldorado, because smoke threaded from chimneys. But as far as Prophet could tell, the citizens of Juniper were staying inside.

The town had the air of a town under siege. Likely, everyone here who fondly remembered the hell-roaring days of Helldorado had joined Miguel's gang east of the opera house. The newer, more civilized folks — those with families — were staying inside until the storm passed and, hopefully, another town tamer was brought in to restore Juniper to civility.

Working his way over to the Golden Slipper rising like a colorful bird beyond the gray and stately opera house, Prophet saw five horses tethered to the hitchrack out front of the gaudy place. Windows were lit against the day's dingy light and the looming night, but mostly only the large, curtained windows of the downstairs saloon and restaurant had lights in them. If any law-abiders remained in the hotel — traveling stock buyers and sellers and drummers — they were likely hunkered down, quiet as church mice. Most had probably cleared out to wait for better days.

Prophet made his way around to the hotel's backside, found a set of unlocked double doors that opened on a store room that smelled of flour and molasses and cured meat, and fumbled his way through the shadows to another door that opened onto a carpeted hall beneath the stairs at the back of the hotel's saloon.

Prophet slipped into the hall and, hearing men's voices and the clink of glasses and bottles and the chink of poker chips, found a narrow back stairway probably used by housekeepers, then climbed to the third story.

All the rooms opened onto a balcony that opened over the saloon hall, so he stayed close to the wall on his left, away from the rail and the possible discovery of the men downstairs, who were laughing and sending tobacco smoke toward the enormous crystal chandelier hanging to Prophet's right.

He spied Sivvy's door and headed for it. He was ten feet away when the latch clicked and he slipped into a recessed doorway two doors down from Sivvy's room. Pressing his back against the door, Prophet heard the actress's door squawk open, its bottom whispering across the deep pile carpet, and a man's voice say, "I'll see you later on. Gotta go keep an eye on things. Wouldn't want any of your boys runnin' away with the gold!"

"My boys are loyal as the king's navy!" Prophet heard Sivvy laugh, her voice more distant than the one he recognized as Miguel Encina's.

Miguel chuckled as he stepped into the hall. There was the smack of a kiss. "Don't you do anything naughty to that ingot, now, Miss O'Shay. Wait for me!"

He laughed. The door raked closed, then clicked as the latch caught.

Prophet tipped his head forward just enough that he could see Miguel don his crisp brown bowler hat as he turned and started off in the opposite direction along the hall, striding toward the stairs, the tails of his clawhammer coat swishing out behind him. The flaps of the brown coat were drawn back behind two pistols positioned for the cross draw high on his lean hips.

He turned and started down the stairs, his footsteps muffled by the carpet.

"Ah, there's the mayor of Helldorado now!" whooped one of the men in the saloon. "Didn't think you was ever gonna come back. Havin' too damn much fun up there, was ya, Mr. Mayor?"

"What can I say, fellas?" Miguel said above the soft thuds of his boots and the slight squawk of the stairs. "Them showgirls can really distract a fella!"

He and the others laughed. The conversation quieted as Miguel approached the men's table. Finally, Miguel's voice rose again as he told the men to keep the cards warm and that he'd be back after he'd checked on a few things around town.

When he left, the other men continued their card game, one saying with a sarcastic snort, "The work of the mayor is just never done, is it, boys?"

They all snickered. Cards were shuffled and coins and chips clinked softly on a baize-covered table.

Prophet strode out from the recessed doorway and, brushing his left shoulder against the wall, stole down the hall to Sivvy's room. He set his hand on the knob and prayed it wasn't locked. It wasn't. The latch clicked softly, and Prophet pushed the door open quickly, stepped inside, and closed the door behind him.

Sivvy didn't see him at first. She had her back to him, rummaging around in a dresser against the opposite wall, between the two tall windows. When she turned from the dresser with her hands full of frilly lace underwear and started toward the canopied bed, she stopped suddenly and gasped, dropping the underwear and pressing both hands against her chest.

She just stood there, staring at him, her eyes wide and glassy. Slowly, tears drew over them like a filmy, glittering curtain.

"What's the matter, Sivvy?" Prophet growled. "You see a ghost?"

"Oh, Lou!" She ran across the room to him, threw her arms around his neck, and buried her face in his chest.

He stood with his hands at his sides, looking grimly down at her. She pushed away from him, threw her red hair back over her head, and looked up at him, beseeching in her red-rimmed, sorrowful eyes as she threw an arm out toward the bed.

"Lou, it's gold!"

Prophet looked at the bed. There was a gold ingot on it. It lay amongst the gowns and blouses and silk wraps and underwear she'd tossed there and which she was obviously intending to pack into the steamer trunk that lay open on the floor. There amongst all that silk and lace the ingot resembled a pretty gold doll in swaddling clothes.

"Why, Sivvy? You were such a dear, sweet thing back in Dakota."

"Back in Dakota I thought I had a future." She pressed her hands flat against Prophet's bulging pectoral muscles and stared up at him, her eyes now enraged with self-righteousness, self-pity. "You know what that future was? It was trying to be an actress in front of pretty halls teeming with drunken men yelling catcalls and jeering and demanding I take my clothes off!"

Prophet felt sick to his stomach. He reached up and removed the girl's hands from his chest, and she gave another sob, went to the bed and sat down on the edge of it, knees together, feet out, hands hanging limp in her lap. Her head hung, red hair cascading down around her shoulders and hiding her face.

Prophet sagged down in a brocade-upholstered chair whose arms were carved in the shapes of fiddles, beside a round oak table in the room's middle. "How'd you hook up with Miguel?"

Prophet dug his makings sack out of his shirt pocket and tossed it onto the table. Sivvy reached up with one hand and carelessly threw her hair back from her face. "In the dining room here. He's a handsome devil, Lou — you gotta admit that."

"Yeah, he's a devil, all right. I seen what he did to Severin. You see that?"

Sivvy stared at him. She looked a good ten years older than she had when he'd last seen her, and she looked as though she hadn't slept in a week. The frilly wrap she wore billowed out from her chest, half exposing her pale breasts and the pearl necklace that was wrapped around them.

When she didn't answer his question, Prophet pulled rolling papers from the hide pouch on the table. "Where's his father? Dead, probably?"

Sivvy dropped her eyes and pursed her lips. She nodded weakly. Tears dribbled down her cheeks, and she sniffed. "I didn't buy chips in that game, Lou. I provided six men I knew from the mining camps I'd performed in. But I didn't buy chips in the high-stakes game this turned out to be."

"I reckon the men you provided weren't church deacons. What kinda game did you expect?"

"I thought we were just going to rob a gold shipment with his men and my men and the guards he bought — Hitt and the others — and we'd hightail it for Frisco!"

"A nice, clean getaway."

"He never told me about killin' Severin and his father until just the other day." Sivvy shook her head and pressed her hands to her temples, mashing one pale, bare foot down atop the other on the floor. "Jesus . . . I never seen such a thing."

"How many wolves you two turn loose on the town?"

"I brought in six men. Boys who owed me a favor. Miguel had six more from an old gang of his, plus the other four gold guards. They're all workin' for a share of the gold. We're gonna split it all up in the mornin' and fork our trails."

As Prophet rolled his quirley closed, he glanced at the steamer trunk on the floor, half filled with red and black lace and high-heeled shoes. "And then you're pullin' out."

"That's right." She stared at him. Her eyes were dry, but her face was wet. "Don't try to stop us, Lou. He'll kill you. We have sixteen men between the both of us. More cold-steel artists have ridden into town over the past few days. I bet a lot of them don't like you much."

"The smell of a gut wagon carries far and wide."

"I didn't mean for you to get hurt."

Prophet chuckled as he scratched a match to life on his thumbnail. "What'd you think was gonna happen when me and Louisa signed on for that gold run? The one you and ole Miguel and your so-called guards was gonna steal?"

"I don't know," Sivvy said. "It all happened so fast — you showin' up so unexpectedly."

"Not too fast for you to have me and Louisa bushwhacked."

"That was Miguel's doin', Lou." She frowned, shook her head. "I had nothin' to do with that."

"What about you callin' me up here the other night, after your performance?"

"I was going to tell you the whole plan, beg you to either throw in with us or get out of town. But I realized, after we'd been together awhile, there was no way I was going to turn you into an outlaw." She sighed, shrugged. "So I had to just let things follow their natural course. There was certainly no changing any of our plans, not with all those men already in place."

Prophet was leaning back in his chair, legs straight out before him, boots crossed. He held his quirley between the thumb and index finger of his right hand, that elbow propped on the table beside him. He regarded Sivvy with bunched brows, the planes of his large, suntanned, broken-nosed face hard as weathered rock.

But inside, his gut ached.

He was remembering the sweet, tender girl he'd spent a long Dakota winter with. It was the only time in his life he'd toyed with the idea of marrying, living a settled-down life.

"Lou?"

Prophet took another drag off the cigarette, blew smoke at a curtained window.

"Don't try to stop us."

"I am gonna stop you. There ain't no one else here to do it. And you both need stoppin'."

He got up to grab an ashtray off one of the room's several bureaus. His ears suddenly felt as though an ice pick had been rammed through them, and he swung around to see Sivvy standing beside the bed, chin raised, mouth open, loosing a shrill shriek toward the vaulted ceiling.

She kept that practiced voice going for a good five seconds, until Prophet thought his back teeth would crack and every glass in the room would break, before she suddenly closed her mouth, lowered her chin, and turned to him sadly.

Downstairs, men yelled and scurried, and then boots were thumping dully on the stairs.

"I'm sorry, Lou," Sivvy said. "You leave me no choice. You see, I just can't let anything or anyone — even you — come between Miguel and Miss Gleneanne O'Shay . . . and the comforts she deserves."

She smiled a bittersweet smile.

The boot thumps grew louder. Men grunted and growled, and spurs rang. There was the ratcheting click of cocking gun hammers.

"It's tough all over," Prophet growled, dropping his quirley on the floor and grabbing his shotgun from behind his back as he squared his shoulders at the door. His heart thumped, and that witch was digging her razor-edged fingernail into his neck. "But I sure as hell wish you hadn't done that."

27

"Here! In here!" Sivvy cried, as the boot thumps grew louder in the hall outside her door.

Prophet stood angled in front of the door, about ten feet away from it, holding the ten-gauge out in front of him.

"Miss O'Shay!" shouted a deep, burly voice — a big man judging by how the floor shook under his thudding boots.

"In here — it's Prophet!" She turned to the bounty hunter, who thumbed both the barn blaster's hammers back. "Give yourself up, Lou. There's too many of them. You won't have a chance. I'll make sure they don't kill you!"

"Miss O'Shay?" the deep voice thundered in the hall, right outside the door.

The doorknob turned. The door came partway open. A big, square, bearded head slid through the three-foot gap.

The dark eyes found Prophet and widened.

The door flew open, and the big man started to raise a Buntline Special in his right hand and a Schofield in his left while another, smaller man shoved into the room behind him, bringing up a carbine.

Prophet tripped both the shotgun's triggers.

Ka-boooommmm!

The big man and the little man flew back out of the room as though they'd been lassoed from behind. They both bellowed like poleaxed bulls as they flew over the balcony rail and disappeared. From below there rose a booming thud almost as loud as the report of Prophet's coach gun.

The building quaked. The crystal chandelier jingled and danced.

"Nooooo!" Sivvy bellowed, clapping her hands over her mouth.

Breeching the shotgun and plucking out both smoking wads, Prophet said, "Well, that's two. How many I got left — a few eggs shy of a dozen?"

Sivvy sagged down on the edge of the bed, hanging her head and sobbing.

From downstairs, a female voice said, "Lou? That you up there?"

Louisa's voice echoed around the cavernous ceiling over the balcony.

Prophet clicked the shotgun closed as he stepped into the hall and peered over the rail. The big man and the dead man lay unmoving on the lobby floor, blood pooling out around them. Between them, Louisa stood looking straight up at Prophet. She had both her cocked Colts in her hands.

"Thought I heard you up there."

"Any more sons o' bitches down there?"

Louisa looked around then back up at Prophet. "It's quiet as a church down here. Likely not for long, though. Your gut shredder tends to announce itself."

"There's so much shootin' in town of late, no one's likely to notice. Wait there. I'll be down in a minute."

Prophet strode back into the room. Sivvy remained where she'd been, arms crossed on her belly, one foot atop the other. She was no longer sobbing, however.

She glared at Prophet defiantly. "You're right, Lou. You got two of 'em. But there's a whole lot more where they came from. You're not gonna ruin this for me. I've been through too much to let you take this from me."

"Yeah, well, we'll see."

"What are you doing?"

Prophet was rummaging through the

341

clothes on her bed. He grabbed a long, cotton nightgown, held it out in front of him, and twisted it into a ball. "Gonna keep you tied up for a while. Quiet as a church mouse."

"No!"

Sivvy bounded up from the bed and started running to the door. Prophet grabbed her by the arm and jerked her back to him.

"Sorry about this."

He slapped her hard with the back of his hand. She sagged in his arms, her wrapper slipping off a shoulder and revealing all of one large, pale breast.

"Well, not really," he grunted, tossing her onto the bed.

When he had her wrists and ankles tied to the bedposts and a pair of her frilly underwear tied around her head, gagging her, he went out and, hearing her stirring, closed and locked the door behind him. He stopped in the hall, looking straight out over the lobby, listening.

The building was silent. Most of Sivvy and Miguel's men were likely holed up with whores or swilling hooch in the saloons and cantinas.

Prophet found Louisa sitting in a quilted leather chair by a potted palm near the

342

vacant hotel desk. She had her legs crossed under her skirt, and she'd holstered her pistols. She could have been waiting for a bellboy to bring her bags down and load them onto a stagecoach.

Prophet said, "What're you doing here?"

"Couldn't sit still. I followed you." She jerked her head toward the ceiling. "Who's up there?"

"Miss Gleneanne O'Shay."

"The actress?"

"Yeah. A damn good one."

"That who Miguel was seeing, too?" Louisa asked. "I saw him leaving the hotel on my way in."

Prophet sighed.

"Men," Louisa said.

Prophet tramped to a front window and stared out. The drizzle had turned to a light rain, and thunder rumbled. It was late in the afternoon, but it was as dark as early evening. Everything looked washed out and gray, and only a few of the shop windows were lit.

Prophet watched a weary-looking saddle tramp leave a small mercantile with two tow sacks tied together with rope. He flung the sacks over his horse's rump, mounted up, and headed on out of town at a sweeping trot.

When the saddle tramp had disappeared, Prophet said, "Which way was the new mayor of Helldorado headed?"

"Toward the bank. Quite a bit of activity over there. I saw Hitt and the other guards staggering that way from one of the cantinas."

Prophet walked over to the hotel desk and set the barn blaster on top of it. He poked his hat brim off his forehead.

He and Louisa were in a pickle, sure enough. But they'd been in pickles before. He had no idea how to proceed, how to start getting Juniper on its feet again. It wasn't really his fight, when you got right down to it. But he'd had his tail twisted.

Hell, Miguel, Sivvy, and their worthless lot had almost killed him and Louisa, and they'd killed a good friend of Prophet's. Whatever Hell-Bringin' Hiram had become in his final days, he hadn't deserved to have half his hide ripped off behind a galloping horse.

Miguel Encina had a reckoning coming. And Prophet was gonna make sure he got it. Him and the other scalawags on his roll.

Easier said than done.

Prophet looked at Louisa. She was staring at him, her hands folded primly in her lap, the pearl grips of her twin Colts jutting above her hips. She seemed to be reading his mind, fully understanding they were in a box canyon with a bear trap at every turn.

Prophet just wanted to see how she saw it. "This isn't really our fight, you know."

"Of course it is."

Prophet chuckled. He picked up his barn blaster and swung it over his shoulder. "Let's head on over to the bank, check on business."

Louisa shrugged, rising from her chair. She picked up her rifle, which she'd had leaning against the chair, and levered a fresh round into the chamber. "Can't say I have any better ideas. If there weren't still some innocent folks hanging around, hiding out from the long-coulee riders who seem to have been lured here like stray dogs to a fresh gut pile, I'd say we oughta find a stash of miner's dynamite and blow the whole damn town to smithereens."

Prophet stared down at her staring up at him with her choirgirl's innocent face. "Sometimes you scare the holy hell out of me."

She rose up on the toes of her boots and brushed her lips against his. "Good."

They headed out.

Heavy thunderheads rumbled, and a night-like darkness descended over Juniper as Prophet and Louisa made their way around behind the opera house. They saw the gold wagon, its canvas top raised against the weather, pulled up to the rear of the bank, with several saddled horses around it. The bank's rear door was open. They scuttled up to the bank's wall facing the opera house, hoping that the darkness and driving rain would conceal them from anyone looking out the single side window.

They each took a side of the window.

Prophet glanced into the bank — a quick look before jerking his head back behind the wall. He frowned at Louisa through the rain sluicing off his funnel-brimmed hat. She pressed her back against the stout stone wall, holding a pearl-gripped Colt in each hand. Rain sluiced off her own hat brim, and the gaze she cast Prophet through the rain and across the window had a question in it.

She answered her own question when she turned to slide her own gaze around the edge of the window and into the bank. Between the two red curtains, she had a good view of the bank's center and the gold ingots stacked in a miniature pyramid on top of it, a few feet from the window.

Beyond the gold, Miguel Encina lounged

346

back in a chair behind the loan officer's broad desk and under a ticking clock on the wall above him. In his lap sat a girl who was as good as completely naked, since the open, wine-red wrap hanging off her shoulders and trailing onto the floor beneath Miguel's chair constituted no attire at all.

She had a long, creamy body with full breasts. Her legs hung over Miguel's as she sat back against him, his chin resting on the top of her head. His hands were on her breasts, cupping them, his thumbs rubbing her nipples. The girl had a dreamy, glazed look as she stared across the gold at the wall somewhere to Louisa's left.

Louisa had seen that look before, and the slack-eyed stare. It could usually be attributed to either marijuana or opium.

Between Louisa and Miguel and the naked girl, Orrie Hitt, Bronco Brewster, Juventino Casol, and Royal Sawrod were grabbing bars off the top of the pyramid and carrying them to the rear of the room, likely hauling them out the open back door and into the wagon.

There were a couple of bottles on the table, and the men were laughing and talking loudly and smoking good cigars, having a good time as they worked. Beneath the din and the intermittent thunder claps, Louisa could hear Miguel say, "Fellas, I think I'm gonna take Miss Madrid here with me to South America. What do you think about that?"

"I thought you was takin' that actress girl," said Hitt, puffing a long, thin cheroot between his teeth as he took two gold bars off the table and handed one to Brewster, another to Casol.

"No, no, no!" Miguel laughed, nuzzling the naked girl's long, fine neck. "That's what I told you I told *her* I was doin'. But no. I see no reason to burden myself with a bad actress. I gave her an ingot. That'll set her up for a few months before she can find her another saloon to kick her legs in."

He cupped the naked girl's breasts, kissed the side of the left one. "But Miss Madrid here . . . there's just somethin' about this sportin' girl I really like, and I ain't always been so fond of whores."

The naked girl responded by smiling dreamily, reaching up and placing a hand on Miguel's cheek, and then lifting her face to press her lips to his chin. Miguel tipped her head back farther and closed his mouth over hers.

Louisa pulled back from the window, then, with another cautious glance inside, slipped on past it to stand beside Prophet.

"They got another double cross on," Louisa said, loudly enough for the bounty hunter to hear her above the driving rain.

"Yeah, it seems ole Miguel's just full of double crosses. Gonna take advantage of the bad weather to pull out tonight. Just him and the guards, while his other men and Sivvy's are likely ridin' out the storm in a whorehouse."

Louisa squinted her eyes. "This oughta be real easy. Only problem is, what are we gonna do with the wagon?"

"We'll drive it on out of town, then come back in for the rest of Miguel's killers." Prophet paused then added regretfully, "And for Miss O'Shay, too."

"Shall we?" Louisa started toward the rear of the bank.

Prophet grabbed her arm. "Hell, let's let 'em finish loadin'!"

Louisa shrugged. Prophet hunkered down beneath the window, doffing his hat and letting the rain hammer him as he watched Miguel's men haul the gold off the table while Miguel himself played patty-cake with the hop-headed whore. When the table was finally cleared, Hitt turned to Miguel.

"All right — let's go. If the rain keeps up, them others'll never be able to track us even if they find we've lit a shuck." The big man rubbed his palms together hungrily. "Let's head to Mexico!"

"One more kiss," Miguel said, tipping the naked girl's head back.

Prophet rolled his eyes and pressed his back against the wall beside Louisa. "Let's dance."

Holding his shotgun in one hand, he slid his Colt from its holster with the other, then tramped to the bank's rear corner. He glanced around the corner at the wagon around which Brewster, Casol, and Sawrod were all gathered with four saddle horses.

When Hitt came out, shrugging into a rain slicker and taking his reins from Casol, Prophet glanced once more at Louisa standing behind him, then started moving toward the wagon, holding his shotgun straight out in front of him.

He stopped suddenly, and Louisa ran into him, and then he swung around and pushed her back around the corner to where they'd been a second ago, his big bulk nearly throwing the Colt-wielding girl to the ground.

Louisa snapped her eyes at him, exasperated. "What're you doing, you big ape?"

Prophet pressed her against the bank's wall, held a finger to her lips, then, hearing a raised voice above the rain and intermittent thunder blasts, doffed his hat once more and stole another look around the corner.

Six horseback riders had ridden up to form a half circle between the back of the wagon and the bank's rear wall. They were all dressed in yellow slickers, and they all had rifles to their shoulders, aiming at the four gold guards. Miguel was out there now, too, wearing a slicker of his own and holding a pistol straight down at his sides.

Orrie Hitt was shouting at Miguel, pointing at him, "We had a deal, you son of a bitch!" He jerked his pointing arm at the six rifle-wielding riders sitting their soaked horses grimly before the guards, who were all looking around warily, angrily. "These boys here weren't no part of it!"

"No, you see, Orrie," Miguel yelled, "all you fellas were part of was loadin' the gold onto the wagon for us. Beyond that, you never were part of anything . . . 'cept dyin'!"

Prophet drew his head back behind the bank as the first gun spoke.

Hitt bellowed.

His horse screamed.

Then the other men screamed and there was a fusillade that for about ten short seconds drowned out the clapping thunder and rushing rain. All four of the guards' horses galloped, buck-kicking, off past Prophet and Louisa, one nipping another one's ass in his mindless fear and fury, their ribbons bouncing through the rain-pelted puddles behind them.

They disappeared past the opera house, angling south toward the main street.

When the rifles fell silent, a couple of the guards — Prophet assumed it was the guards, for he and Louisa were both down on their haunches, pressing their backs against the bank — were still screaming. Two more quick shots and then one more as if an afterthought silenced the screams, so that now there was only the sound of the storm and the nickering of the riflemen's frightened mounts.

Behind the bank, Miguel said, "Where's Abrams and Ned and Sivvy's other pals?"

"At the Spade Bit cantina," one of the riflemen shouted. "Upstairs with the whores. They think we're pullin' out in the morning, but by then, *knowin' them,* they'll be too drunk to stir until *noon!*"

Prophet glanced at Louisa hunkered to his left, resting both her guns on her upraised knees. "Well, we lost four but gained six," he said just loudly enough that only she could hear him above the rain.

Louisa lifted a shoulder. "Not bad odds,

considering we'll be surprising them."

Prophet nodded. He started to rise, then settled back down on his bootheels as one of the men behind the bank said, "What the hell you bringin' a girl for?"

Miguel's voice said, "Don't worry — you can have her when I'm finished."

Louisa must have heard, too, because when Prophet looked at her, she was grinding her jaws. "Now what are we going to do?"

Behind the bank, hooves clomped and there was the clank of the wagon's brake being released. Prophet jerked his head, and he and Louisa both rose and jogged along the side of the bank to the front, where the veranda's roof gave them shelter from the storm.

Prophet glanced back along the side of the building, ran his sleeve across his dripping nose. They couldn't bear down on Miguel's gang now without risking the hopheaded whore's life, for whatever it was worth.

The wagon bolted out from behind the bank, and Prophet pushed Louisa back against the bank's front wall, out of sight. He doffed his hat and peered around the front corner to watch the wagon, driven by Miguel and flanked by the six rifle-wielding cutthroats in yellow slickers, disappear behind the opera house, taking the same course as the runaway horses.

When the wagon and the men were gone, heading west out of town, Louisa doffed her wet hat and slapped it against her thigh. Her blond hair hung limp across her shoulders, and the rain streaked her tanned face. Her hazel eyes were sharp.

"We'll just have to run 'em down — that's all!" She started off the veranda. "Let's fetch our horses."

Prophet grabbed her arm. "Wait a minute, Miss Bonnyventure."

"How many times do I have to tell you, you big idiot — there's no 'y'!"

"Why do all the work ourselves?"

Louisa just stared at him, wide-eyed with incredulity, holding her hat down by her side.

"I mean — shit," Prophet said, tossing his head toward the saloons and cantinas and whorehouses on the east side of town. "There's six more been double-crossed, ain't there?"

Louisa narrowed one eye as though his meaning was still as cloudy as one of the growing puddles around them.

Prophet waited for thunder to finish clapping, then yelled, grinning devilishly, "I bet them six ain't gonna like it one bit when they find out Miguel and the other six just rode out of here with about a million dollars in gold!"

28

The Chinaman perched on a stool behind the counter of the Spade Bit cantina puffed a brass pipe trimmed with jade.

He blinked slowly, catlike, as he stared through the sweet smoke hovering around him at the two sopping strangers. Only, his eyes were molasses black and shiny. The smoke had a bitter tang that caught in Prophet's throat like pepper.

There probably hadn't been many opium dens in town when Hell-Bringin' Hiram was running things. Likely, the Chinaman had kept it upstairs for his girls — sporting girls were always more sporting when in the grips of the Eastern spices — and started smoking freely again himself when Hiram and his deputies had been so unceremoniously unseated from their positions.

Pouring the rain from his hat onto the worn wooden floor and tramping wearily, boots squeaking wetly, toward the bar,

Prophet knew where Miguel's comely whore had acquired such a glazed and peaceful look even stark naked on a cold, rainy day.

The Chinaman wore a black silk cap and a purple kimono. There was no backbar behind him but a large oil painting of an Indian chief dressed in full regalia, though Prophet had never seen any Indians dressed that way except in oil paintings.

On the other side of the narrow room, there was a trophy head of an albino buffalo and a small chalkboard with the Chinaman's five working girls priced out according to age. Nothing else adorned the shabby, smoky place's walls except cracked plaster and bullet holes.

Prophet and Louisa were the only two besides the Chinaman in the saloon's dingy main hall, if you could call it a hall, but Prophet heard grumbling and hushed voices from the ceiling above his head.

Prophet dropped his wet hat on the bar and pointed at the ceiling. "You got business upstairs?"

"Upstairs?" the Chinaman said in a heavy accent, showing a cracked front tooth as a perfect smoke doughnut rolled out of his mouth. "Girls upstairs. Busy now. Come back later."

Prophet glanced at Louisa then said to

the Chinaman, "How many men upstairs?" He held up six fingers. "Six?"

"Five girls," the Chinaman said, pointing at the chalkboard on the other side of the room, beneath the white buffalo head. "Five girls — all busy now. Come back later. Or stay and have whiskey." He hauled a bottle from a shelf below him and grabbed a cloudy glass off a pyramid in front of him.

"Sure, sure." Prophet unknotted his soaked neckerchief and wrung it out on the floor. "Set me up, partner. Sarsaparilla for the girl."

The Chinaman froze with the whiskey bottle tipped over Prophet's glass, frowning curiously.

"Never mind. Two whiskeys."

"You know I don't imbibe," Louisa told him, leaning forward and wringing out her wet, blond hair around her boots.

"Might do you some good. Warm you up. Besides, I'll drink what you don't. Set 'em up, partner." Prophet showed the Chinaman two fingers. "Two whiskeys. Best diamondback venom in the territory, no doubt — yes?"

"Yes!" The Chinaman poured out two drinks. "Oh, yes. Ver good wheeskey! Fifty cenz unless you wan girl. Yes? Girl? You both wan girl?"

"No. We'll just settle for the whiskey and a warm place over here by your stove."

Prophet glanced at Louisa. "Pay the man."

As she rolled her eyes at him, Prophet took both drinks over to the stove that creaked in the room's middle and around which feather sticks and sawdust lay around an empty peach crate lined with yellow newspapers. He plopped down in the chair and shivered when the stove heat hit him.

He was soaked from head to toe. It would sure be nice to crawl into a big, soft bed and sleep for a day or two. But he doubted he'd sleep well again until Miguel Encina's neck was stretched and his rancid carcass was swinging from a cottonwood limb. He and Louisa would retrieve the gold and get it back in the bank where it belonged, until Jose Encina's investors seated another president.

Louisa winced as she eased her lithe frame into her own chair to Prophet's left, the damp clothes tightening across her body. She set her hat on the table, and Prophet, sipping his own whiskey, set hers in front of her.

"Not bad," he said, smacking his lips.

The voices from above grew louder, and the timbers creaked as men moved around, boots hammering. Jinglebobs clattered like loose coins in a pocket. Louisa glanced at the ceiling, then turned to Prophet, strands of her wet blond hair plastered to her cheeks.

"How we gonna play this one?"

Prophet threw back the rest of his shot and sighed as the strong brew seared his tonsils. "Some things are best not so much played as winged."

He set his shot glass down and picked up Louisa's glass.

"You're gonna wing it drunk?"

"I wing it best drunk."

"Why do you suppose Miguel left the six upstairs alive? If there are six upstairs, that is."

Prophet shrugged as he eased back in his chair, feeling the whiskey soften and warm his aging joints. "Maybe they're better shooters, even drunk, than the other six. I don't know. I stopped trying to crawl into the minds of folks like Miguel — and Miss Gleneanne O'Shay — a long goddamn time ago."

Louisa reached over and picked up her glass from which Prophet had not yet sipped. She lifted it to her nose, made a face, then closed her lips over the rim, tipping the glass back slightly.

"Hmmm." She set the glass back down in

front of Prophet. She'd probably taken a half a teaspoon of it. "Not bad."

Prophet chuffed, lifted the glass, then set it back down half empty.

"Who was this actress to you, Lou?" Louisa wanted to know.

Prophet remembered those long winter nights back in Dakota, nights that he and Sivvy Hallenbach had warmed considerably for hours on end, and gave another wry chuff, slanting his mouth devilishly. "That, Miss Bonnyventure, is a story for another time and another place."

"You're pathetic."

"I've risen a notch, then."

Louisa reached over for the shot glass and took another miniscule sip before boots sounded at the top of the stairs, and a man laughed and a girl gave a little fearful squeal.

Making another face as she swallowed, Louisa set the glass down and stretched her gaze to the plank-board stairs rising into the second-story shadows at the room's smoky rear. Prophet looked in the same direction and reached down and freed the keeper thong over the hammer of his .45.

"Shit."

Louisa slid her eyes to him, but he said nothing as he watched the man descend the stairs, wobbling as though his feet were rubber holding a small, black-haired girl on his shoulders. The girl squealed and laughed, clinging to the man's shirt, tugging at his collar, as she ground her bare heels into his triceps.

The man said, "Ouch! That hurts!" without passion and then, by turns holding the girl's legs and the rickety rails on either side of the groaning, sagging, swaying stairs, clomped down toward the saloon.

When the man and the girl — Prophet had recognized the face when the man had lifted his head a few minutes ago — were halfway down, the Chinaman scrambled out from behind his bar and shook a finger at the man. "No-no! You treat nice! She ver young! Young Chinee girl! Very hard to come by!"

"I'm treatin' her right," the obviously drunk cutthroat said, his voice pitched high with jovial indignance. "Shit, I'm givin' her a fuckin' ride down the stairs, ain't I?"

He laughed, and just then he leaned to one side, releasing the girl's right leg to grab the rail with a gasp. The girl screamed as she sagged dangerously in the same direction, and then the cutthroat overcompensated in the other direction, and the girl screamed again as the man spun, stumbled down the quaking stairs, and did a little, graceless pirouette as he came to a stop before the Chinaman haranguing him in Chinese.

"Holy shit!" the man intoned, visibly shaken and letting the Chinaman help the girl down from his shoulders. "That was close. Little Irene, I don't give a shit how cute you are — next time I'm gonna let you *walk* down that death trap of a goddamn stairway!"

Prophet regarded the man with a sneer on his lips as the cutthroat lifted his black hat, ran a hand through his uncombed, coal-black hair, then dragged heels to a near table. "For that, bring me a whiskey, Irene. Bring the whole damn bottle. Looks like we got a long, rainy . . ."

He had turned to the front of the room, and he let his voice trail off when he saw Prophet and Louisa. His eyes had hooked on Louisa as most male eyes did, and then they brightened. But when they slid to Prophet, they only just started to slide away before sliding back quickly. The light left the man's gaze, and his cheeks hardened.

"Well, well," he said, kicking a chair out of his way and sauntering toward Prophet's table. "Look what the old bobcat dragged in outta the storm!"

As the cutthroat moved between tables,

kicking more chairs out of his way, his right hand dropped to subtly free the keeper thong from the heavy Remington jutting from the holster tied low on his right thigh. He swept a hand across his long nose and stopped three feet in front of Prophet, hooking his thumbs behind his cartridge belt.

"Well, if it ain't my ole friend Charlie Sparrow," Prophet said with false friendliness, glancing at Louisa who glowered across the table at the man.

"I don't know what you're here for, Prophet, but if it's me, you can go take a running jump down a privy hole."

"I thought you was doin' time in New Mexico."

"Pshaw! I did two weeks in the Jicarilla pen you took me to, and when they was sendin' me to the federal pen for killin' them two circuit judges — the ones that hanged my brothers — I broke out of their damn jail wagon. After killin' the guards, I mean."

He smiled, and his eyes became as slanted as those of the little Chinese girl scampering over from the bar with a bottle and a shot glass and sliding apprehensive looks between Prophet and the killer Charlie Sparrow. "That was two years ago. I hear there's a reward on my head. But I tell you,

Lou, whatever it is, it ain't enough."

He leaned forward, planting his big, brown fists on the table and glancing down at the barn blaster lying in front of Prophet's empty shot glass.

Prophet entwined his hands behind his head, and smiled. "If there's a reward on your worthless carcass, Charlie, I'll likely collect it one of these days. For now, though, you're no more interestin' to me than that pile of dog plop on the porch step out yonder. I'm here for your boss, Miss Gleneanne O'Shay and her double-crossing cohort, Miguel Encina. I got the actress all bound up in her room over at the Golden Slipper, but it appears Miguel's lit off for sundry points west and south."

Charlie Sparrow chuckled as he picked up his bottle and shot glass. The girl, seeing that she wasn't wanted at the moment, straddled a near chair backward and watched the three with vague fascination, her chin resting atop her chair back.

"What the hell're you talkin' about, Proph? We got it all sewed up here. More gold than . . ." Sparrow frowned as Prophet's words started sinking in. He filled his glass only halfway, then let the bottle hang down at his side.

"What you mean you got Miss Gleneanne

bound up in . . . ?" The lines above the killer's nose cut deep as stab wounds. "Double cross?" Sparrow's face turned red as sandstone bricks at sunset, and his eyes got darker. "What're you talkin' about, you bounty-huntin' scalawag? What kind a trick you tryin' to pull?"

"Encina's the one pullin' the trick. Or was that part of the plan — him and his six pards gunnin' down Hitt and the other gold guards in the bank, then lightin' out in this crazy weather with the gold?"

When Sparrow just stared at them, eyes mantled by his bushy black brows, Louisa said, "I think they mentioned Mexico and South America — didn't they, Lou?"

"I believe you're right, Miss Bonnyventure — they did mention Old Mejico and South America. Prob'ly real hard to track 'em down there. Since you and your own pards, Charlie, would be gettin' such a late start and all. And with all this rain. Hell, them wagon tracks'll be done washed away in another ten, fifteen minutes. If they ain't already."

Slowly, Sparrow raised his arm, pointing an accusing finger at Prophet. "If this is a trick . . ."

"Oh, it's a trick, all right," Louisa said. "But we ain't the ones pulling it."

Still extending his arm at Prophet, Sparrow backed up to the foot of the stairs, then wheeled, clomping up to the second story three steps at a time, the risers leaping beneath his hammering boots. Upstairs, he started pounding on doors and yelling. Girls started screaming. Prophet and Louisa sat back in their chairs in quiet contentment, listening to Sparrow's cohorts arguing as they stumbled around, dressing.

Meanwhile, the rain streaked the Spade Bit's front windows, and thunder rumbled angrily, shaking the hanging coal oil lamps, sharp lightning flashing.

The little Chinese whore — who couldn't have been much over twelve, if that — glanced at the Chinaman who'd retaken his place behind the bar, repacking his pipe from a small, delicately carved box.

The girl glanced at the ceiling. The Chinaman shrugged and told her something in their strange tongue, and then she slid off the chair, grabbed a hide coat hanging off a peg near the bottom of the stairs, and disappeared through a curtained doorway.

The din above their heads became concentrated at the top of the stairs — men shouting and clomping and doors slamming — and then they started bounding down the stairs. They came so fast and with so much fury, some still dressing or wrapping shell belts around their waists, that the rickety stairs looked like a swaying and jostling rope bridge over a wide canyon.

Prophet was sure it would give way, but he was wrong. They all made it, a blond at the top of the stairs yelling, "You said you was gonna give me an extra cartwheel for them French lessons, Rigsby, you bastard!"

Five cutthroats hustled out into the storm.

The sixth, Charlie Sparrow, stopped suddenly halfway across the room and turned to Prophet. "Why didn't you go after that gold your own self?"

"Why should I?" Prophet said. "When I got someone around as capable as you to run it down for me?"

Spreading his feet, Sparrow switched his Henry rifle to his left hand and held his right hand over his Remy's grips, curling his upper lip with menace.

"I oughta kill you now, you son of a bitch."

Prophet was lounging back in his chair, enjoying the show, a boot hiked on a knee. "You best not try it, Charlie."

"Why not?"

" 'Cause my partner has her twin Colts cocked beneath the table, each aimed at one of your oysters."

Sparrow slid his skeptical glance to Louisa.

Bam! Bam!

The table jumped with each concussion, which sounded like cannon blasts in the close quarters.

Sparrow leaped back with a yelp. He looked down at his crotch.

Each of the .45 rounds had torn a small swatch of tobacco-brown tweed from the upper inside of Sparrow's thighs, about two inches south of soprano country, so that Sparrow's red longhandles shone through the holes.

Terror flashed in Sparrow's eyes as he looked up at Louisa, who re-cocked her Colts under the table with loud, ratcheting clicks. Smoke billowed out from the table's edge.

Lower jaw hanging anxiously, Sparrow raised his right hand in supplication above his holstered Remington. With his other hand, he held his rifle far out to his left as he sidestepped around Prophet's and Louisa's table as though around an unsprung bear trap and stumbled backward out the saloon's double doors.

Thunder crashed.

"Some other time, you son of a bitch!"

Sparrow's boots thumped across the veranda, and he was gone.

29

Prophet saw no reason to hurry after the cutthroats.

It would take Charlie Sparrow's drunken crew a couple of hours to catch up to Encina's bunch. And when they did run them down there was bound to be a prolonged lead storm, cutthroat shooting cutthroat in the dark of a rainy Wyoming night.

Sparrow's bunch might not even light onto Encina's until morning. Hell, it could be another twenty-four hours before Prophet and Louisa's dirty work had been done for them, at least done enough for the bounty hunters to swoop in and finish off whomever was left, if anyone, and to fetch the gold wagon back to Juniper, with relative ease.

So Prophet and Louisa spent a leisurely evening in Juniper, mingling with the dozen or so hard cases who'd been haunting the nearby hills and flocked to the town like vultures when word had spread that Hell-Bringin' Hiram was out of commission. Playing poker in one of the saloons around ten o'clock that night, Prophet thought he recognized at least four of the visages around him — playing faro or stud or sparking the doves — from wanted dodgers he'd seen posted outside Wells Fargo offices over the past year.

Encina's cutthroats might have pulled their picket pins from Juniper, but the town still had a raggedy-edged, wild air due in no small part to the lawmen who'd been left to molder in the mud of the town's main drag. Prophet and Louisa were about to risk drawing unwanted attention to themselves by dragging the carcasses over to the undertaker's when they saw the undertaker himself loading Jose Encina and the deputies into a wagon — after picking their pockets and piling their guns and other valuables under the driver's seat of his old buckboard.

Give the town another week or so, Prophet thought as he watched the buckboard head for the sheriff's office — likely intending to fetch the body of Hell-Bringin' Hiram himself — and pulling Juniper back out of the jaws of Helldorado would be one hell of a feat. Even the bona fide businessmen who now ventured from their shops and houses and back into the saloons seemed to have acquired a shiny-eyed, devil-may-care air as they laughed a little louder than they might have a few days ago when out on the town. They gambled with a little more daring and acted a little more brash with the painted ladies than the old town tamer, not to mention their wives, would have approved of.

The storm continued throughout the night, the thunder occasionally drowning out the intermittent bursts of gunfire issuing from the saloons, as well as the shouts and screams of the all-night revelers.

Just before heading to bed at the Muleskinner's Inn, Prophet thought of Sivvy. He'd left her bound and gagged at the Golden Slipper. Forget her, he told himself. She'd probably spit the gag out by now, and a night tied to the bed would do her good. He'd throw her sorry hide in Severin's jail come morning and hire a local odd-job-Joe to toss her feed and water now and then.

Prophet woke the next morning at dawn with Louisa virtually sprawled on top of him.

She'd had one of her bad dreams during the night — one of the dreams in which she relived her family's horrific demise at the hands of the Handsome Dave Duvall gang — and when she had one of those she couldn't get close enough to Prophet, it seemed.

He'd soothed her, made slow, gentle love to her, and hummed a little song he remembered from the north Georgia mountains until she'd fallen into a peaceful slumber. But she must have had another bad dream afterward, he thought now as he eased her willowy, warm, naked body onto the bed beside him.

She groaned and buried a cheek in her pillow.

Prophet leaned down and kissed the pale half-moon of a tender breast bulging slightly out from her side, then spanked her bare rump through the sheet. "Come on, you oyster-shootin' pistolera. We gotta fetch us some gold."

When he'd finished dressing, she turned onto her back to show him those wonderful breasts, and he had to clamp his jaws against his lust.

"I'll meet you at the livery barn in a half hour," he said, donning his ragged hat and turning away from her with effort.

Louisa looked around groggily. "Where you going, Lou?"

"Gonna haul my friend Sivvy over to the hoosegow."

He went out and tramped through the

soggy, dawn street that was as quiet as a graveyard over to the Golden Slipper. He opened Sivvy's door, turned to the bed, and cursed. She and the gold bar were gone, leaving a rumpled bed covered with frilly women's undergarments.

A voice echoed from downstairs: "Are you looking for Miss O'Shay?"

Prophet stepped into the hall, peered over the balcony rail and down into the lobby at the pale, mustached face of the gent who ran the place staring up at him. "Where the hell is she?"

"I turned her loose, of course. What was I supposed to do — leave a naked girl tied to her bed all night, screaming?"

"I could think of worse ways to spend a rainy evenin'," Prophet quipped in spite of his frustration. "When you'd turn that little ringtail loose?"

"Heavens," the man said. "Early last night. She was screaming so loud I thought she would shatter my chandeliers!"

Prophet snorted another curse, but it was his own fault. He should have tracked down whoever had been manning the joint yesterday and told him to leave the actress where she was. Or hauled her over to the hoosegow pronto. But it had been hard to decide what to do with her at the time, in the eye of the outlaw storm. Something in him had recoiled against the idea of throwing his old pal Sivvy into a stony, dark cell.

He could do it now, however, having mulled over all she'd done, her part in so many killings.

Prophet tramped down to the lobby, his double-bore coach gun swinging from its lanyard against his back. "You know where she went?"

"I am not her keeper, sir!"

Prophet growled and went out into the still-quiet street and tramped through the mud and the fresh, cool, post-storm air — the sun hadn't yet risen over the mountains, but it looked to be a clear day — and over to the livery barn where he and Louisa had stabled their horses.

Two hours west of Helldorado, Prophet and Louisa found the wagon on the backside of a steep mountain pass.

It had been ridden off the right side of the trail, into rocks and stubby cedars, and it was turned over on one side. The mules had wrenched free of their hitch, gone.

The canvas sheeting had been torn off the ash bows; it lay like a blown-down tent in the rocks and brush, and the gold ingots that had apparently been riding free in the box were sprawled across it like jewels spilled from heaven. The lockbox was there, too, still chained and padlocked but hanging precariously over a steep cutbank.

Prophet and Louisa both saw the body at the same time. It lay just beyond the wagon. At least, it looked like a body.

As they spurred their horses ahead and held up beside the trail, and Louisa leaped down and dropped her reins and jogged into the brush and rocks, it was clear that the girl Miguel had had sitting on his lap in the bank had reached the end of her trail.

Prophet remained mounted while Louisa dropped to a knee and turned the girl onto her back. She wore only the sheer wrapper she'd worn before, and a long, men's denim jacket. She'd been shot in the forehead from point-blank range, likely to get her out of the way when Sivvy's gang had run the wagon to ground. There were no other bodies around, but there were plenty of hoofprints and spent cartridge casings along the trail.

Louisa eased the dead girl back against the ground, looked up at Prophet, and hardened her jaws. "Miguel's mine, Lou."

Prophet nodded. Just then a rifle snapped from ahead along the trail that curved across the top of the rocky pass before dropping into another valley farther on. Louisa jerked her head in the direction of the shot.

Several more sounded, echoing faintly.

Prophet shucked his own Winchester from its boot, cocked it one-handed, and set it across his saddlebows. "Let's get after it. We'll bury the girl later!"

Louisa leaped onto her mount with the quickness and ease of a wild-assed Indian brave, and they booted their mounts into instant, ground-eating gallops, spraying rocks and sand out behind them. Prophet hunkered low in his saddle and tipped his hat over his eyes.

They raced down the twisting trail, pines of the lower slopes pushing up around them. The rifle bursts grew louder. Just before they gained the broad valley at the bottom of the pass, Prophet began to hear men yelling above the thuds of Mean and Ugly's hammering hooves.

The valley was broad and open, carpeted in tall, green grass, and there were several knolls scattered across the way. It was beyond one such knoll, on the trail's right side, that the guns were blasting and men were shouting and hollering.

Louisa read the play the same way Prophet did, and they turned their horses off the trail at the same time, checked them down to skidding stops, leaped out of their saddles, and threw down their reins.

They ran up the side of the knoll, dropped to hands and knees several feet from the top, and crawled until, doffing their hats, they edged cautious looks over the crest of the low hill.

A log cabin hunkered about a hundred yards from the base of the knoll and quartering to Prophet's right. Two bodies were slumped belly down in the grass at various distances from the cabin. Another hung out a side window, arms dangling down the front wall. The dead man's hat lay in the grass beneath his bald head, and his rifle lay not far from the hat.

A creek sheathed in wolf willows meandered along to Prophet's left, about forty yards from the front of the cabin and disappeared in a snaking, lime-green line against the far ridge.

Smoke puffed amongst the willows. A couple of hats bobbed there as well. Smoke also wafted from the cabin's two front windows, the shutters of which were thrown back against the wall. Guns blazed bright red in the golden sunshine.

Bullets fired from the creek hammered the cabin with loud, resolute *whaps!* Slivers and doggets of wood flew away from the window casings. Return fire from the cabin cracked into the brush along the creek or spanged shrilly off rocks.

Men from both quarters screamed and yelled, cursing each other like sailors on competing, seagoing vessels.

"Hey, Miguel!" one man shouted, his resonant voice rising clearly above the din. "I'm gonna blow your right eye out with this next shot. I'm gonna blow your *left* eye out with the one after that!"

Someone in the cabin laughed.

Guns roared. In the willows, a girl shrieked shrilly and followed it up with an even shriller curse.

Prophet ran a gloved index finger across his lower lip. Sivvy.

"Miguel!" she bellowed. "I'm gonna kill you, you double-crossing snipe! And then I'm gonna take all your gold and fuck all these men out here *over your swollen, bleedin' carcass!*"

She laughed loudly, maniacally, and the men in the willows laughed then, too, as they triggered one shot after another at the cabin.

"They could have each other pinned down for days," Louisa said.

"Let's flank the greedy sons o' bitches,

and put an end to this fandango once and for all."

"Miguel's in the cabin." She favored Prophet with a hard, determined gaze.

"All right — take the cabin. I'll sneak up behind Sivvy's gang, and we'll all say a little prayer together." Prophet offered a grim smile. "Louisa?"

She looked at him, grass brushing against her smooth, tanned cheeks, hazel eyes clear with purpose.

"Try to take the bastard alive. I know he don't deserve it, but . . ."

"I know, I know. You start playing judge and executioner, and everything just goes to hell in a handbasket."

Prophet grinned. Louisa crabbed back down the knoll, then stood and ran crouching straight out toward the northern ridge to circle around behind the cabin.

"Be careful," Prophet called after her. "There's a lotta lead buzzin' around over there!"

30

Prophet worked his way slowly toward the southern ridge, keeping knolls and brush clumps between him and the two sets of shooters, so he wouldn't be spotted by either those in the cabin or by Sivvy's gang holed up along the creek.

When he got across the creek, nearly losing his boots in the muddy hummocks along the two-foot-wide span of gently flowing water, the willows gave him good cover as, following the creek, he made his way west toward the hammering fusillade.

When, judging by the pitch and volume of the rifle fire, he figured he was within thirty yards of Sivvy's shooters, he got down on his hands and knees and crawled, wincing as several errant shots from the cabin thumped into the ground around him, pruning shrubs and throwing up mud.

He continued crawling, staying as low as he could. The willows parted before him.

Gradually, four figures showed through the shrub leaves and nimble branches — three men and a woman lying up along the creek's opposite bank, shooting over the top of the bank toward the cabin. One man lay facedown in the creek, unmoving, blood glistening from bullet holes. Another lay back against the bank, his hat off, lifting his chin and wide-open eyes as if taking some sun on his face. His hands hung limp in his lap, and his Winchester was negligently cradled in one arm.

Blood dribbled from the bullet hole in the left side of his forehead. The other three men and Sivvy were sending empty cartridge casings rolling down the bank behind them, flinching occasionally when a slug slung from the cabin whistled around their heads. Prophet snaked his Winchester out before him, pressed his cheek against the stock.

"Hold it there, you privy snipes!"

He triggered a shot into the bank just left of the hip of the man beyond Sivvy. The hard case jerked and swung his head around so quickly that his hat fell off his head, and Charlie Sparrow looked furious.

Sivvy turned toward Prophet then, too, and the other two shooters followed suit. Only Sparrow had spotted Prophet in the brush; the others were jerking their heads around, trying to pick him out of the bending willows.

"All of ya drop those shootin' irons or get ready to meet Ole Scratch at the smokin' gates of perdition!"

Sivvy squinted her eyes as she cast her befuddled gaze somewhere just over Prophet's right shoulder. "Lou?"

"You too, Miss O'Shay," Prophet ordered. "Throw down that carbine and reach for a cloud. You don't think I'd shoot you, but I will if I have to."

Sivvy turned the corners of her mouth down. "Even after Dakota?"

"Dakota was a long goddamn time ago."

"Lou," she said, her eyes finally finding him in the brush just upstream from her and on the other side of the creek. "Imagine all that gold back there . . . split up five ways. We'd be millionaires — every one of us!"

"Forget that horseshit!" In the periphery of his vision, Prophet saw Sparrow jerk his rifle around. The cutthroat bellowed savagely as he racked a fresh cartridge into his Henry and leveled the barrel at Prophet.

Prophet triggered twice, showing no mercy for the crazy cutthroat. The first bullet slammed Sparrow's head back while the second punched through his breastbone with a solid *whunk,* blowing up dust as it smashed the cutbank behind him.

Sivvy screamed.

Leaving her rifle on top of the bank and turning full around toward Prophet, she buried her head in her arms.

The other three men, on the opposite side of her from Charlie Sparrow, made their moves at the same time guns blasted inside the cabin. Levering and firing his leaping, roaring Winchester, Prophet dispatched all three of Sivvy's men with only one getting off a shot that cracked through the willows above his head.

The middle man, wounded in the belly, dropped his rifle and scrambled to his feet, running toward Prophet and clawing a Smith & Wesson from one of his two low-slung holsters. Prophet's last round left the gent blowing red bubbles facedown in the creek.

A man's scream rose from the cabin. Two more shots from inside.

The bounty hunter climbed wearily to his feet, glancing toward the cabin. The gunfire had died there as it had here. The cabin sat eerily hunched and silent, the one dead man hanging out a side window.

Prophet looked at Sivvy. He lowered his

empty Winchester and slipped his Colt Peacemaker from its holster. "Hold it, Miss O'Shay." To him, she'd never be Sivvy Hallenbach again.

She'd slipped a double-bore derringer from a hiding place in the simple, purple dress she was wearing, with a white wool sweater covering her shoulders, and half boots with three-inch heels on her feet. "You might have at least considered the offer, Lou. For old time's sake, anyways."

"Put it down, Sivvy."

"Oh, it's not for you, silly."

Prophet's gut tightened as she gave a funny little mocking smile. He grimaced and closed his eyes when he saw her slip the popper's barrel into her mouth.

He turned away as he heard the muffled explosion.

Reloading his Winchester from his cartridge belt, Prophet crossed the creek and moved through its ten-foot buffer of willows and into the clearing. The cabin was thirty yards away. Voices sounded from inside, and Prophet froze as Miguel Encina staggered into the doorway, holding his shoulder with the same hand he clutched a Remington revolver.

He winced, shouted, "Bitch!" at the tops

of his lungs, and staggered out into the yard.

Prophet was nearly straight out in front of the young banker, but he didn't appear to see the bounty hunter.

Louisa appeared in the doorway, boots spread wide across the threshold. Her face was hard beneath her hat brim, and one smoking Colt hung low in her right hand. Miguel dropped to his knees, twisted around, and screamed back at her, "We could've been rich, you simple-minded bitch! You and me — together and richer than you could ever dream about!"

"That'd be a rather tricky relationship, don't you think?" Louisa said. "Seeing as how you've been trying to kill me — me and Lou — since we first rode into town."

"I didn't order that. Yeah, Big Dick Broadstreet worked for me, but him and his boys set up that ambush themselves. They must have recognized you, figured you'd be trouble and wanted to get you out of the way pronto." Miguel stared at Louisa with false sincerity. "I was hoping we'd be together, Louisa. We still could be . . . if you killed him."

Miguel looked at Prophet, hardening his gaze again.

Louisa clucked her disdain and moved out away from the cabin, striding purposefully, challengingly toward Miguel.

Prophet held his ground and didn't say anything. He knew what would happen. Miguel screamed another enraged curse and raised his Remy.

Louisa didn't let him get it half raised before she blew the top of his head off and left him jerking there in the sage, turning nearly a complete circle on his back, dust rising around him.

Louisa stared down at him. When the shaking stopped, she looked up at Prophet and blinked. She flicked open her Colt's loading gate, shook out the spent shells, and replaced them with fresh.

"Anyone alive back there?" she asked.

Prophet was looking in the cabin in which Miguel's men lay sprawled in pools of their own blood.

"What do you think?"

"Want to bury 'em?"

"I'm gonna bury Miss O'Shay. Not sure why — old-time's sake, I reckon. Then we'll go up and bury that girl and the gold. No point in takin' it back to Juniper with no banker, no law around." Prophet turned away from the cabin, lowered his Winchester, stretched his back. "Shit, I'm tired."

"We just gonna leave Miguel and the others out here like this?"

Prophet kicked Miguel's Remy away from his dead fingers. "I see no point in wastin' time . . ."

". . . Burying killers," Louisa finished for him. "When the hawks and coyotes are right hungry."

"There you go," Prophet said and began tramping back toward the wagon.

The next morning, when Sivvy and the girl had been buried, Prophet and Louisa buried the gold well off the trail. They weren't sure what to do with it yet, but they couldn't return it to Juniper. Not with how wide-open the town had become in the past few days. Likely, they'd send a telegram to the mines it had come from, let the owners know where it was so they could dig it up and do with it what they would. It was theirs, after all.

Prophet mounted Mean and Ugly and looked around at the cabin sitting quiet in the morning's golden, high-country sunshine.

"Well, what's next?" Louisa said.

Prophet rubbed his chin, thoughtful. "How 'bout Denver?"

"What about Denver?"

"Have you been to Denver lately? It's a right nice town. There's churches there and folks' livin' peaceable, younkers goin' to school. We could ride on in, get you some nice duds to wear, find you a nice —"

"Lou?"

Prophet looked at her.

"Shut up."

Prophet glowered at her. "It ain't nice, tellin' a man to shut up who's only lookin' out for your purty little hide."

"Shut up."

Prophet sighed and shook his head with futility.

"Let's go back to Juniper," Louisa said. "Get the town on its leash again, collect the bounties on those hard cases still skulking around. Then get the gold back in the bank. Hell, in one or two days we could make several thousand dollars, enough to get us through another Mexican winter if you keep the whoring down and don't blow it all on cards and tequila."

Prophet blinked at her. "Mexico?"

"I wouldn't want to spend the winter in Canada."

Prophet stared at her. He thought of Montoya, but something in the girl's eyes — the bright, shiny confidence of the resolute huntress — told him she'd put the prison behind her.

"I ain't never gonna see you in a church

dress, am I?"

"What do you think?"

"Shit."

Louisa turned her pinto around and spurred him into a ground-chewing gallop. She cast a devilish glance over her shoulder. "Race you back to Helldorado!"

"Ah, shit," Prophet said again. He heeled Mean and Ugly up the trail, the eager horse lunging off its rear hooves and spraying gravel in his wake. "Here we go, Mean and Ugly!"

And for some reason, while he and the Mean and Ugly hammerhead raced up the trail behind Louisa, Prophet felt his spirits rise like spread wings, and he broke into loud, bellowing song: "Jeff Davis built a wagon, and on it put his name, and Beauregard was driver of Secession's lovely frame!"

ABOUT THE AUTHOR

Peter Brandvold was born and raised in North Dakota. Currently a full-time RVer, he writes Westerns under his own name as well as his pen name of Frank Leslie, as he travels around the West. Send him an e-mail at peterbrandvold@gmail.com.

The employees of Thorndike Press hope you have enjoyed this Large Print book. All our Thorndike, Wheeler, and Kennebec Large Print titles are designed for easy reading, and all our books are made to last. Other Thorndike Press Large Print books are available at your library, through selected bookstores, or directly from us.

For information about titles, please call:
  (800) 223-1244

or visit our Web site at:
  http://gale.cengage.com/thorndike

To share your comments, please write:
  Publisher
  Thorndike Press
  295 Kennedy Memorial Drive
  Waterville, ME 04901